TAKING THE HEAT

PAUL McDERMOTT

Beaten Track
www. beatentrackpublishing.com

Taking the Heat

First published 2021 by Beaten Track Publishing
Copyright © 2021 Paul McDermott

Paperback ISBN: 978 1 78645 501 7
eBook ISBN: 978 1 78645 502 4

Cover Design: Siobhan McDermott and Debbie McGowan

Beaten Track Publishing,
Burscough. Lancashire.
www. beatentrackpublishing.com

TAKING THE HEAT

CHAPTER ONE

Doctor Joey Hart looked around the fifty or more drinkers gathered for the evening in the Ship & Mitre, and nodded. "Not bad, for a Tuesday," he remarked to his assistant, Katherine, who had been responsible for organising the event.

"Best turnout in the three months we've been running the Sci-Bar project," she agreed. "Let's hope it means that enough people actually care about this month's discussion topic."

Amongst the 'spinoff' benefits of Liverpool's successful year as European Capital of Culture had been the groups starting up in pubs throughout the city centre, from rambling clubs and barber-shop quartets to reading groups, drama clubs and a vociferous body who had decided to promote 'Philosophy in Pubs'.

Perhaps as a direct response to this, the Sci-Bar series of talks followed by discussion on a range of scientific topics had proved a real crowd magnet, comfortably filling the Higher Room above the popular city centre CAMRA pub.

"Best make a start!"

He tapped a few times on the side of his half-full glass. The hum of excited anticipation from those present swelled momentarily, then subsided.

"Thanks for showing your interest in this evening's discussion topic. It would be very encouraging to think the ordinary man or woman in the street might one day have as much influence as our political leaders. They disappointed us yet again last week when they failed to reach any agreement on what we're discussing tonight—global warming..."

Joey preferred to speak without notes, and the constant asides and wisecracks which peppered his address appealed to his audience. The free-flowing rounds of drinks loosened tongues and inhibitions too, but without the evening deteriorating into a drunken shouting match.

"Fascinating subject, Doctor Hart. Thank you seems inadequate, somehow."

"Glad you enjoyed it, Mr...?"

"Whelan. Dave Whelan, and this is my wife, Brenda."

"Off duty like this, I'm Joey. What brought you along?"

"The beer." Dave grinned. The Ship & Mitre had a reputation for quality beers. "Seriously, though, we were here purely by chance the first time the Sci-Bar evening was held, and we enjoyed it so much I made a point of writing the dates into my diary."

Brenda raised her glass, to attract Joey's attention. "I teach global warming to my Year Six—I've lost count of how many times one of them has said, 'Two degrees isn't a big difference, Miss.' Sometimes I wonder if they're right. Like you said yourself, temperatures in general have risen by that much since the earliest records we have, and that's... how many years? A hundred and sixty?"

Joey nodded. "Nice to know someone was paying attention. Yes, which takes us back to Victorian times— around 1850—roughly when the Industrial Revolution was taking off in Britain, and people only had a vague idea what pollution meant. But think of all those 'dark, satanic mills' and how they poisoned the atmosphere, the rivers and everything else they touched.

"Despite that, the industry of that particular period did very little to affect the climate. In fact, more than half the rise in global temperatures has happened since roughly the mid-twentieth century, which is over a hundred years after the period we generally accept as the time the Industrial Revolution started."

Dave frowned. "So, the fact that our noble leaders have agreed to try to limit global temperature rises to no more than two degrees—"

"Isn't worth the paper it's written on!" snorted Joey dismissively. "Apart from anything else, it's not even an agreement per se, and it's only been put forward by a very small number of those taking part—and of those, the only real culprit, as far as carbon emissions is concerned, is the USA. Now, if they'd got China to agree to make an effort, it might have been worthwhile. If you want pollution control, you have to start with the worst offender. Makes sense, yes?"

"You certainly opened my eyes to a few facts tonight, Doctor...Joey," Dave corrected himself as the guest speaker looked at him sharply.

"But is there anything we ordinary folk can do?" Brenda persisted. "I mean, beyond recycling, switching off unused lights and all that. Something which might make a real difference?"

Joey fished in a pocket and passed her a business card. "Talk to friends. Get in touch with me if you'd like to organise some sort of structured evening, debate, or something of that nature. Can't promise I'll be available, but if I can come, I will."

Dave looked at the bottom of his pint and decided not to chance another if he wanted to drive home with a clear conscience. "We might just do that, Joey, but it won't be until after we come back from our holidays."

"I'll be at the college address. I'm using the summer break to do some long-overdue research, so I won't be going home."

* * *

"Eddie, that's your own fault! What on earth made you decide to follow the sheep to the Costa Fortune for your hols?" ... "Yeah, I bet it's raining, that was a given! Haven't you noticed how people have stopped going to the Med resorts these last few years? Never thought to ask why?"

Dave transferred his phone to his right hand and swiped his left on a towel that was already damp with sweat. He continued to rag his friend mercilessly as he took another gulp from the frost-rimmed cocktail glass at the side of his lounger.

The volume of Eddie's complaint increased again and now sounded like a full swarm of angry wasps rudely shaken from their nest and looking for their tormentor. Dave thought he really ought to show some sympathy for his friend, who sounded as if he was having a disastrous holiday break in Spain.

"Yeah, okay." ... "Listen, Ed, I didn't really mean all that." ... "No, honest! I wouldn't wish a bad holiday on anyone, no matter who! But you know, if you'd checked the weather reports, you might have had second thoughts." ... "No, seriously. It's all there for anyone to read on the internet.

"The stats are there to be read, Eddie. Over the last seven years, each UK summer has been longer and hotter than the one before. Did you know, there are parts of Devon and Cornwall where last summer's ban on using hosepipes was never lifted? They were so short of reserves they had to keep it on through autumn and winter. This year, they were on the back foot and piping water in from South Wales even before the summer started, so assuming the weather 'dahn sahf' is similar to what we're having here in Southport, they're guaranteed in dire straits already and it's only mid-flaming-June!"

Alternating between casual holiday chat and surfing the endless information pages on the web, Dave and Eddie lost track of the passage of time. It was only when the early afternoon sun wandered beyond the rim of the awning above Dave at the poolside and caused him to squint against its ferocity that he was brought back to reality.

"I'm telling you, Ed. I can't turn on a news programme these days—radio or TV—without some expert wanting to talk about global warming and how the clock's ticking and we've got to do something about it, and yadda-yadda, usually followed by a weepy plea for more money to research whatever it is said expert happens to specialise in, surprise, surprise! And the gravy train chuffs off to its next stop down the line!" ... "What, moi? Cynical?? Now, whatever gives you that impression?" ... "Yeah, we must get together when you're home. It's ages since last time. We can continue this discussion then...

"Brenda? She was smart, she went indoors for a siesta. It's way too hot to do anything other than sit by the pool—it was twenty-one degrees when we left home this morning. You can imagine what it was like by midday, and it only took us an hour to get here by train. No airports, no passports, no queues." ... "Yeah, you too. Listen, this might be what they call urban legend, but for what it's worth, it's a good idea to stay well away from the drains in Spain." ... "Yes, I said drains and that's what I meant! Apparently, they weren't built to cope with large amounts of rainfall, and they're ancient, falling apart—certainly not suited for the heavy rain you're getting. Result—backflow, and a very real chance of diseases and suchlike spreading like wildfire.

"Now, tell me again—when did you say you were going to check out and head home?" ... "Look on the bright side— at least it wasn't a package deal. You'd lose a fortune by cutting the holiday short. You've got the car, you can do it in stages through France, stop where it suits you, and still have a holiday of sorts."

After a few closing remarks, Dave ended the call and shut down his laptop as he prepared to go into the hotel and wake Brenda. With just a suggestion of regret, he reflected that Ed's unfortunate experiences with the weather must inevitably affect many others too. Hotter summers combined with very mild winters had become more noticeable—a direct result of the global warming which everyone seemed so anxious to talk about. It was a shame nobody seemed to have figured out an effective solution to the problem.

In their hotel, Dave discovered Brenda had opted to shower on returning from the beach and had flaked out in her bikini, on a wicker terrace lounger, rather than dressing or drying herself in order to siesta on the bed.

Dave eased the door open and entered, silent as a cat as he crossed the room. Brenda's eyes were closed, her breathing regular, her features relaxed. He paused and gazed at her, taking this rare opportunity to lose himself in her beauty. What on earth had he done to deserve someone so wonderful as a soul mate?

She'd always had the same effect on him, right from the first time she'd walked into his life. He felt it happening again; his breathing quickened, his heart laid down a thudding bass rhythm he was sure had to be loud enough to rouse her. His throat ached, painfully dry. He longed to kiss her tenderly until she woke and he could drown in her violet-blue eyes.

As if in answer to his silent plea, Brenda's eyelids fluttered open. There was a secretive smile about her eyes. Dave surrendered himself willingly, falling into their depths once more. She raised a hand in languid greeting; he caught it with the tips of his fingers and brushed his lips against her perfectly manicured nails.

"Had a good nap?"

"Mmm-hmm. Don't think I slept. Too hot, really."

"Just had a call from Eddie. He's run into monsoon weather. Not a happy bunny!"

Brenda swung her legs off the lounger and snuggled close to Dave's chest as he sat next to her.

"Monsoons in Spain? They used to be much further south. The tea crops in Sri Lanka and India depend on torrential rain."

"Yeah, I thought that," Dave murmured, absently stroking Brenda's golden hair. He felt her tense under his fingers and waited patiently for her to put her thoughts into words.

"So, we're now getting the sort of summers which made Spain popular with tourists—"

"While they're getting storms like they've never seen before," Dave finished.

"Makes you wonder what's happening further south..."

"Maybe I could look it up on t'internet." Weekend away or not, he was beginning to think there might be something in this line of thought. "But there's also this..." He kissed her earlobe, then placed his hand under her chin and eased very slightly away from her to a comfortable focal distance. "If weather patterns are changing—and from what you've just said, it seems they are—what's happening further north from here, if the weather patterns we used to have until about ten years ago are moving that way?

"Unlike you, I was never much cop at geography in school, but I remember Batty Roberts telling us that the UK was in the temperate climate zone. We never had summers like this. The summers we had as kids—when we got so used to 'rain stopped play' right through the cricket season. Even that sort of climate change would have a major effect on the ice fields up around the Arctic Circle, and isn't the world two-thirds water to start with?"

"It's nearer three-quarters," Brenda said. "But yes, point taken."

Dave suddenly became aware that during this interchange of thoughts, they'd somehow managed to stand away from the lounger without either of them being fully conscious of any decision to do so. Standing so close, the kiss was inevitable, and it was followed by several more, each lasting longer, more full of commitment than the one before. Pieces of his 'n' hers swimwear, all slightly damp—though not from being in the hotel pool—landed in a tangled heap on the floor as Dave swept Brenda into his arms and carried her into the cool shadows of the bedroom.

CHAPTER TWO

THE NARROW STRIP of pure white, sun-bleached sand between the esplanade and the surf line reflected a blinding glare which made sunblock and dark, matte-black lenses in your Ray-Bans not fashion accessories, just basic survival equipment.

No traffic had been allowed on the tarmac strip which ran parallel with the beach for several years, making this two-mile stretch a quiet zone: a child-friendly, safe area where those who simply wished to lie and soak in the sun could set out their picnics and scatter blankets, allowing young children to play, knowing there was no danger of them being involved in traffic accidents. Further north, beyond Southport's iconic, several times rebuilt Victorian pier, there was another beach of similar size which had become the most suitable place for more energetic sun-worshippers to indulge in games of beach volleyball, cricket, or a pick-up skins-vs-shirts soccer match. As the coastline curved gently beyond that, the current and tides had turned the extreme northern end of the bay into a venue where the cream of Europe's best surfers believed they had died and truly gone to heaven.

"Turned out nice again," Dave murmured, faking an atrocious parody of what he imagined a Lancashire Woollyback ought to sound like as he massaged another liberal helping of factor-twenty onto Brenda's shoulders.

Brenda rolled onto her stomach and eased the straps of her bikini down her arms so Dave could oil her skin without missing a spot.

9

"Where does that come from?" she asked, not really caring what the answer was. His cultured tenor voice was one of the first things which had attracted her to him, and she loved listening to him speak, whatever the occasion, regardless of what he happened to be talking about. She had a pretty good idea there would be a musical reference somewhere in the background. Musical cues and hints were part and parcel of Dave's everyday speech, and frequently made the difference between winning and losing a close-fought pub trivia quiz, something which he took seriously.

He didn't disappoint her.

"It's from something my granddad told me, a famous star of the music halls almost a hundred years ago. Bloke who lived not far from here. George Formby, his name was. They even made a film with that song title...can't remember if I ever heard it sung, though. Don't think so. There! That should stop you burning up—as long as you don't fry in all this oil."

"Mmm, thanks!" Brenda rolled again, onto her back, and adjusted the parasol.

Being their only full day away, they'd decided to do nothing more energetic than laze in the quiet zone for an hour or two before it got too hot, then shoot off somewhere for an early pub lunch. As a result, they were almost the only people on that part of the beach who appeared to be on the 'right side' of fifty. None of the radios were particularly loud or intrusive, and seemed to be tuned to Radio 4 rather than pumping out brash, aggressive and eminently forgettable Radio 1 grunge.

Dave stretched and glanced in both directions as he massaged a few drops of surplus sunblock over both wrists. Although they'd left the hotel in time to make the beach before it got too crowded, they'd barely managed to find a speck big enough for their modest stakeout.

Between blankets, sunbeds, inflatable mattresses and picnic tables, there was precious little of the fine, pure white sand visible as far as the eye could see.

"Just as well we weren't planning to come back after lunch," he said as he eased himself back down. "This spot won't stay empty for too long once we leave, and it's not even eleven o'clock yet. I can't imagine how these...older people stick it out, lying in the sun all day. I bet half of them look like lobsters by the time they go home, even with max factor!"

"That's a brand name, Dave, not a strength guide."

He chuckled. "I know. I was just checking to see if you're paying attention!"

"If I could be bothered, I'd throw something at you," Brenda warned mock-seriously.

"I figured you'd find it too much effort."

"Consider yourself thrown at, then."

"You usually miss anyway." Dave turned and took the last two drinks out of the cool box: Cain's beer for himself and a cherry Coke for Brenda. The ice in the box had melted to mush. "These aren't especially cold anymore, sweetheart. We should think about that early lunch once we've finished them. I'd better buy some ice when we refill the cool box."

* * *

The timber-framed terrazzo was blindingly, spotlessly white, and the noon sun seemed to bounce off, making it possible to sit comfortably in the shade created by the straw thatch overhead. The weakest hint of a current of air tried to circulate from time to time, without success.

"When I think of how crowded that strip of beach was this morning... My grandfather always said Southport was known as 'the seaside without the sea' when he was growing up," Brenda said, stirring a swizzle stick in her aperitif.

"Did he say why?" Dave was trying to resist the overwhelming temptation to empty his ice-cold Magners in a single swallow, and his resolve was weakening by the second.

"It's to do with local tides and currents. At low tide, if you stood on the road, you could only just see the sea."

"But it can still come all the way up to the road. Remember the damage the winter storms caused last year?"

"Yeah. That caught everyone on the hop, didn't it? Of course, we've had so many mild winters on the trot, everyone's assumed it was going to carry on the same way."

"People will always tend to go with the flow when it's a good news week." Dave paused and shot Brenda a quick glance, but something warned him that it would be better not to improvise a bar of the old sixties hit at this point. He sipped his drink to cover the hitch and continued. "I mean, if they like the idea, they'll use any excuse to believe it's gospel. Which is only human nature, I suppose— Yes, please."

He gave in to temptation and emptied his glass as the waiter approached with their tapas and a mixed-salad platter, ordering refills for both glasses. As a token gesture, they had both put an absolute minimum layer of clothing over their swimwear before settling at the nearest open-air restaurant that was reasonably busy.

"If a place is crowded, it's usually because they serve decent food," was Dave's argument, and looking at what they were being served, Brenda thought he was probably right. The restaurant was across a footbridge spanning the miniature railway which had been one of Southport's tourist attractions from time immemorial. Following the decision to pedestrianise the road which served the beaches, the railway had been developed and expanded to cater for elderly and infirm visitors or anyone who didn't want to rent a bicycle or quad bike in the centre of town. Those were permitted on the road; separate cycle lanes had been marked out, wide enough for emergency services vehicles to use as and when needed.

"So you think these people who shout the odds about global warming are misguided doom-and-gloom merchants, then?" Brenda finished the last of her salad and nodded to Dave that he was welcome to polish off what was left.

"Hard to say, love. I don't know enough about it to have an informed opinion, but if the science johnnies think there's something to worry about..." He shrugged and speared the final king prawn from the platter, continuing thoughtfully, "Since there's such a narrow strip of beach above the waterline now, it's reasonable to assume the water level overall must be higher than it used to be. It's a very flat beach, without much of a slope, which I'm guessing is the reason there used to be such a big difference between high- and low-tide marks."

"Which also means the tide comes in and goes out very quickly," Brenda added. She wasn't sure if it was relevant or important in any way, but she'd opted for an education-and-languages route through sixth form and later university. Minor details of that nature were part of her make-up, even in her leisure time. She enjoyed the rough-and-tumble of a competitive pub trivia quiz as much as Dave did, and if they both managed to get themselves onto the same team, it quite often won the cash pot.

"Okay, I know it's only pin money," Dave always reasoned, "but it pays for the evening's drinks—and I've no wish to go on *Mastermind* and make a prat of myself!"

Occasionally, Brenda wondered what it would be like to take part in one of the other, less academic TV quiz programmes and give her brain a break, but she was happy to see Dave enjoying the relaxed atmosphere and friendly banter of the pub quiz circuit, and equally glad to share the amateur scene with him.

"Anything you fancy doing this afternoon?"

Brenda glanced at her watch before replying. It was just turned one-thirty; the hottest part of the day was still ahead. "Nothing too strenuous, not in this weather," she answered with a grin. "And we should be a bit careful not to burn while we're out and about, but the thought of being indoors..." She shuddered.

"Well, at least the supermarket is air-conditioned, and we'll need drinks whatever we're doing."

"And ice. You said you'd buy ice."

"Your wish is my command, oh mistress mine! I hadn't forgotten, but it's where to go afterwards. D'you think it would be cooler if we go down to Marine Lake and either hire a boat, or see if there's a couple of seats on one of the cruise ships? I fancy going on that big paddle steamer. I hear they have live jazz bands."

CHAPTER THREE

Errol Dwight popped a match with his thumbnail and touched it to his trademark black cheroot. He had fifteen minutes of freedom before he had to duck back inside and blow that horn for another two hours on the return trip, but these few minutes were his precious time alone, and he'd worked hard for it.

From Stetson to boots, he cut an imposing figure in white with discreet gold thread embroidered on strategically chosen seams. The colour was a deliberate choice in this weather. It reflected most of the heat, or so the experts assured him, but the laundry bills were ridiculous. Every single sweat mark showed, and there were plenty of them. Everything he touched or even brushed against unawares seemed to leave a permanent mark. He had four identical jackets and five pairs of pants, and spent over an hour each evening cleaning his boots just to maintain the image he had as one of the best jazz trumpeters in North West England—which, for all practical purposes, meant the best in the UK.

The drummer, Max, pushed through the saloon door carrying two tall, slender glasses covered in rime frost and decorated with an outrageous number of slices of fresh fruit. Anyone seeing it could be forgiven for assuming that these trad jazz players were hard-drinkin' good ol' boys; in fact, none of the band drank alcohol when they were being paid to play—though what they did in their spare time and during rehearsals was another matter altogether.

Was it an overworked imagination, or did Errol really hear a hiss of evaporation as the ice-cold lemonade hit the back of his throat? He almost convinced himself he'd seen the faintest suggestion of a cloud of steam issuing from his own lips, just at the very edge of his field of vision.

Max chugged at his glass as eagerly as Errol, who was still listening intently, trying to decide if the lemonade was evaporating against superheated tonsils or if it was a more mundane *hiss* caused by the simple act of decanting a fizzy drink.

"What you looking at?" Max asked, hugging his glass protectively to his chest as he noticed Errol's interest.

Shamefacedly, Errol admitted his momentary indecisiveness between hiss and fizz.

"Mmmmm." Max fished pieces of fruit from his glass with a cocktail skewer. "I doubt global warming's that much of a problem, Errol. Not yet, anyway."

Errol sent his cheroot butt spinning into the clear blue waters off the starboard bow. The ship's engine note altered slightly as she prepared to make a long, smooth loop to steam back east to Southport's marina. "Even out here on deck, there's hardly a breath of air," he muttered. "It's going to be murder in the sweatbox on the way back."

"Look on the bright side," Max consoled, "at least we get to sit down for the next coupla hours. I think if I tried to dance the way some of the punters do, I'd dribble off the floor in a pool o' sweat!"

"Best get down there, all the same. We've still got to play all the way home."

***

"This was a brilliant idea, Brenda! We've got an air-conditioned bar, and it's a damn sight cooler out here than it would have been back on land."

"And aah do dee-clare I've got the best mint julep aah eva tas-ted!" Brenda drawled, twirling her glass as she caught Dave's mood. As soon as they'd seen the vessel, they'd decided to enter the spirit of the day and hired 1930s costumes from a fancy-dress shop not far from the ferry terminal. On boarding, they'd been pleased to discover they were far from the only passengers to do so; long chains of imitation pearls and Charleston dresses swirled around the floor, escorted by gentlemen with Brylcreemed hair, false mutton-chop whiskers and straw boaters.

They'd danced most of the way on the 'out' leg, and Dave had made a tactical raid on the bar just before the band took a well-earned breather. As a result, they had fresh cocktails to enjoy on the shaded afterdeck without having to suffer in the scrum which developed immediately the band announced the break.

"Sounds like the band's tuning up," Dave said, tossing back the last drops from his highball glass—memories of a Manhattan which, by now, contained only tiny splinters of what had once been ice cubes. "I'm still thirsty. I need a long drink. That's the only problem with cocktails, I can't afford to buy them in pint glasses."

They wandered back inside, appreciating the air conditioning despite only being on deck for a few minutes. A slow blues number was being played.

"Want to dance?" Without waiting for an answer, Dave led Brenda onto the floor, straight into a relaxed, sinuous rumba. A sprinkling of other couples were already dancing, but there was plenty of room for everyone, and Dave was a good, easy lead to follow.

After a few more slow numbers, the band went up-tempo, and one or two of the couples on the floor began an energetic jive, but Dave shook his head and took Brenda's arm, heading for the bar.

"That sort of jazz is too hot for me. I haven't got the energy to jive."

"That goes for me, too," Brenda agreed. "Even with the air conditioning in here, anything more strenuous than a rumba's out of the question. I can't imagine where they get the energy from!"

Dave hesitated for a second before opting for the fresh, clean taste of ice-cold cider. Brenda nodded her approval and asked for the same.

"This is for you, Eddie—wherever you are," murmured Dave, holding his glass at eye level before tasting it.

Brenda lifted her glass and added her silent toast to absent friends. "Is he going to drop in, once he gets home?"

Dave nodded. "I told him to phone us when he gets here, maybe we can go out for a meal. I think he'd like to meet Doctor Hart, you know. He's always been keen on environmental issues."

"Are you planning to follow up on this, then?"

Brenda's tone carried neither approval nor the opposite as she asked the question, but Dave saw from her eyes that she needed a proper answer, rather than the facetious, flippant nonsense that had been on the tip of his tongue. He took a sip at his glass to buy a few seconds while he rapidly rearranged his thoughts.

"If our national leaders won't tackle the problem, I think it's time we try something different. Doc Hart seems to know what he's talking about."

"It's going to need some organising, though."

"If enough people want to get involved, there's bound to be someone with the experience. I mean, look how many wanted to buttonhole him after that talk he gave. And if Ed's keen on doing something practical about global warming and protecting the environment..."

"I'll bet he can drag in a few more," Brenda said. "He could talk the hind legs off a donkey!"

"Pardon me, ma'am. I just love the word pictures you Brits paint in everyday speech. It's hard to believe y'all speak the same language we do."

Dave raised his gaze beyond Brenda's shoulder. The cultured, slow drawl of the Southern States came from an apparition in white waiting to be served. With a leisurely gesture, he tipped his hat gravely to Brenda before offering Dave his hand.

"Errol Dwight, honoured guest in your country these past five years. Like a permanent vacation."

"Dave Whelan, and this is my wife, Brenda. You play a mean horn, Mr. Dwight," Dave said approvingly. "I've often wished I'd learnt to play as a kid."

"Why, thank you, sir," Errol said with a grin. "But as for playing, I always said it's something in the blood. You're born with it. Yeah, lessons are important, but they're mostly for the classical gas pro boys. You wanna talk jazz, blues, soul, it's gotta come from inside. But don't let me get started or I'll be talkin' the hind leg off somethin' or other."

"Still, playing brass must need some real effort. Every jazz band I've ever seen, the trumpet player always seems to be the first one to become wet through—even at an outdoor venue," said Dave, with just a hint of an upward query inflection on the last two words of the sentence.

Errol nodded. "Said as much to our drummer out on deck a few minutes ago. 'Least this room's air-conditioned. You don't need to persuade me the weather's going crazy. Far as global warming's concerned, we're in the deep-brown stuff—my cleaning bill's proof enough of that."

He glanced around as if to make sure nobody else was watching before unbuttoning his jacket to reveal large telltale sweat patches darkening his shirt from both shoulder yokes, creeping insidiously towards the centre of his chest. He quickly buttoned up again and leaned closer.

"I wasn't purposely eavesdropping, but I couldn't help overhearing. Now, I bet you're thinking, *Damn Yankee, can't keep his nose outta other people's business!*"

Errol's order arrived, which appeared to consist of a half-gallon jug of ice cubes topped with a minimum amount of water. He signalled for four clean glasses and turned away from the bar.

"Talk to y'all later? Got a few questions I'd like to ask."

Dave nodded. "We'll wait for you to pack away after we dock. Perhaps we could grab a bite somewhere?"

CHAPTER FOUR

"G OT A SORRY-LOOKING card from Eddie in this morning's post, Dave."

"Sorry? That's not like him. Is he still depressed about the weather on the Costa Fortune?"

"No, I mean literally sorry-looking—the card itself, not what he's written. It looks as if it's been through a couple of car washes instead of sorting offices."

"I thought he'd already left, heading for the subtropical North?"

"He has. At least, the card has a French stamp on it, but a lot of what he's written is runny, blurred—here, see for yourself."

Brenda passed the card over. Sure enough, Eddie's scrawl was more difficult to read than normal, and the original postmark was completely illegible.

"*Weather seems to be...fall...no, following me. Fill...feel like the CB cartoon, always...something...raincl—smudge.*" He turned the card back and forth. "Let's try again.

"*Weather seems to be following me. Like the Charlie Brown cartoon, always under raincloud. Sleep in car, no hotel rooms, campsites total losses. Wine harvest destroyed according to press, other crops equally bad prospects. Expect price rises on basic foods. Home when I get there. Eddie.*"

"Definitely not a happy bunny, then."

"You're right, Brenda. And typical for him to close with a comment about the effect on food prices."

"He's a banker, Dave, and single. Some would say he barely qualifies as a human being."

"He might not be the easiest person to get along with, but he's all right if you get to know him, love."

"Sorry, darling, there's just something about him which makes me uneasy. Still, I really think you'd find something positive to say about the devil himself if he came knocking on the door."

* * *

At that moment, Eddie was at least as wet as he had been at any time during the twelve days of non-stop rain which had been the one constant feature of his vacation to date. He'd stopped for something to eat and discovered far too late that he'd apparently chosen the one bistro in the whole of France totally incapable of providing any food at all that could be described as edible. Further, it seemed they also had a policy of employing the rudest possible staff, determined to make a virtue out of ignoring customers.

He'd picked at his *déjeuner* and left almost the whole of it on the plate. Then he stepped in a puddle up over his ankles on the way back to the car. It shouldn't really have surprised him at that point to discover he had a flat tyre to change. Sometimes Murphy's Law kicked in with a spiteful glee, and when he had to turn the ignition key three times before the engine caught, he was very close to losing control altogether.

A day such as this could only end one way, and of course, he missed the 18:00 Calais departure by less than ten minutes. It gave him no pleasure to watch it leave from his position at the front of the queue for the next crossing. He'd already been warned that without a reservation he wasn't guaranteed passage on his open-return ticket.

"That is one reason the open tickets are inexpensive," the clerk at the ticket desk had explained in laboured and heavily accented English. Eddie could curse as fluently as any Parisian *garçon* or street urchin, but by this time, he was in no mood to cooperate or feel in any way kindly disposed towards *la belle France* or her citizens.

There was no way he was going to be refused on the following departure two hours later, but he was still forced to wait to one side until every vehicle with advance reservation had been called forward and parked. He was then assigned a dark, narrow and inconvenient space as far as possible from a stairwell leading to the main deck. Once there, a swift glance at the outrageous price tariffs in all the restaurants was enough for him to refuse to contribute more than the price of a cup of indifferent coffee towards the early repayment of the country's national debt. Futile, perhaps, but Eddie felt it was his only opportunity to make any sort of protest against that unmistakeably French *raison d'être*, xenophobia.

* * *

"Eddie's written again, Brenda. You should come and hear what he says."

There was something in Dave's tone of voice, something Brenda had never heard before, and it caused her to choke back the vague, unsolidified but negative feelings Eddie's name always inspired in her. She nodded and sat with Dave at the kitchen table.

"Not a postcard this time, and not an email, either!" Dave waved the evidence in the air, a quality pale-blue envelope with a discreet but distinctive watermark and carrying a first-class UK stamp. He already had the contents of the envelope in his hand.

Dear Dave, Brenda,

I'm guessing that you won't have expected a second mailing from me while I'm making a relatively short trip back from mid-France.

I value my friends, particularly because I'm not easy to get along with. I know this for a fact. With neither family nor siblings to confide in, I need to tell someone this, so nobody starts an unnecessary manhunt.

I'm doing this by snail mail for two reasons.

First, I'm old-fashioned enough to enjoy sending and receiving what I consider proper letters once in a while. Emails might be faster and more efficient, but like the song says, they 'don't got no soul'.

Second, the extra day or so before you receive this will give me more time to think about what I'm doing...

Which, you'll be relieved to hear, is neither illegal nor dangerous!

Recent lurid headlines about extravagant, unjustified bonuses paid to certain (senior) bankers have told one side of a story that needed to be told. Unfortunately, the situation for someone such as myself in a relatively *junior* position is nowhere even remotely close to being a bed of fragrant roses, caviar and champagne.

I got the bullet a couple of days before I was due to go on holiday. With no family to talk with, I kept my mouth shut. It was too late to cancel anyway, so I thought I'd give myself time to think. I'm convinced I'm being hung out to dry along with other juniors. I managed to check higher up the food chain, and there're no casualties amongst the senior partners. Make of that what you will. I know how it feels to me!

At least the redundancy pay's generous enough to cover me for a few months. I just want you to know that I'll be travelling most of the time, and as I've no job to come home to, I might not bother coming back to Liverpool immediately if I get prompted to turn aside and go wherever my wanderlust takes me. Mortgage and utilities are all on the drip feed at the bank, but can I ask you to check the house for mail occasionally? There's a spare key to the back door in a tobacco tin on the workbench in my garage (I think I always knew I'd bottle it and end up asking this favour by post!)

Don't worry if you don't hear from me for some time. I'm not feeling suicidal. I won't do anything stupid, and considering my lack of any family to keep in touch with, there really isn't anyone else I can turn to.

As ever,
Eddie

Dave surprised himself by managing to read the full letter aloud to Brenda without welling up in floods of tears or losing his voice entirely for other emotional reasons. He generally succeeded in presenting a cheerful, practical façade to the world, but he didn't fool Brenda as often as he fondly imagined in this respect. She cut him some slack in this tiniest of attempts at deception. She had to. Her opinion of 'Loner Eddie' had altered, positively and permanently, with every phrase of his letter.

"That must have been really, really difficult for him to write," she said, after a few moments of thoughtful silence.

"Amazing. I really thought I knew whatever there was to know about Eddie," Dave said. "Just goes to show, people always have the capacity to surprise and amaze you!"

"I have to agree." Brenda felt a little embarrassed that she'd quite possibly misjudged someone she'd never understood properly until now. "What was that he said about wanderlust and going off the radar?"

Dave took the letter out again. "He says not to worry if we don't hear from him for a while. If he thinks he's got enough in his suitcase to cover his immediate needs, there's no compelling reason for him to come back. It's the height of the holiday season, and we've already agreed the weather's better in the UK than it is anywhere else in Europe at the moment."

* * *

Eddie would definitely have argued about that statement. He'd been on deck as the ferry approached Dover, and he'd been appalled to see the irreversible damage done to the famous White Cliffs by violent, unpredictable winter storms gouging deep ravines, carved by a greedy giant in his favourite local cheese. The cliffs were being undercut and one day would just collapse into the sea.

He then had to endure the further inconvenience resulting from the treatment he had been subjected to by the French authorities, which meant he was one of the last to disembark. Inevitably, he was in the longest and slowest queue to be inspected at Customs, and when the driver of the vehicle immediately in front of him appeared to have mislaid some—or possibly all—of his documents, it didn't surprise Eddie in the least.

It was well into the afternoon before he left the port and pulled into the first filling station he came to. He hadn't yet decided where he was going, but he wasn't paying motorway prices for fuel, and he wasn't heading north, either. Nothing personal. He hadn't suddenly developed a hatred for his birthplace, but Liverpool seemed far too *boo-ooring* for words just now. Mentally, he flipped a coin.

Heads. West.

At the cash desk, he glanced to his left, and on impulse added a road map of Devon and Cornwall to his fuel bill. He knew nothing of the region, but he had a vague memory of something to do with…was it Arthur, the whole Camelot thing? Fact or fiction, myth or reality, it lifted his spirits a fraction, and he drove onwards in a much better mood, despite the weather.

CHAPTER FIVE

"Wぃ HAT'S THE SCI-BAR topic tonight, Joey?"
Dave and Brenda generally made an effort to arrive early on Philosophy in Pubs evenings. Dave insisted on using the bus so he could drink in his favourite CAMRA pub with a clear conscience.

Joey was setting up a couple of visual aids. "Believe it or not, I've got some evidence from our very own facilities at Bidston Hill showing earth tremors which have been recorded *this week* at no less than four different places here on the UK mainland!"

"You're joking! Earthquakes? Surely not!"

Joey grinned. "We aren't exactly sitting over a major fault, like the tectonic plates grinding at each other in the Pacific or the San Andreas Fault in the States, but the bedrock beneath the UK is, in geological terms, relatively young, and there can be half a dozen in any given week. Almost all of them are too small to notice—we only know about them from the extremely sensitive seismic recorders we have available. Still, the graphs don't lie. They're all here, from all over the country."

"There's one here in Cumbria—that's not too far away!" Dave said.

"Yes. It happened while I was watching the dials yesterday afternoon, but it was so small I might not have noticed it at all if I hadn't been online at the time."

The week's selection of amateur philosophers began to fill up the Higher Room. Brenda secured a table and Dave trotted back downstairs to refill their glasses.

"Guess who walked in while I was getting served!"

Brenda had no difficulty guessing the answer to her husband's conundrum. Measured to the apex of his Stetson, a seven-foot apparition of white leather had followed Dave up the stairs.

"We played a set at a pub in Liverpool last night, and some guy said this place sells the best beer in town, soooooo…"

"Well, that's true enough, Errol. And it gives me the chance to return the very generous Southern hospitality you showed us last Sunday evening."

"So, what's this all about? Some sort of club? A meeting? It's not AA or something o' that nature, is it?" The twinkle in Errol's eyes showed he didn't think that for a second.

"Well, it's a sort of a club, I suppose," Dave said. "Think of it as an informal way of making science interesting for Joe Public. And the speaker's brought some actual footage, evidence of earthquakes, believe it or not, one of them quite close by during the past week."

"Hey, the place ain't gonna fall down 'round our ears, is it?"

Hearing this, Joey strolled over to welcome Errol personally. "Relax, friend! Earth tremors they may be in name, but they're nowhere near the strength and severity of world disaster scenes. You're more than welcome tonight— we don't very often have guests from over the pond at the Ship!"

"Errol Dwight—came to England about five years back on vacation and forgot to go home, I guess. Don't get beer like this back in Arkansas, I can tell ya!"

"Although he's too modest to tell you how well he plays trumpet," Dave added. "He fronts the Magnolia Jazz Orchestra—we met up last week in Southport."

Joey nodded. "Heard you on the radio once or twice. I don't get out to concerts much, I'm afraid, but jazz is easy listening when I work late at night. Anyway, I think we can make a start." He turned and walked back to the end of the room. "Good evening, all, and thanks for coming! For those who don't know, I'm Doctor Joey Hart..."

* * *

"So, is there any danger we could experience a major quake—or seismic event, I think you called it—here in the UK?" The question came from the back of the room.

Joey took off his glasses and polished them for a couple of seconds before answering. "It would be a very brave man who dared say 'never' to that, but if we look at all the written records we have, we're living in a pretty stable part of the world.

"The UK sits comfortably on bedrock, which is quite young, geologically speaking. The tremors we've measured are small change compared to the headline-grabbing disasters reported elsewhere, but by studying them, we can figure out how to tackle more violent quakes. Ideally, we would then be in a position to assist with an emergency anywhere in the world."

It might have been the mellow feeling generated by the consumption of alcohol, or the very British tendency to sympathise with the underdog or anyone less fortunate, but Joey's suggestion that there were humanitarian reasons for studying the effects of earthquakes and other tremors was warmly applauded, and the meeting dissolved into smaller discussion groups loosely based on each table in the room.

"There's only one problem with setting up a response team to deal with emergencies, Joey."

"One problem, Errol? I can think of half a dozen straight off the top of my head."

"I'm thinking more along practical lines—perhaps thousands might be more accurate."

"Aha! Filthy lucre raises its ugly head again, I see! Yes, Errol, cash is always the problem we can't walk away from."

"Do you have any idea how much you'd need to seed your scheme?"

Joey almost dropped his glass and stared at Errol. "There didn't seem much point. We're probably talking telephone numbers, quite honestly, and it's not going to happen overnight."

"Humour me anyway." Errol's lazy Southern drawl demanded an answer. Joey scratched his head.

"First and foremost, there's manpower, the people who make up the team, or teams—I can't see a team of less than six being effective in dealing with any emergency."

"And you can't hope to provide just the one team because misfortunes never come singly. So two, maybe three teams, and they'll all need training to deal with a variety of different situations, basic first aid, firefighting and half a dozen other scenarios—"

"Is there some point in this, Errol? All we're doing is adding more and more to the cost of the project."

"Joey, you need to for-ma-late a business plan if you ever want to go ahead with this, and the most important item on a BP is the cost."

"That's true enough, I suppose."

"Now, I ain't on the Forbes List, but I ain't broke either. How'd you think I afford to be on a five-year vacation and cover the cost of running a jazz orchestra?" Errol placed his glass on the table and locked his gaze with Joey's. "Give me a figure—a realistic one—and maybe we can make a deal. You talk about telephone-number accounts. The Dwight family is what we in the Confederacy still call old money, and the number of zeroes on the page won't necessarily be a problem."

Joey stared right back at Errol, speechless. "You're serious."

Errol shrugged. "People tell me you can't take it with you, and I'm never gonna spend all I inherited. If I find a worthy cause I think deserves a few dollars to give it a helping hand…"

"But we've only met this evening, for the very first time. You know nothing about me! I could be the most devious con-man in Liverpool."

"Snake oil salesmen don't go 'round setting up emergency response teams to react to natural disasters. Nor do they lecture in the science department of a major British university, so let's get serious for a minute." A business card appeared from nowhere. "Gimme some kind of ballpark figures and we can discuss it the detail. Now, what's a man gotta do to get a drink 'round here?"

A few rounds of real ale later, Dave and Brenda found they'd been conscripted to accompany Errol on a visit to the Bidston Hill Observatory at Joey's invitation, to get a closer look at the research facilities available.

"It isn't just quakes and tremors we're watching," Joey said as they ended the evening. "We're looking at the overall pattern of weather changes, trying to see if it's possible to predict potential problems before they develop, prevention being better than cure, as the saying goes. But it's not easy. There are too many variables."

"Let's take it one step at a time," Errol suggested. "Starting tomorrow—mid-morning okay with you, Joey? Dave, Brenda, I can pick you up. I've got the station wagon. We won't need more than the one car."

CHAPTER SIX

"YOU GOT SOME real nice knickknacks and gewgaws in this observatory, Joey!"

Errol leaned back as the group settled around an outdoor patio table after Joey's guided tour of the research centre and coffee was poured. "Anybody mind?" He held up an etui, and when nobody objected, he lit a cheroot. "Joey, this is clearly a much bigger picture than just chasing shadows and recording details of minor rumblings deep underground. You showed us details of research being done all over the world—volcanic activity in Iceland and Italy, strong tides in Australasia, that disastrous earthquake last year in Haiti... Now, remember that none of us—" he nodded to include Dave and Brenda "—are science majors. Do you think there's any possibility that these events are connected? Or did I read too many DC science fiction disaster comics when I was growing up?"

"I really wish there was an easy answer to that one, Errol," Joey said ruefully. "Unfortunately, at the moment, we don't have sufficient data to make even a qualified guess. Take the volcanoes, for example. We know the one in Iceland erupts roughly every hundred years, and there have been some suggestions of pressure building underground over the last twelve months. It may well blow soon—but 'soon' in geological terms doesn't even guarantee it'll happen in our lifetime!

"There are several volcanoes in Italy which erupt regularly, and more often than the one in Iceland. These we've learnt to contain and control, so as long as they don't go completely off the scale, we should be able to cope. Once again, the problem is getting an idea of *when* they might sound off.

"The earthquake that hit Haiti last year is a different matter, and we have to look some distance from the island group to understand where the problem came from.

"Several hundred miles from Haiti, deep below the South Pacific, the plates of bedrock beneath Asia and Australasia have been pressing against each other for millennia. When the pressure reaches a critical point, one slips slightly *under* the other to relieve the stress. Now, basic science has to be mentioned, I'm afraid—remember the phrase 'action and equal and opposite reaction' from your schooldays?"

Nods all around. Joey was relieved.

"Good! That means I don't have to explain in detail. Essentially, the energy released when the two plates slip fractionally is translated into a motion wave, which starts travelling in a straight line. Because most of our planet is water, this most often sets up a tidal wave, sometimes a tsunami, which is even more destructive. From time to time, depending on various factors, it can also result in an earthquake. There doesn't seem to be a way of knowing for certain exactly what the result is going to be in any given situation."

"So the place the quake starts from can be some distance from the area affected? Is that right?" Dave asked.

Joey nodded. "That seems to be the case. Having some idea of what parts of the world are under threat *before* disaster strikes would be fantastic, but as it stands..." He glanced back into the workshop; something had caught his attention. "Back in a minute—there's an alert light on one of the weather screens."

The visitors followed Joey back indoors, and he indicated the alert light.

"It's not that far away—looks like it could be an aftershock from the one in Cumbria last week."

"Can you pinpoint it, Joey? Should we be feeling it here?"

"Give me a minute." He made a few minor adjustments. "It happened yesterday, apparently. The station isn't manned, so it's only now been logged. It's from a weather station outside Blackpool. Strength just about a two on the Richter scale, depth five to ten klicks—sorry, kilometres. Barely enough to rattle a few teacups, but typical of the twenty or so tremors we log in the UK each week."

"Really? As many as that?" Dave was palpably surprised.

"With the sensitive equipment we have available these days, I'd have expected to pick up more than that. On a geological scale, it's still a relatively short time since this island of ours broke off the Central European landmass. We're still in the bedding-down process, if you care to look at it that way."

"Is it possible to work out if there's any connection between these tremors and the reports of extreme weather affecting mainland Europe?" Brenda asked, then blushed as three pairs of eyes focused on her. "I was only thinking of what Eddie said in his card and the letter we got last Tuesday," she added defensively.

"There's no probable cause to link the two, I wouldn't think," Joey mused, "but that's not the same as saying there isn't a connection. I'd need to write a whole new programme to feed The Beast, and I'd have to have a lot more data at my fingertips before I could begin to interpret whatever results it *might* throw up."

"Hope that was a Freudian slip, not just an unfortunate choice of words." Dave made a comical pantomime of someone vomiting.

Joey chuckled. "What, you mean GIGO—garbage in, garbage out? No, I think we've progressed beyond the stage of using poor-quality data and trying to guess at possibilities. With the internet, it's become far easier to access accurate and up-to-date records on just about anything happening all over the world, and usually within seconds of it being posted—that is, of course, if it's not sensitive data and protected by a battery of security tags."

Dave looked at Brenda. "Poor Eddie. He'll be developing a Jonah complex if this continues."

That comment earned blank stares from Errol and Joey. Dave felt obliged to explain their friend's disastrous summer break in the South of France. Discreetly, he avoided mentioning Eddie's employment prospects.

"Here's one hot off the press!" Joey said as a ticker-tape message marched across the base of the screen. "*Tremor recorded, Richter 2, 25km N of Taunton, Somerset.* Now, let's play the sceptic scientist who doesn't believe the word coincidence should exist other than as an entry in the Oxford dictionary."

Rubbing his hands together, clearly in his element, he crossed to one of the long walls of the room and picked up a pointer rod which had quite possibly seen active service in the same office when it had been used as a World War II plotting room.

"Looking at this North Europe map, I can compare the time lapse between the *first* rumble in Cumbria—"

"Sounds like the blurb for a heavyweight boxing match," Dave interrupted, but the joke fell flat. "Sorry, Joey! 'Open mouth, insert foot' should be my motto! Please, carry on. You'll hear no more facetious remarks from me!"

"That's nice to know," Joey answered but without malice. He'd sensed early on that humour was Dave's way of dealing with tense situations, and he was closer to the truth than he perhaps realised. He continued.

"We have exact figures for the timing and the distance between the epicentres of the Cumbrian quake and the Blackpool tremor, and then again the data comparing the timing and size of both incidents with the one in Somerset. That gives me a handle on the time/distance vector for the two UK events. Sooo, if—and it's a big if—but all the same..." He scribbled a few lengthy equations on a notepad before continuing, "*If* the available data for the speed and distance travelled by the storms moving our way from Europe can be downloaded from somewhere, we could have a value for the weather front heading north. It's just possible!"

He spun on his heel. "Brenda, your question suddenly seems to be the *right* one to ask! Maybe us science 'geeks' need a non-scientist around to ask the obvious questions from time to time."

"Someone who lives in the real world, you mean?" Errol drawled.

Joey nodded his agreement, then frowned. "There are far too many variables I need to know—temperatures, prevailing wind directions, paleo-history—"

"Whoa! Stop! You've lost me already!" Dave protested.

"Sorry! Habit, I'm afraid. I don't get out much. Most of my conversations recently have been with other geeks and freaks who love to talk shop."

He took a breath and let his eyes flicker onto his scratchpad. "Paleo-history is shorthand for what we learn from a study of the stone and strata which the landmasses of the continents rest upon. The only thing you need to appreciate for the moment is the *timescale* involved—time periods involving millions of years as an insignificant third planet circling a relatively small sun on the outer rim of a not particularly large galaxy somewhere in a star system called the Milky Way.

"Nothing of any consequence has happened here in the last couple of hundred thousand years, which on a galactic scale is the time between the moment you decide to completely empty your lungs and the beginning of taking a deep breath.

You need to bear this in mind—the casual reference to a period of hundreds of millions of years, and distances measured in billions or trillions of light years can be daunting for ordinary folk to even begin to understand."

"So measuring a few hundred miles, and times which I guess are being measured in minutes rather than how far light can travel in the time it takes us to plod our way once around the sun..." Dave's tone implied the question.

"Is like using a jackhammer to mend your watch or performing eye surgery with a machete!" Joey answered with no trace of flippancy or humour. Dave felt the acknowledged expert in his field had erred on the side of caution, understating the case rather than exaggerating to impress.

"On the other hand," Joey continued in a much more positive tone of voice, "we've over fifty years of experience behind us here at Bidston Hill, and when the new 'scope being built in Oz comes online next year, we'll be controlling it from here because we've got the best qualified staff in the world."

"How's a telescope—no matter how fancy or expensive it is—going to help with weather studies?"

"We can't judge weather as a local phenomenon anymore. We have to look at the general climate of the world, and to understand this, we sometimes have to take into account outside influences, such as the effects of sunspots and solar winds. Believe it or not, this next generation of radio telescope is as close as science has yet come to building a time machine. It works by tracking the radiation travelling across space and plotting its course."

"Okay, that's more than enough," Brenda interjected. "You've got my head spinning!" Dave nodded his support.

"That makes three of us non-science boffins, Joey," Errol said. "I'd say you're outnumbered! Now, how does this link to predicting when a tremor might show on the screens down south—Somerset, did you say?".

"That's not something I could even begin to explain without using a lot of scientific jargon. Let's just say, assuming a constant speed from Cumbria to Blackpool and continuing south..." He frowned and checked his figures. "If these are right, the shock wave heading south won't get that far before tomorrow. What's on the screen right now can only be from the shock rumbling north from the European mainland."

Joey reached for a phone as he spoke, dialling a number he evidently used often enough to know by heart.

"Brian, it's me, Joey." ... "Fine, thanks." ... "Listen, we can gab another time, I need a favour, and you might be a bit pushed for time! I need exact—and I mean *exact*—times on some seismic readings you've already got, and some on the way from up north in the next few hours. I particularly need data on the figures you haven't got yet—I need to compare it with what I've taken here at the source. And, Brian? Keep this under wraps for now. I'll let you in on what's going down ASAP, but for the moment, I'm depending on you trusting my calls." ... "Good on yer, mate. I knew I could rely on you!" ... "Promise, you'll be the first to know!"

Dave beckoned for Joey's attention. "There seem to be several different—what should I call them? Events? They're all happening more or less at the same time. How can we be sure there isn't some sort of connection between them?"

Joey paused a moment. His hand strayed towards his scratchpad and biro but stopped short, as if he'd changed his mind. "As I said to Brenda a few minutes ago, it might be useful for every researcher to have a non-scientist around to ask the obvious questions a specialist wouldn't. As it stands, Dave, I haven't got enough data. In fact, I'm not sure how to phrase the question, and until I can do that, there's no chance of any sort of an answer."

"Forty-two," Brenda muttered and immediately flushed as her *sotto voce* comment plopped into an unexpected pool of total silence.

Sensing she was right, Dave grinned at Joey and Errol. "If you get to a pub quiz once in a while, you'd know this is a literary reference! Never heard of Douglas Adams?"

Neither the scientist nor the musician had.

"Your loss. He won't be writing anymore—he died recently. In his best-known work, *The Hitchhiker's Guide to the Galaxy*, scientists build a machine to discover the Ultimate Answer to Life, the Universe, and Everything. The machine tells them the answer is forty-two, and they must now build an even bigger machine."

"To work out what the Ultimate Question was?" Joey guessed, slapping himself on the forehead as Dave confirmed his suspicions.

"He didn't have a serious take on life, really," Dave went on, despite the apparently irrelevant pathway of his thoughts. "But as I said to my class when it came up for GCSE studies this year, he sometimes makes a throwaway remark and you think, 'Hey, I can relate to that.'"

A few seconds passed while Joey and Errol considered this. Errol broke the tableau by reaching for a pen.

"I'll have a look for that book—sounds interesting! Brenda, has Dave...?"

She nodded. As usual, her soul mate had expressed in simple language exactly what she'd been thinking.

Joey glanced at them both; this time, his hand managed to reach as far as the scratchpad, and he scribbled a memo nobody else could have deciphered.

"Looks like I'm going to be busy writing the Ultimate Question or, at least, one which strays far enough outside the scientific box to include as many as possible of the random facts which need to be considered."

CHAPTER SEVEN

E DDIE WASN'T HAPPY. Not only had the bad weather
which had ruined his Mediterranean break followed
him throughout his flight north, it had decided to dump a
month's worth of withheld rain on him and him alone as he
motored along what had become in recent years the English
equivalent of the Riviera resorts along the south coast.

Something he hadn't taken into account was the fact
that, as a consequence of the changing weather patterns,
many more people had opted to stay home for their summer
holidays rather than head for the traditional resorts in
Europe. He'd had no luck whatsoever finding a hotel or even
a humble B&B that could offer him a room for the night,
and by the time he reached Taunton, he was exhausted, cold
and very hungry.

At least I can get a decent meal at a pub somewhere, he
thought to himself as he parked in a council-run car park.
Here he had his first piece of good luck for several hours.
He'd arrived just after six p.m. and discovered that parking
was free until the following morning. There was a scattering
of other vehicles dotted about. As long as the local lowlife
didn't amuse themselves by wrecking unattended vehicles,
it might be safe to leave it there overnight, although if he
couldn't find a hotel room, he could rough it for one night in
the car and at the same time protect his sole form of transport
from said hypothetical scallies.

Another thought struck him and had him rooting through
the contents of his glovebox. He was sure he'd kept it...*yes!*

There it is! In a free magazine he'd picked up in his local pub, there was a piece about a new brewery acquisition opening in Taunton. That was one place he knew he could get a decent meal...strike two, he could actually *see* the pub, off to one side of the car park. Fate, karma, kismet or coincidence, Eddie didn't necessarily give any of those much credence, but right then, all he wanted was the excuse to freshen up in the Gents' at the pub while his evening meal was being cooked. He slung a change of clothes and a razor into a discreet bag he could carry without arousing undue comment or notice and strolled across the car park.

***

There had always been a Coal Orchard in Taunton since records were first kept. Originally it had been an apple orchard, famous for its crop of cider apples; later, it had become the centre of a busy harbour in the days when coal was king and most heavy goods transport was carried out by canal boat rather than by road. There was an ambience of understated solidity about the present building, sited on the banks of the River Tone, despite being less than a decade old.

As he walked through the door, none of this was of immediate significance to Eddie, as he was most interested in the guest ales available. He might strike lucky with a dependable favourite, but he was confident that the menu would be familiar. He was about to pick one up en route to the bar when his nose reminded him what day it was. His choice was made for him: the Curry Night that ran across the brewery's pubs every Thursday evening was a treat which was not to be sniffed at.

At the bar, there were difficult decisions to be made, and it took Eddie almost two whole minutes to settle on a pint of Wobbly Bob while his lamb biriani was prepared. As he deposited his glass on a table in a quiet corner and headed for the Gents', he told himself that, as he had no intention of driving further that evening, he could indulge in as many guest ales as he wanted with and after the meal. There were definite advantages to drinking at CAMRA establishments.

The pump with a handwritten label which simply stated 'Local Cider' seemed a logical choice for something different following the meal. It had very little head and few bubbles. It was slightly cloudy and stood on the bar, trying hard to persuade him it was an innocuous non-alcoholic apple juice. Eddie wasn't fooled. He'd heard far too many stories about the ABV of scrumpies and other locally brewed ciders from this part of the country. When ripples began to appear on the foam-free surface without him even touching the glass, he was puzzled. There was no obvious cause. The pub was quiet, without even loud music or raised voices to set up vibrations on the bar.

The ripples swiftly became a series of regularly spaced concentric circles which appeared to start from the centre of the glass and spread outwards. The bartender was still standing close, waiting for payment. Eddie caught his gaze and knew he wasn't seeing things.

"No oidea what's caused thaa', Sirr." The syrupy Somerset syllables seemed fitting, somehow, to the as-yet unexplained phenomenon.

Eddie paid for his drink but continued to watch the glass rather than pick it up. As he received his change, the lights flickered, and several tankards hanging above the bar began swaying, slightly but rhythmically, some touching and sounding a gentle chime. Both men looked up at the new distraction.

"What now?" Eddie's question was rhetorical. He didn't expect an answer, but the bartender had apparently been thinking along similar lines.

"We sometimes 'ave problems with the 'lectrics in storms," he said, slowly, pronouncing the last word with a languid *z* at both ends rather than an *s*, "but weather ain't 'nuff to call a storm, least, not in these parts."

"Looks like it's settled now, anyway," Eddie commented, as the tankards settled back on their hooks and the surface of his pint returned to a placid state, punctuated by a final few bubbles of effervescence.

The bartender glanced at his wristwatch and switched the pub's sound system from the quiet background music to the local radio station. "Almos' the hour. If summat's happened, mebbe we'll hear on the local news."

Eddie took a pull at his drink, enjoying the richness of liquid apple on his palate, both sweet and powerful and a refreshing change to the hoppy taste of his usual choice of traditionally brewed bitter ale.

The five-minute news summary was rounded off, as usual, with the local weather news.

"*...the storms which have swept north from mainland Europe have caused every available lifeboat along the south coast to be launched with at least fifteen different vessels in difficulty.*

"*There are reports from coastguard stations that powerful waves are pounding on the famous white cliffs around Dover, eroding the fragile chalk. Experts are concerned that large sections of the cliffs may collapse into the Channel.*

"*There are also reports of a minor earth tremor, recorded at one point nine on the Richter scale. At the moment, it has not been established if there is a link between this and the bad weather approaching from the south, but the possibility is being investigated.*"

"We'm 'ad a few trembles here the last few years, right enough!" said the barman, as the news ended, "but I ain't noticed it so clear as that affore!"

"I've a friend at home who knows a bit about these things," Eddie mused, barely aware that he was speaking his thoughts out loud. "I wonder what he thinks about it all."

"You here on holiday? The weather's not been kind t'ye if y'are!"

"Well, it was worse when I started!"

Without meaning to, Eddie found himself regaling the publican's sympathetic ear with the main disasters of his intended break in the French Riviera and his equally luckless drive back north.

"I don't imagine it can get worse," he concluded, "but since I've nothing urgent to hurry home for, I thought I'd take each day as it comes and lose myself along the way."

He had a feeling it was probably against some obscure bylaw or other to sleep the night in a council car park and deliberately omitted to mention the matter. Bidding *mine host* a cheerful good evening, he finished his pint and wandered back to the car park and a few hours' rest.

He noted the time on the dashboard clock as he settled on the passenger seat, fully extended and reclined almost to a horizontal plane; this wasn't the first time he'd been obliged to spend a night in his car. It wanted two or three minutes to midnight: he decided to see if there was any update on the weather and possible earth tremors.

"*...ships which sent out distress calls have been accounted for. Every lifeboat has now returned to their stations, and there are no reports of fatalities.*

"*It has now been confirmed that the weak tremor which registered one point nine on the Richter scale about nine p.m. this evening was in fact an early warning riding ahead of the storm. Police are advising everyone who lives within two miles or three point five kilometres of the south coast to be prepared to move further inland. As reported earlier, wave action is washing away large sections of the chalk-based white cliffs, and there will be some damage and erosion."*

Conscious of possible battery drain, Eddie turned off the radio and sat for a few moments in the subdued light of the car park. It was easy for him to imagine farms along the south coast suddenly losing fields full of livestock or crops as they slid into the storm-lashed Channel separating Britain from mainland Europe, and it didn't require a great deal of imagination to picture himself gazing down from the passenger seat in a small plane, watching new, small islands form from the washed-away remnants of the famous cliffs while the coastline of Britain was radically altered, forever.

Another thought struck him, one which made him very uneasy.

If this was typical of the damage that could be caused by inclement weather in the narrow, normally placid waters of the English Channel, how much damage might be caused elsewhere? For example, a storm building in the west had several thousand miles of open water to cross before pouncing on the west coast of Ireland as the only warning prior to venting its fury on North West England.

Sleep didn't come easy to Eddie that night.

CHAPTER EIGHT

JOEY HART HAD been close to the literal truth when he'd joked with his visitors about not getting out much. He wasn't averse to a bit of company, but he preferred to work alone.

He'd developed a habit of reserving one of the monitors in the workshop for its original purpose of receiving a TV signal, and it was permanently tuned to the twenty-four-hour BBC News Channel. He didn't allow it to distract him from his work, but there was a continuous low level of speech from it which created a much better environment than the alternative—a sterile silence broken only by the chink and click of scientific instruments and Joey's muttered comments and curses intended for nobody other than himself.

The word 'Australia' finally registered on Joey's inner ear. Glancing up at the News Channel, he realised it must have been mentioned several times already, as the scenes on the screen were evidently part of a longer report. He stopped what he was doing and poured a coffee.

"...police and coastguard are advising people to move away from the coast and head for higher ground. Several major rivers have already burst their banks, and the next high tide along the east coast in about eight hours will be one of the fullest ever recorded, with a strong current following it and a force ten or eleven gale behind it."

Nobody likes a smartass, Joey thought to himself, *and I certainly don't want to be the one to jump up and shout, "What'd I tell you?" but...*

His computer Morsed the receipt of a text message. It was from Dave. Joey read it and called without allowing his attention to wander from the dramatic pictures on the News Channel.

"Hello, Dave?" ... "Yes, thanks. I noticed it when it came up a few minutes ago." ... "Really? No, I didn't know, I've only just—" ... "Someone said the next high tide's in about eight hours. Is that live or recorded comment, I wonder? Not that we're in a position to do anything useful from this distance, anyway." ... "Yes, I'm aware of that—though I'm not especially happy to be proved right on this occasion. I'd much have preferred to be wrong!"

"Joey, I just needed to ask—how serious d'you reckon this could become? If you remember, I told you we've relatives Down Under, both in Oz *and* in New Zealand."

"No need to panic, Dave. Australia's not going to be washed off the world map. But if they can move away from the coast, they'll be a lot safer on higher ground. As far as New Zealand's concerned, there's still some doubt about how long it's likely to be before the stresses start building in that direction, but again, if your relatives are on reasonably high ground rather than along the coastline, they shouldn't be in too much danger."

"Joey, things seem to be moving along just as you predicted and maybe a damn sight faster. Is there anyone you can think of might be able to verify your figures? I don't mean steal your thunder or plunder your research, but we may be talking about saving lives here."

"I might be able to call in a favour or two. An uplink to the weather satellites would be a good start—that's public domain anyway. I'll call you back."

* * *

Joey checked the data spread on his desk one more time.

"There's something not quite kosher in this," he muttered to himself, "but I'm damned if I can spot it!"

Gathering the printouts which showed the tracks followed by the orbiting weather stations, he squared them all off neatly, ready to stack them on one side, then frowned and fanned them once more.

"Let's try something a bit different." He arranged the shots according to their orbital order. There were twelve in all: he dealt them out in a clock-face formation and stood back to look at them once more.

The photographs at one and seven o'clock were slightly out of line, he decided, and moved back to adjust them. No, they *weren't* out of line. He took a tape measure, marked a point exactly in the centre of the chart table and re-laid the still shots at precise intervals and with meticulous care.

His eyes told him that the discrepancy was still there, a fact confirmed by the traditional cartographer's standby: a pair of dividers.

"I'm emailing you the schematics right now, Rob. How close are you to doing some beta-tests on the new radioscope? I know the building's a couple of months from finished yet, but how about the lens itself? Is it in place?"

"Tell me what you want to look for, Joey, and I'll tell you if it's possible."

Rob Jones's Aussie twang seemed to bounce all around the lab at Bidston Hill, unaffected by being transmitted halfway around the world.

"There are twelve shots. Lay 'em out in a clock formation, starting with the station marked 'Cancer' at one o'clock, 'Leo' at two and so on in the order they pass.

"Look at what happens to the orbit of *every* satellite as it passes through the one o'clock position and *again* when it gets to seven o'clock.

"What I need from you is the most accurate data you can supply for me. The best 'scopes I have available aren't sensitive enough, as these satellites are orbiting at a height which makes small variations difficult to measure. What seems to be happening is, every time one of them reaches a position which—for *me* in the UK—corresponds to one o'clock, it deviates *away* from the plotted orbit. It's a minute deviation, compared with the overall flight path, but it looks like it's exactly the same magnitude every time and, as far as I can judge at exactly the same point every time a satellite passes through.

"One hundred and eighty degrees away, at seven o'clock, the corresponding satellite dips by a corresponding fraction of a degree *towards* Earth, and the deviation appears to match with its oppo, both the timing and the deviation itself. I need to confirm that the two are identical. That way, I can be certain there's a connection, and I'll know I'm not going to be wasting my time chasing shadows."

"And you want some results, when?"

"Yesterday would have been nice, but..."

"Nothing new there, then. Are the cops involved?"

"Not as far as I know."

"I need something with a bit of meat on the bones to run a real programme," Rob said. "Give me three hours. Four, tops. But I can't promise anything."

***

"Cross-Channel ferry services will be disrupted, possibly suspended for several days while the damage caused by last night's storms is assessed and shipping lanes cleared. The local authorities have requested help from the army to deal with the collapse of large sections of the famous white cliffs around Dover, where fragile calcium deposits were eroded away and resulted in several significant landslips."

Dave and Brenda listened in silence to the BBC news report, which was accompanied by live camera shots taken from the air. The helicopter was buffeted by strong winds, and the heavy rain was making the images grainy, but the damage was clearly visible. A flotilla of sturdy British tugs, workhorses of the Channel accustomed to every sort of foul weather imaginable, could be seen bobbing amongst countless small islands which hadn't been there the previous day, a ragged line of obstacles preventing any traffic from entering or leaving harbours along the south coast. Dover and Folkestone were the worst affected.

"The main problem is, we don't have dredging equipment suitable for working at the sort of depths we're dealing with," a spokesman for Dover Harbour explained for the interviewer.

"Dredging is a basic daily chore in every harbour. Most harbours are constructed around the natural depth of the river mouth, and we have records of how deep they are. Outside the harbour, however, the depth of the water increases sharply, and our cables and tools aren't designed to function in open sea.

"For the moment, all we can do is break up the deposits of cliff face, along with the additional soil and other detritus which has fallen around the coastline. Some of this may have to be removed by setting off controlled explosions and waiting for the rubble created to sink to a depth where it will no longer present a problem for shipping. Along the shoreline, we're liaising with REME and the Territorials to clear deposits at or above the high tide point on the beaches to get them carried away. For the time being, we're keeping this stored as ballast. It's possible we may use it to construct emergency dykes as protection against flooding if we experience more severe storms in the immediate future.

"Several farmers and smallholders have suffered losses of land and livestock. An emergency number they can contact will appear on-screen shortly, and the relevant local authorities will ensure that nobody will suffer financially. There have been no reports of any loss of human life, but we advise everyone to be extra careful if you must travel while these storms persist. If you have an elderly or infirm neighbour, look in and see if they are all right or if they need anything from the shops. Little things like this mean a lot."

"Hello, Dave."

"Eddie!" Dave muted the TV. "Good to hear your voice. We were getting worried!"

"Yeah, well at least I made it back to GB—have you seen the news? I swear that storm's followed me through Europe. I'm in Taunton now, but the ferry straight after mine was cancelled. You wouldn't believe the damage that's been done all along the south coast."

"There were some scary pictures on the national news this morning, so I've got a good idea. What're your plans now?"

"In view of the fact that I've no boss howling for me to get my ass back in the chair, I'm going to mosey 'round a few places along the way—you know, the kind of places you tell yourself, 'Must go there sometime,' but you never do. No timetable, and I'm reasonably flush for a while…"

"Don't let it get you down, Eddie."

Despite the barrage of light insults and banter which was normal between them, Dave was aware of Eddie's habit of concealing his emotions.

"Dave, I reckon I've earned a decent holiday, even if this isn't the way I imagined I'd be taking it. I promise, I won't do anything stupid. There's always someone who needs a number-cruncher, so I'm not bothered about job prospects whenever I'm ready to put my shoulder to the wheel again."

"That's the spirit, mate! Listen, have a pint o' scrumpy for me while you're there."

"Ahead of you on that one, mate. Had a very nice pint last night—handwritten label on the pump, brewed in the pub cellar, I was told."

"Jammy sod! You always seem to fall on your feet that way. Well, if you're passing Stonehenge, kill me a Druid or two on the way."

"Since I haven't decided on any travel plan, Stonehenge sounds as good as anywhere else to stop off."

* * *

"He seems to be in reasonable spirits," Brenda remarked after Dave had ended the call.

"Yeah. Eddie's a bit of a worrier, but he'll get by. He always does, somehow. I wish I was as laid-back as him." Dave reached for the TV remote and unmuted the sound. Reports were still coming in from the south coast, and the extent of the storm damage shocked him. The clean-up operations involving naval and other vessels of every conceivable size and shape seemed pitiful, futile efforts to deal with a task of truly Herculean proportions.

"Wonder if Joey's contact 'dahn sahf' managed to get any useful data for him?" Brenda mused, fascinated by the scenes of devastation on the small screen yet feeling that it was somehow wrong to take a vicarious thrill from this. What was that German term used to describe the emotion? *Schadenfreude*? A word that needed a complete sentence to translate it into English: 'taking pleasure from the misfortunes of others' was as close as she could come.

"He's probably too busy working on trying to predict where these storms will strike next."

Dave's practical comment brought her out of her guilt trip. She sighed. "You're probably right, and it looks as if they need all the help they can get right now."

CHAPTER NINE

"Did you have any gut feeling about what was off base in this data you sent me, Joey?"

"I just felt there was something about what I spotted in the orbit of the weather satellites—a one o'clock wobble? Not a very professional term, I'll grant you, but it'll do for now!"

"We can argue semantics another time, once we've got the problem licked."

"So we agree there *is* a problem, Rob? Has your new, expensive Christmas toy found something interesting?"

"That little hiccup in the orbit—as you thought, it's balanced on the opposite side. There's no measurable difference, and it needs more investigation. There has to be a reason behind it."

"Any possibility it could be down to fluctuations in the Earth's magnetic field or something of that nature? We're measuring these orbits in thousands of miles—millions, in fact. It wouldn't take much of a variation to create a noticeable difference at that distance from the planet's surface."

"Mmm. Not convinced. That could only be due to something or other further out—*beyond* the orbiting satellites if it was going to affect their flight path—and it would have to be both large enough and close enough to show up on every radar screen in the world."

""Yeah, and even a transient comet or something else passing through would have been spotted long ago."

"Agreed. So, logically, we have to look *inwards...*"

"Changes of some sort here at ground level?"

"Or maybe even deeper. We might just be into *your* special field, quakes and other subterra stresses and strains. We need to be—what's the hip phrase people use these days? That's it. We need to be thinking outside the box."

"My old Jesuit teacher called it lateral thinking, Rob, but I take your point. I've got lots of data, pretty much up to the minute. Thanks to the web, there's more than enough to dig into if I know what I'm looking for."

Joey glanced up at the BBC News Channel, which continued to run with the sound muted. Updates of the salvage work going on along the south coast were still the central news item.

"Rob, bear with me a moment. I'm thinking out loud."

"Go ahead."

"I'm looking at this one o'clock wobble again. It's not too far off what we use as magnetic north, and we already know that tends to vary a little from one year to another."

"Yeah. Every so often, we have to allow for it in map updates. Go on."

"If we're looking at global changes, one thing we *have* been able to measure, especially since we've all become more aware of the environment over the past decade, is the erosion and melting of both polar ice caps. Since ice is denser than water—"

"The volume of water which has melted down as a result of global warming *must* have had some effect. Joey, you're onto something here, I'm certain of it. How long will it take you to get some sort of corroborating evidence?"

"—and since about three-quarters of the planet's water, that should be easy enough."

This was the kind of data Joey was accustomed to handling, and he continued with confidence, "So even small variations in the alignment of the magnetic pole could have made a significant difference to the gravitational pull on the weather satellites."

"Joey, one more thing. The mass of the volume of water sloshin' about in the oceans—the runoff from the melting ice caps—*has* to make a difference to the rotation of the Earth itself."

Joey was feeling dry from the long, technical conversation and reached for a glass, fumbling as he concentrated on what Rob was suggesting. The glass tilted dangerously, but he managed not to spill it on the desk. "Rob, this might sound crazy but hear me out."

"Crazy sounds good right now, cobber."

"Don't go all Oz on me, mate. Listen to this."

He rolled the glass in his free hand and watched the water ripple along the inner surface. "Suppose the extra volume of water—which has the same *weight* as the ice it once was, but now occupies a greater *space*—"

"Or *mass*, due to being less dense," Rob corrected.

"My point exactly, and yes, you're right. Because we know that matter cannot be created or destroyed. It can only be exchanged."

"Your point, Joey?"

Joey swirled the glass once more and watched the contents move sluggishly before letting it settle. He was certain now that he was on to something.

"If the extra mass of the released water reaches a point at which it can be measured, it's going to start flowing. With the constant spin of the Earth's rotation, that's inevitable."

"So it's going to flow in a certain direction, and since it would be meaningless to talk of it flowing downhill, as a stream or river would *above* sea level, it has to be a lateral—sideways movement, right? And if it's aligned itself somewhere close to the axis of the magnetic pole…"

"It could have been going on for years and we wouldn't have noticed anything untoward until now."

"It might even provide us with the data we need to link the quakes and storms we've been recently monitoring all around the world. It might even point us in the right direction to finding a way of dealing with them. Rob, if we're right…"

"This could be the breakthrough we need. I'll get on to it from my end and leave you to do what you do best. Keep me in the loop, okay?"

"Another tag line I don't care for, but I'll certainly keep in touch. Must be about bedtime for you Aussies, but I've got the full day ahead of me."

Joey broke the connection without giving his friend the chance to reply with a final withering insult and turned back to his research notes. Somewhere in the data he already had available at the stroke of a key on his laptop, he was convinced there was an answer to be found. All he had to do was find it.

CHAPTER TEN

THE VAST, IMMEASURABLE gargantuans had opposed each other for countless millennia. Like ring-weary bare-knuckle fighters, they had circled and feinted, leant on each other, dealing fearsome blows occasionally before easing back to assess from a safe distance what damage their handiwork might have caused the opponent.

It was the perfect example of the irresistible force meeting an immovable object. The groans and grindings of the tectonic plates poised where they met beneath the deepest section of the South Pacific were like the snarling of the forwards in a surreal submarine rugby match played between rival teams of colossi, each eager to taste the other's blood on their teeth, or the battle cry of their more carefully armoured counterparts, the line of scrimmage players in a game of American Football.

It was inevitable; something had to give. Thanks to their sensitive aural faculties, the whales had long since given the area a wide berth. The creaks and crashings had developed far beyond being a mild inconvenience, becoming a loud, terrifying warning of impending doom. At such depths, the early warning systems deployed by nature were effectively muffled, silenced by the soundproofing blanket of the sea, and went unheard.

As the pressures built, the screams and agonies of the opposing armies of stone became louder and more prolonged until even the totally deaf and least sensitive living organisms capable of independent movement had taken the hint and followed the savant whales, moving north and south, far from the region of the seabed where the fault lowered across the scrimmage and locked shoulders. A breath, a microsecond of eye contact representing at least one full generation of human life expectancy, and the gigantic shoulders of the scrum prop heaved forwards.

The southern plate, emulating the superiority of the all-conquering rugby masters known as the New Zealand All Blacks, gained the upper hand and forced their opponents to give a begrudged half inch. The balance had shifted; the war was won. The stresses were resolved for at least the next few centuries, possibly even millennia. At a safe distance of several thousand miles, the whales would be the first to sense that, for them at least, the danger had passed, and they could begin their long, slow journey back to their preferred feeding grounds and the fresh supply of plankton which the underwater collision had made available.

The line of scrimmage stretched for thousands of miles, roughly northwest and southeast of the point at which the source of the battle was centred. A microscopic few molecules of water shimmered and took on a degree of the kinetic energy released by the battling giants, energy which they swiftly and efficiently transferred to their immediate neighbours. The ripple spread in a geometric progression, doubling and redoubling, growing to an unimaginably powerful mass, until finally, it developed momentum. Mere centimetres in height, it had a leading edge of over seven thousand miles, and as it began to move, drawing more water along with it, the height and the speed of the ripple increased as more and more water was drawn into motion. Unseen and unheard, the ripple became a current and grew from moment to moment, a powerful, uncontrolled force too deep to register on even the most sensitive meteorological instruments but now with a definite directionality.

A less powerful counterflow had been produced, the last gesture of defiance from the vanquished northern rugby giants, sending a weaker ripple back towards the Antipodes, a barely detectable current which would never achieve any dangerous proportions in the comparatively short distance it would cover before encountering landmasses upon which to cast itself. The northbound wave had time and open sea in its favour, with the potential to develop into a far more potent threat to anything it confronted before reaching the small fishing villages dotted along the eastern seaboard of Japan.

* * *

"These bloody flood tides would be a lot more use out west." Fire Chief Billy Randall muttered as he sculled another fortunate housetop refugee from the half-submerged property which had recently been a semi-detached house. An emergency centre had been established on the top seven floors of the local hospital. The access point was through a hole in the wall, which had once been a goods lift shaft, Jerry-rigged by the ingenuity of the local Queensland Territorials and transformed into a rough but serviceable dock.

While the east coast of Australia was being pounded by a combination of torrential rain and extreme high tides, bush fires were raging out of control in the thinly populated and difficult to reach outback.

"Billy, we're getting reports of flooding affecting the north coast—could be we've seen the worst of it here."

"Pray that you're right, Ged. It wouldn't surprise me if it's spreading rather than moving on."

Ged Hanlon had been on duty for the same thirty-six hours as his boss, and they had both long since passed the point of exhaustion. They were running on a mixture of adrenaline and caffeine. Relief crews were out of the question.

Every man with a full set of limbs had been conscripted into the rescue efforts already.

The latest casualty was a walking wounded and managed to disembark more or less unaided. Billy and Ged reversed from the makeshift jetty and turned to go in search of another flood victim.

Billy glanced at the dark, lowering storm clouds overhead. "The wind's still in the east, Ged. I reckon the floods in the north have to be a separate issue."

"Doesn't sound good. We could be fighting on two separate fronts."

"Three, Ged—don't forget the bush fires. If only there was a way to send 'em some of our excess. I could cope with the floods if we were free of the rain. It would be a godsend to them as well as us."

They were approaching another house where a survivor was standing waiting. As they got in close, Billy could see that the man was waving something over his head. When they pulled alongside, he discovered it was not a mobile phone but a small, working radio with enough battery power to transmit the news.

"Thanks for pickin' me up, mate. Have you heard the latest?"

Billy and Ged both shook their heads, and Billy said, "The only news we've had time for these last two days is what we've been making ourselves."

"But we've heard a prelim about more storms affecting the north shore," Ged added.

"There may be a link," the homeowner said. He seemed better dressed against the elements and much better prepared than anyone else Billy and Ged had come across so far. As well as a radio, he was the first victim to have a well-stuffed tucker bag at his feet, which he swung into the rescue craft before stepping down himself.

"I guess you need my name, for hospital records," he said, "and I'm grateful to see you, by the by. Paul McCann, on a rare town visit. Most of my worldly goods are in that swag bag."

"What keeps you out of town, Mr. McCann? You a farmer, maybe?"

"I draw maps. Do you have any idea how little of the Aussie outback has been properly surveyed at close quarters? Aerial photography is all very well, but there are some things you still have to get up close and personal to see."

"If you were thinking of heading back west..."

McCann shrugged. A tired half-grin flickered and was gone. "Not much point right now. Even if I could persuade a duster or a sky-jock to take me most of the way, I doubt I'd find a reliable mount for the last stage. And the news I've just heard wasn't from out west, anyway. The opposite, in fact."

He turned up the volume on his transistor. They heard the unmistakable received-pronunciation vowels of a seasoned BBC announcer's voice.

"Christchurch on the North Island of New Zealand was hit today by an earthquake which measured close to eight on the Richter scale. It struck at about five a.m. local time, and initial reports suggest that there was considerable structural damage but relatively few casualties. These figures, however, are expected to rise..."

Paul turned down the volume again and looked up at his rescuers. "It's not my specialist field, but you get to be a bit of a jack-of-all-trades when you spend most of the year on your own, living out of a bag. And basic geology tells me a shock wave that ripples off from a quake that size in New Zealand is likely to have some sort of aftershock effect down here before too many hours have passed. Here on the east coast—and also along the north coast—I'd say we were more or less right in the firing line."

"I'm no scientist, either," Billy admitted, "but it certainly fits the facts as they stand. Listen, Paul, I hate to ask, but we could really do with every able-bodied man we can muster to keep the effort going. Are you carrying an injury? Have you been out there long? I know I've got a cheek to ask, but you're just the type of assistance we could use."

"Happy to help, mate. As it happens, I wasn't out in the weather a great deal. I saw this bloody great wave heading my way, and I ran for cover. The door was open, but there was no car on the drive. I can only think the family who lived there must have scarpered already. I just had time to slam the door and get to the upper floor before the waters burst in. Lucky for me, I could get into the attic and through a skylight. I'd guess I was on the rooftop twenty minutes, tops, before you turned up. I reckon I'm fit for the game, but I suppose I should get checked out to be on the safe side— especially as I don't have what anyone'd call a fixed address most of the year. I'm not even sure when was the last time I had any medical treatment."

Paul swung his tucker bag over his shoulder as they pulled up to the hospital's temporary emergency entrance and stepped onto the jetty with a confident, easy balance.

"I'll tell them I've arranged to help out here with the reception of patients. That way, I should be reasonably easy for you to find."

* * *

When Billy and Ged returned from yet another search-and-rescue mission, Paul was at the jetty, having been duly processed and declared fit for work.

"News from New Zealand isn't good," was his first comment as he helped them negotiate an injured child onto a stretcher board. "There's a lot of structural damage, and the casualty list is growing rapidly."

"How's our own casualty tally going?" Billy asked.

"We're coping. The hospital's not reached capacity yet, and there's still room for admissions, but the doctors are working flat out."

"I've a mate in Christchurch," Ged suddenly broke in with a worried scowl.

"That's where it's hit hardest, I'm afraid," Paul said.

Ged grimaced. "I'd better give him a call, then. No point waiting until the morning."

"It *is* morning," Billy said, glancing at the sky. "Not that you'd know it from that lot up there."

CHAPTER ELEVEN

J OEY, I'M SORRY to get you out of bed..."
"What makes you think I've *been* to bed, Rob?"

"In that case, I'm twice as sorry. But there's more bad news—another major quake in Christchurch, New Zealand, about four, five hours ago. Richter eight, they say. Plenty of structural damage, I guess casualties are inevitable. At the time it happened, most people would have been in bed."

Joey cursed fluently for several minutes before he began to repeat himself and paused for breath.

"Rob, that might be our first hint of a clue. There's a region of the South Pacific where two major tectonic plates meet. We've known about them for years, and we've also monitored stresses in the area. What we need right now is a set of photos—it doesn't matter if they're stills or a video recording—from the weather satellites which were nearest the South Pacific region from, let's say two to eight hours *before* the first quake was felt in Christchurch. Can you get that data for me?"

"Might be a bit tricky if it's under NATO jurisdiction. They're going to have kittens about compromising security and need-to-know. I can only try, I suppose, but I don't have a lot of military clout."

"Call me if you get stonewalled by some officious uniformed jobsworth. I'll get a result. See if I don't."

Joey banged the phone back on its cradle and scribbled furiously on a notepad. Phones started ringing, but he managed to ignore all of them. The new data was from a direction he'd anticipated, and if his gut feeling was even close to what his figures suggested, the worst-case scenario was looming uncomfortably close.

He checked his figures for a third time, with growing unease. There were no errors that he could see in the data. With great reluctance, he took a metre rule to a wall chart showing the South Pacific and plotted the information on the map with a water-soluble whiteboard marker. There was no possible doubt. He felt physically sick as he crossed to a locked cabinet and fumbled for a specific key on his fob, one which he had hoped he would never have to use.

Amongst other documents and government publications, the cabinet contained a slim volume of emergency telephone numbers, which were updated regularly. The number he needed was close to the top of the very first page.

The telephone was answered in the middle of its first double trill. Joey kept calm by following a reporting procedure he'd had to study and agree to before he was granted security clearance. Without preamble or introduction, he spoke two words, a rank and a name, and waited to be connected.

"Brigadier Groth."

"Meteorologist Hart, reporting Region Eight. This is not an exercise. Condition Red, I repeat, Condition Red. Affected area South Pacific. Weather front currently approaching Japan from southeast. ETA 1100 Zulu. Latest available data suggests combined earthquake Richter scale nine or greater accompanied by tsunami, heading directly for Fukushima, northeast Japan. Sending confirmation details by email."

"Region Eight, message received, including email confirmation. Evacuation will be recommended immediately to reduce fatalities."

"Sir, I estimate two hours maximum to impact."

"Thank you, Doctor Hart. Evacuation is not our main concern. There is a major nuclear power plant on the coast at Fukushima, which is likely to become the ground zero of a potential disaster zone. All we can do is advise the Japanese authorities, hope they can perform a damage-limitation exercise and have troops available to offer assistance as soon as we are asked."

Joey was left listening to a dial tone: Brigadier Groth had ended the call without signing off. The dial tone stopped ten seconds later, and Joey realised it had to be a secure line that cut off automatically when not in use.

He had also signed the Official Secrets Act and knew what this entailed. He was alone in the observatory—a situation he'd taken some trouble to 'arrange' by encouraging all his staff to take time off, on the pretext of wanting to do some private research. It was an offence for him to speak to anyone other than his superior about the impending catastrophe, and technically, at least, the observatory itself was on lockdown. Nobody—especially not civilians—was allowed to enter or leave without a direct order from the Home Office or the Ministry of Defence.

At least there were clear instructions to be followed in an emergency, and the present circumstances seemed to fit that description. He crossed to a wall safe and opened it, extracting the combination by accessing the orders of the day.

Supplies of dried and preserved food were kept in store against the possibility of such an occasion, and there was direct access to an underground spring, which was supposed to guarantee pure, uncontaminated water. He had to trust this held true. He had no idea how long he would be isolated in the basement of the observatory, where standing orders insisted he should transfer daily operations until further notice. In truth, he had no idea of when, or even if, he might have someone else to work with, bounce ideas off. There was nothing in standing orders which covered the lifting of a lockdown. He consoled himself with the thought that the procedures had been formulated to combat a worst possible scenario of imminent disaster or warfare affecting the UK, rather than a climatic event on the opposite side of the globe. Surely, he could expect to have some assistants and staff allowed in within a day or two?

Still, he could use this rare opportunity of total, unlimited access to the impressive range of instruments and other 'big boys' toys' available at one of the UK's best-equipped research facilities. There was nobody to share the workload, true, but at the same time, there was nobody to pull the plug and tell him it would be a good idea to take a break, eat, get some sleep or any one of a hundred other pointless, boring hindrances to pure research. Without consciously planning his movements he discovered he was in the galley area, and grinned. One thing he knew for certain: NATO and the NAAFI could be depended on to provide an endless supply of proper, strong coffee. Anticipating the taste was enough to send a jolt of adrenaline coursing through his veins. The tiredness which had begun to affect him dropped off like a discarded cape as he prepared a brew of Lava Java.

* * *

With instantaneous internet news connections, the impending disaster sweeping towards Japan's east coast was common knowledge before it hit. Mercifully, warnings had reached a majority of shipping in time for tankers, cruise liners and other larger vessels to escape the direct line of the building wave.

The hundreds, possibly thousands, of fishermen who carved out a precarious existence in small fishing craft based in tiny villages along the coastline were generally too poor to afford radios. They had no warning that the tsunami was coming until it darkened the horizon, bearing down on them before they had an opportunity to save themselves.

The speed at which the waters gathered was terrifying, inexorable, but the earthquake outstripped it, striking the coastline at Fukushima, where the country's first nuclear power plant, now thirty years old, took a direct hit.

Though none of the buildings collapsed, the damage was devastating. The tsunami swept an estimated thirty kilometres inland before losing its momentum, carrying cars, lorries, railway locomotives and even ocean-going ships with it, depositing some of the latter on the roofs of tall office blocks. Many buildings had been constructed to survive earthquakes, which Japanese architects had known about and phlegmatically accepted as a fact of life when designing them. Nonetheless, it seemed amazing to the rest of the world that a surprisingly high number of buildings shown on TV news reports during rescue operations had remained more or less intact, a tribute to Japanese design, technology and workmanship.

"Although access to the centre of Fukushima is limited to the emergency services, we do know that at least some people living in the immediate vicinity of the nuclear plant received a warning of sorts, and many of them managed to flee before the earthquake and tsunami struck. There is no indication yet of how many reached relative safety on higher ground, but all employees at the nuclear plant were evacuated. Fires have started in at least two of the plant's four reactors, and emergency services are unable to get close enough to combat them. There will inevitably be some radiation leakage, but at the present time, there is no way of inspecting the extent of the damage, or of making any assessment of how serious the leakage might be."

CHAPTER TWELVE

D AMN."
Dave slung the phone back in its cradle.

Brenda came through from the kitchen with a mug of coffee.

"What's the matter, love?"

"I've been trying Joey Hart's number—thought I'd ask a pro if he's got any inside info on this freaky weather which they aren't telling us in the news, but all I get is a recorded message and a click to voicemail."

"Perhaps he went away for the weekend. It's still the holidays as far as lectures at Liverpool Uni are concerned. He might even have taken a long weekend away to do some research."

"I somehow got the impression he's a bit of a workaholic, though. I can't imagine him sagging off work. He doesn't strike me as a Monday-morning-blues type."

"I'll agree with you on that." Brenda nodded. "Have you tried his mobile number? I'm pretty sure I added it to my list at the pub that first night, just in case...yes. Here it is."

She punched the speed-dial button and handed the phone across the table.

Dave sat and waited while the phone rang. He was about to give up and pass it back when it was answered.

"Hello?" It *sounded* like Joey Hart, but there was something in his voice, an element of...tension? Perhaps even a hint of suspicion?

"I hope that's you, Joey. Dave here. Dave and Brenda Whelan?"

"Yes, Dave, it's me. Sorry if I sound a bit…I've been busy."

"That's all right. But I could only get your voicemail on the landline."

"I've been…away over the weekend. Working, unfortunately."

"I was wondering if you had any inside-track weather gen—anything the news media aren't telling us?"

"Dave, before we continue this conversation, I'm working on a government issue, and it's classified. I assume you know what that means."

"Enough to respect the fact that you may not be able to—"

"Answer all your questions. It's as well you had this number, but I'll have to ask you to let me call you in future."

"That's okay, Joey. Is there anything your conscience *will* allow you to say?"

"I can't even tell you where I am, and I don't know how long I'm going to be here. I can tell you I'm on my own and under a lockdown order. Nobody's allowed in *or* out until further notice."

"Understood. Can I assume it's connected with the weather conditions?"

"You can assume that much. I can't stop you doing that, but I can't comment."

"I won't put you on the spot, Joey. I'll leave it at that, but remember we're here if there's anything at all you need."

"I'll remember, Dave. I may need your help, and I'll keep in touch if I can."

Brenda looked at Dave with concern in her eyes. She clasped the phone as he handed it back to her.

"Cloak-and-dagger stuff? Joey Hart?"

"Uh-huh. Sometimes it's the quiet, unremarkable guy nobody notices who makes the most effective secret agent."

"Still, if he was serious about 'I may need your help', he can't be *too* far from home, can he?"

"Like a certain observatory we visited recently, you mean?"

Dave nodded. "My thoughts exactly. But we have to let *him* call us when he feels he can."

* * *

"Juliet Bravo. Weather update for Central Command."

"Brigadier Groth. Go ahead, Juliet Bravo."

"No significant seismic activity recorded at the sites in Cumbria and Cornwall. Initial assessment suggests the forces giving rise to these events, originating mid-France in the south and somewhere north of the Scottish Highlands, have effectively cancelled each other out. The accompanying storm from the south has also blown itself out. Wind direction veered west overnight and dispersed over open sea."

"Prognosis? Weather window for tomorrow?"

"Settled. No further storms expected. Mean temperatures will continue at around twenty-eight degrees Celsius, possibly more. No rain imminent."

"Received and understood, Juliet Bravo. Lockdown is now lifted. You can make arrangements for your staff to resume work, but until further notice, only those with highest security clearance are to enter the observatory. Please acknowledge."

"Acknowledged and understood, Command. Over."

"Over and out."

Joey replaced the phone receiver and rubbed a hand over his unshaven jaws. Coming down off his caffeine high, he realised how long it had been since he last slept, and he had to force himself to remain on his feet. If he sat down now, just as the tension which had kept him going was released, he'd keel over and sleep wherever he collapsed. He picked up an unfinished cup of cold coffee and wandered into the office to start ringing around the few staff with the required level of security clearance. Fortunately, the first-choice team he wanted all had this.

By midday, the Bidston Hill Observatory was running on a skeleton crew. Joey had managed to snatch some time from his desk and was back comparing and correlating notes which dealt with different aspects of current and expected weather conditions.

"We've had no further tremors in the past twenty-four hours," he reported. The relief in his voice was clear, especially after several days spent recording aftershocks that followed no discernible pattern.

"Noon temperature's up again," an assistant called. "Local, too. The station on Crosby beach has just posted thirty degrees."

"Same from Cardiff," another chimed in, quickly followed by readings of between 28°C and 29.5°C from other desks.

"One extreme to the other," Joey growled, frustrated both by the fickleness of the weather and the fact that there was no obvious course of action he could take to combat the extreme conditions nature seemed determined to inflict on humanity in general.

His heart felt heavy. He was convinced there was a pattern developing, something which ought to be blindingly obvious. Why couldn't he *see* it?

A flicker of bright colour on one of the TV monitors caught his eye, and he glanced upwards to discover it was an outside broadcast on the BBC News Channel. The scene was vaguely familiar; he looked more closely and read the text at the bottom of the screen. It was identified as Red Moss Nature Reserve, near Horwich. He pointed a remote towards the screen and toggled the mute button.

"...available fire tender in North Manchester has already been deployed. More have been requested from adjoining regions."

Thick, oily smoke hung over the moor. Joey made the connection at once.

"Peat. Dammit, that'll burn forever."

He reached for the nearest phone. It rang before he touched it.

"Juliet Bravo. Are you following the BBC News?"

"Yes, Sir. I was about to contact you. I assume you're referring to the fires?"

"Correct."

"We're dealing with a peat base, Sir. Putting it out is going to be difficult. It's generally deep-seated, perhaps ten metres or more when it's close to the surface. The main problem is likely to be reignition. You think you've put it out and move on to the next blaze, and..."

"Understood. Can we assume this is most likely due to the exceptionally hot and dry weather?"

"More than likely, Sir, unless it's due to deliberate fire-setting or arson?"

"That's always a possibility, of course. Unfortunately, we can't do a great deal about the morons and the antisocial elements of society."

"We have to go deep when we tackle each blaze, Sir, and each incident is going to need monitoring after the fire has—apparently—been extinguished."

"That's going to need extra manpower. Perhaps I should include a general call for the TA to support the Regulars and the Fire Brigade..."

"It would certainly help, Sir."

"Leave that with me. Keep me informed of any developments."

As before, Joey was left listening to the dial tone. Brigadier Groth didn't waste his breath on lengthy goodbyes.

* * *

"Got another hotspot, Joey."

"Go ahead, Brian. Cumbria again, I suppose?"

"Closer to home. The fire's breaking through again in Darwen and near Ormskirk—that's your neck of the woods, too."

"Not good. But I've just been told that the TA Reserves are being mobilised, manning the Green Goddess pumps. They'll be working in tandem with the regular Fire Service. I assume they'll try to put an experienced pro on each tender to help the volunteer crews."

"Anything that helps will be appreciated. Where'd you get that news?"

"Reliable source, but I've got to be cagey. It comes under need-to-know, and the fact that I've signed the Official Secrets Act..."

"Understood. But you know what? I'm not convinced this last rash of hotspots is all down to the weather. Some of these peat beds are incredibly deep. Is it possible there could be a subterranean cause? Strata damage, following the tremors we've been recording in the area?"

"Don't even go there. D'you really want me to lie awake worrying all night, every night?"

"Don't think for one minute I'm not scared shitless myself." Brian snorted. "But you boffins seem to get most of the funding and all the latest, cutest toys to play with. Can't you at least set up some sort of simulation programme, find out if it's possible, at least in theory?"

"Mmm, yeah, probably." Joey wasn't trying to discourage his colleague, but he was already scratching a few figures on a convenient scribble-pad and wasn't giving the conversation his full attention. "Listen, Brian, thanks for the update.

I'm already sketching the bones of a possible programme. I promise you'll be top of the list if I get a result from it."

As Joey worked through page after page of notes and calculations, Brian's reference to strata damage kept returning to distract his thought processes. Every time he factored in another set of variables relating to either of the known sources of disturbances north or south of Bidston Hill, the overall picture which was developing became bleaker. At last, he gathered his scattered notes into some semblance of order and tried to summarise the overall trends they suggested. He gazed at the TV monitors around the room, giving up-to-the-minute data from weather stations all over the world, and was suddenly distracted by a 'breaking news' item on the twenty-four-hour BBC News Channel.

"We're getting reports of two serious earthquakes affecting Lorca in southern Spain. Each measured about five on the Richter scale. They have caused extensive damage, and a significant number of fatalities can be expected."

Joey looked once more at the file relating to information from all points south. Even without using a calculator, the timing of this latest disaster spoke volumes to anyone who had even a minimal understanding of climate conditions. The alarm bells were ringing louder and more discordantly with every report he read.

If we assume the incident in Spain continues the pattern of sending shock waves north and south, as has happened with everything else we've been picking up, the first reports should be arriving soon.

As he thought this, a phone trilled. Instinctively, he reached out but hesitated as he realised it wasn't the landline; it was a Skype call coming through the computer. It had to be a personal call from a friend, but the number on the screen wasn't immediately familiar. Perhaps someone he didn't call very often? Or a relatively recent addition?

"Hello?"

"Joey, it's Dave. Dave and Brenda, remember? Is this a bad time for you?"

"No worse than any other, and I'm glad you called. I'm still under security restrictions, meaning I can't make outgoing calls. I'm not breaking any rules if I say it's been a very lonely weekend, and nothing's changed on *that* score. At least not yet. But I need a break, and I need someone to talk to—talk about anything which isn't climate or earthquake related, that is."

A thought struck him.

"As a matter of fact, I'm still under orders not to contact the outside world. However, *you* called *me*, and I need something to prevent me going round the bend."

"Is there anything practical we can do for you from this end? People we could contact? Anything you're short of or need?"

"I've told my superior the names of a few specialists whose brains I need to pick. He said he'll have to vet them first, but I don't think that's going to be a problem. For the moment, if we can agree that you phone me on this number at the same time each day—nine o'clock, for example—I can have some outside contact without breaking the rules by making a call myself. Is that okay by you?"

"Fine, Joey. Hang on a moment."

Joey could hear a swift, muffled discussion and had to assume Brenda was telling Dave something.

Dave came back on the line. "A friend of ours who had his hols in the South of France ruined by the weather has been in touch. He's back in England, and he decided to use the rest of his vacation time to do a whistle-stop drive home, stopping wherever he happens to be. He says he's being dogged by the weather. He hasn't had a single dry day yet, and he's feeling a bit picked on, if you know what I mean."

"Sounds like he's been really unlucky, but it can only be coincidence. I never heard of anyone being a bad-weather magnet. Did he say how far he's got, or where he's been so far?"

"He said he went from Dover west to Cornwall, and from there to Stonehenge and across into South Wales. He was literally about to toss a coin to decide whether to drive through central Wales or make for Aberystwyth and drive along the coast."

There was nothing in Dave's casual, chatty tone to suggest any hidden agenda or hints of anything with a possible connection to the alarming scenario Joey could see developing all around him. Nonetheless, he felt as if a mule had planted a vicious double heel drop in his stomach.

"Dave. Did you say your friend is still somewhere in South Wales? Can you reach him before he moves off?"

"Probably, if I do it straight away."

"Give him a bell while I check a few figures. It might sound crazy, but he just might be our man on the spot and can do me an enormous favour."

Joey's fingers danced over the computer keyboard, rearranging data. The results pointed to an entirely different prognosis.

The signs were there. Across the country, earth tremors and unseasonal weather at both ends of the scale were being reported and recorded, with strong tides and powerful currents threatening to launch a further assault on the ravaged coastline of Great Britain. Worryingly, the shoreline, especially along most of the south coast, was already showing signs of weakening and crumbling away into the surrounding, relentless sea.

"Still there, Dave?"

"Yeah. Brenda's got him on her mobile. He's a good egg. If there's anything he can do to help, he can be trusted to do it."

"Right. This might sound a bit off the wall, but hear me out. Ask him to take the inland route and stay close to the mountain range. He should keep an eye out for any signs of structural or other damage—fallen trees, maybe evidence of recent shale falls, earth movements, drystone walls which have had a couple of stones dislodged. Tell him I'm looking for signs of any ripple effect heading this way from an earthquake reported in Spain a couple of hours ago. If we can pinpoint time and distance, we can make an educated guess at where and when we might have a situation to deal with."

A few moments passed while Dave relayed this request through Brenda.

"Message passed on, Joey. He wants to know if there's any danger of roads crumbling or rockfall blocking his route?"

"I've got to be honest, Dave. I can't promise anything, but we're talking about the effects of a quake measuring Richter five about two hours ago and an epicentre which is a couple of thou' miles to the south. All I can say is, if it behaves in a similar fashion to other incidents over the past few weeks, the power of the tremor should have tapered off by the time it gets this far—if it's coming our way at all. I can't even confirm that, as yet, unless I get some data which suggests it's heading our way."

"He says that's good enough for him. He's not one for motorway driving at the best of times, so tootling along the lesser roads through mid-Wales suits him down to the ground. He's on his way as we speak."

CHAPTER THIRTEEN

E DDIE TOOK HIS AA book from the glove compartment and thumbed through the map pages. He wasn't particularly familiar with the road network in South Wales and decided it would be a good idea to use a few minutes in preparation before heading north. He'd escaped the monotony of the M4 at Newport; with any luck, he could actually relax and enjoy the rest of the drive. He'd filled the tank and his reserve can after leaving the motorway, avoiding the insane pump prices demanded of captive commuters at motorway services, and bought a sensible selection of snacks and drinks to graze on.

He picked up his mobile and punched Dave's number.

"Hi, mate. Listen, just in case the brown stuff hits the whirly bits, I thought it'd be a good idea if someone knows what route I'm using." ... "No, I'll be careful, but accidents can happen." ... "Okay, here's the plan. I'll head north from here through Pontypool and Abergavenny..."

He looked at the notes he'd made and reeled off the towns along the route, as well as the numbers of the main roads he intended to use. Eddie was a meticulous planner; if there was any possibility he might run into unexpected problems along the way—minor inconveniences such as earthquakes and floods, for example—then he wanted to cover *all* the bases, thank you very much.

"...and then I'll head towards Chester."

He paused, not really for breath, though he suddenly realised he'd been gabbling at a high rate of knots, but more to indicate he'd finished giving his intended itinerary and to allow Dave the opportunity to scribble down anything he needed to record.

"I'll avoid the motorway as far as I can, then over Frodsham and the Runcorn Bridge. I imagine I'll have to use the motorway from there to Liverpool, but I'll keep my eyes open for any signs. That's really why I'm avoiding the motorway."

"Fair enough. But keep in touch. As journeys go, it doesn't sound too bad."

"I'd say three, four hours under normal driving conditions, but you never know. Tell you what, I'll stop and call you once an hour. It's eight-thirty now—I'll call you at nine-thirty. Any excuse to stop for a coffee break."

Not for the first time, Eddie marvelled at the arrow-straight precision of the approach road the occupying Romans had constructed to reach the fortress they had built at Deva, modern-day Chester. It was a far more enjoyable driving experience than the sometimes crowded and invariably boring, monotonous rat race along the northbound M6. He wondered why more people didn't choose other routes but had to concede that the answer was most likely pressure of time. Business meetings, in-house training, web seminars— when he thought about it, he decided that getting the bullet might not be the worst thing that could have happened to him. For the first time in years, he had no pressure ruling his day-to-day routines.

It wanted but a few minutes to ten-thirty as he crossed the ancient iron girder bridge over the River Dee, which he had always recognised as the Wales-England border even if there were no customs officers or passport control to confirm one had entered and exited one of the few remaining bilingual regions of the UK.

Coming to the last section of the bridge, Eddie slowed, aware of the time and his promise to remain in touch.

He decided to pull over at the car park close to the bridge, a spot which provided tourists with an excellent opportunity to photograph the Welsh mountains south and west of sthe river.

As he changed down a gear and indicated left, he felt an odd rumble under his wheels, the sort of judder that comes from crossing a cattle grid a shade too fast for comfort. He glanced automatically in his mirrors, but there was nothing in any of them. Both wing mirrors and the rear-view showed a totally empty road: no other vehicles and no sign of a cattle grid or similar traffic-calming measures. Perhaps he'd hit a dead rabbit or something of that nature. He completed his parking manoeuvre, killed the engine and plucked his mobile from the dashboard charger before getting out to stretch his legs and call Dave. First, though, he checked the car for any signs of a collision with an animal.

Nada. Not so much as a chip of paint or a scratch on either front wing.

Something made him look up and gaze across the river, but rather than being drawn to the majestic sight of the Welsh hills, half-shrouded in mist, his attention was redirected to the middle distance, focusing on the river itself.

This far north, he was back on familiar ground. He'd driven this route many times and it was one of his regular coffee stops if he was in no particular hurry. The River Dee was tidal at this point, and he enjoyed observing the conflicting eddies.

The surge of brackish water carried by the incoming tide was slightly darker than the freshwater of the river's flow. The two forces cancelled each other out immediately downstream of the bridge, where a long, ragged oxbow of a bend had been gradually eroded to form a wide, shallow basin, the surface of which was pocked with random, drifting eddies, some circling clockwise, others in a contrary direction. There was no discernible pattern or logic, suggesting this stretch of river was as close as makes no difference to dead water.

Pouring a coffee from his flask, Eddie strolled across to the edge of the parking area to get a closer look at the ambivalent state of the swirling currents. As he gazed across the river, he felt the faintest tingle in the soles of his feet, no doubt the circulation returning to his legs. Concentric rings appeared on the surface of his coffee, which he'd placed on the security barrier. Eddie frowned, but as he did, something on the edge of his vision demanded his undivided attention.

Beyond the cup but still in the close-to-middle distance, a wavering line of foam was building, yet it moved neither upstream nor down, but from south to north, *across* the river, in defiance of both the natural downhill flow *and* the twice-daily reverse effect imposed by incoming tides. The coffee in his cup was suddenly in danger of spilling over the rim, and the tingling in his feet became more pronounced. A vague, muted rumble caught his ear, and he realised that he wasn't suffering pins and needles at all.

CHAPTER FOURTEEN

A NYTHING IN THE news?" Eddie asked.
Dave shook his head. "Not in the papers, and it's too early for the TV news. I've been listening to local radio—BBC Merseyside—but you've probably been tuned to the same station, since you called from the Welsh border?"

"Sure thing. How about your man at Bidston Hill? I gather he's barred from making outside calls, but have you tried to contact him?"

Dave and Brenda exchanged a glance, which Eddie felt obliged not to notice.

"We didn't want to...abuse his willingness to bend the rules by calling him without a very good reason. He's not exactly an old mate or someone who grew up in the next street. We only met a couple of weeks ago. And I'm not keen to dump him in hot water with the powers-that-be, whoever it is he has to make his reports to. Still, we don't seem to have a lot of options."

Dave punched a shortcut button on his mobile.

"Hello?" ... "Yes. I don't want to compromise your security regs, so I'll be brief. The Prodigal has returned from foreign fields. He's driven up from the south coast in stages—not on the motorway network—and he's got an update, something you might be able to verify with your electronic gizmos."

"Assuming I can get some readings from available equipment here and elsewhere, I can present this to...my superior as if it's something I've monitored myself. If I admit I got the info from an outside source, he'll have my ass and yours. In the circumstances, I can't give you credit for—"

"Big deal!" Dave interrupted. "We're all adults here. Personally, I don't give a monkey's. If this is helpful, and relevant, it could be vital. We still don't know exactly what's happening, and we're looking for a pattern before we can begin to plan for what we might have to deal with next. Hell, we can't even begin to guess the where or when, yet."

"Calm down, calm down."

The popular comedian's tag line delivered in a deliberately over-the-top fake Scouse accent by Joey Hart had the instant and intended effect of easing the tension which was creeping into the illicit phone call. The meteorologist continued in a more normal speaking voice.

"Leave this with me. The military guy who's my only *official* link with the outside world is going to have to cut me some slack. I can't continue to function efficiently without some more staff. I'll find a way of persuading him to let you become involved, somehow. He owes me that much."

* * *

"...and although the data I have from my instruments and various listening posts around the mainland is good, it's not enough. I need more staff back inside the observatory, and I need up-to-date information from real people who witness events as they're happening. As an experienced military man, I'm sure you can appreciate that, Brigadier."

"Mmm. Why do I get the distinct impression you have some specific people on a *very* short list in mind?"

"I wouldn't waste your time by asking if I didn't have a few possibilities, and the people I have in mind aren't likely to be security risks."

"Permission granted for you to liaise with eyewitnesses. I'll consider your request for more staff, Doctor Hart. If the other people involved aren't department employees, that might complicate things, but if you can vouch for them personally, I may be able to arrange limited security clearance."

Joey held in his sigh of relief. He'd known it wouldn't be easy to persuade the brigadier, but in the circumstances, this felt like a major victory. Thanking Brigadier Groth profusely, he kept the remainder of the call as brief as possible. The last thing he wanted at this point was for his superior to have second thoughts.

* * *

"Dave, I know I said I wouldn't *make* a call in case it was traced, but I've had a result—sort of—and I don't think we'll be having security issues from now on. And you can tell your friend his input was very useful as well as timely. Once I knew what I was looking for, I managed to follow the shock wave, small though it was, by plotting it against the timeline.

"It looks as if the brigadier—I still can't tell you his name, sorry—it looks as if he's going to sanction limited security clearance for a few people on my personal guarantee. You're clear to be included as a listening post reporting to me here, but I'll have to make it official. Leave that with me. Listen, I've got a couple of red lights flashing. I'm going to have to call you back."

Joey signed off as abruptly as Brigadier Groth, leaving Dave listening to the open line tone.

Dave looked at the handset in disbelief. Brenda caught the expression on his face and laughed.

"Takes something special to leave *you* lost for words."

"It must have been urgent. Joey's usually one of the most courteous blokes."

* * *

Joey was once again holding the fort on his own and fighting a losing battle. The bank of lights showing 'call waiting' was growing longer. More than half of them had now changed from amber to red as the callers were kept on hold beyond five minutes.

His Skype pinged as he ended a call from an observation point in New York.

"Brigadier! You don't know how glad I am you called."

"Doctor Hart, I realised you had to be snowed under. I've been trying the switchboard for almost half an hour. I'm authorising immediate extra staff for you. They should arrive imminently. For security purposes, you'll have to vet each arrival and let them in. The last thing we need right now is public panic based on guesswork and rumours."

"Brigadier, I'm getting reports from a number of observers, which suggest there may be a link between *some* of the weather phenomena we're currently experiencing. I'm not necessarily limiting this to UK weather patterns either, Sir. I still need some cross-checks to confirm it, but there's a pattern developing. I've plotted a timeline of incidents. I believe the unseasonal weather in the UK can be traced to two separate incidents."

Joey paused and took a deep breath. Somehow, he knew he was only going to get one chance to convince Brigadier Groth to listen to his theory. Even with the data he had in front of him, it seemed far-fetched and preposterous as he attempted to organise his thoughts coherently. It was going to sound even more insane when he dared speak it aloud, but there was no way around it.

"Doctor Hart? Are we still connected?"

"Sorry, Brigadier. I was collecting my thoughts, but I must warn you, this is going to sound completely unlikely. I'm starting from some volcanic activity in Iceland last week, spreading south to affect the UK, combined with the weaker and more distant tremor which started from southern Spain and rippled north a few days later."

Joey gained more confidence as he spoke, thanks to the facts he was able to read off the collection of documents he had before him. Perhaps the brigadier was aware of this, as he allowed the doctor to make his case without interruption.

"How reliable is your data?" Groth's question was neutral. His voice gave no clue of what his personal opinion might be, either for or against.

"The readings from Iceland are very detailed. What we have from Spain and all points south is more recent, but the event itself was much weaker and difficult to measure, so the results aren't as conclusive. It was also further away, and the recording equipment available isn't as sensitive. But the pattern is similar."

"Can you get corroboration from any other sources?"

"Working on it, Sir. I have global contacts in other weather stations who report here regularly, and I believe there's a bigger picture developing. I have a colleague in Australia whose work I can vouch for. He contacted me *before* any of our current problems kicked off. He's convinced there's a common causality for the earthquakes in New Zealand, the floods and fires in Australia, and the tsunami which destroyed the nuclear plant in Japan. He thinks they're all related to the stresses of tectonic plates deep beneath the oceans in the Southern Hemisphere."

In a few short sentences, he described the scenario which had been explained to him, the unthinkable 'immovable object/irresistible force' being fought in a silent no-man's-land, and the potentially catastrophic consequences of one gaining a few millimetres of advantage over the other.

"...but because it takes so long—measured in human lifetimes—for the stresses in these rock strata to develop, we have no personal experience of such events to guide us. In geological terms, it's not long since the last major climate change, which wiped out the dinosaurs almost overnight."

"Doctor Hart, let's assume the statistics you're quoting are accurate. Do you or your colleagues have any suggestions for a solution?"

"I can't answer for any of my contacts around the world. I'm still on my own here, and I haven't had time to think that far ahead, yet. But the priority has to be to develop a plan of action, assume a worst-case scenario and seek some effective countermeasures. If there is indeed a direct connection between the events you're describing, we're facing something far more serious than a temporary shift in weather patterns across the UK."

"My apologies for leaving you isolated for so long, Doctor. I'm prepared to give you a free hand to put together a team—subject to a satisfactory security vetting, of course—and I need some answers ASAP. Can I assume you have a shortlist of people you want on board?"

"Yes, Sir."

Joey hoped he'd managed to keep his elation out of his voice. This was the opportunity he'd barely dared hope for, the chance to bring Dave, Brenda and Errol into the picture without awkward questions being asked.

"I'll need your list at the first opportunity. Start thinking about possible solutions."

Joey glanced at a monitor screen showing CCTV of the main entrance to the observatory. Two or three people were approaching. The cavalry was about to arrive. He took a short breath to relay this information to the brigadier, but as usual, Groth had ended the call without a formal sign-off and Joey was left staring at a 'call ended' message. He shrugged and trudged off to welcome the first of his returning staff, grateful for the prospect of human company, which he missed far more than the assistance he desperately needed. As he greeted each staff member by name and checked them off on the security list, he was suddenly aware of how long it had been since he last had the opportunity to sleep. It would be a while yet before he could allow someone else to oversee operations, but at least he could now look forward to crashing for a few hours.

CHAPTER FIFTEEN

H OW'S TRICKS, JOEY?"
"Frantic, Rob. You managed to drink Oz dry yet?"

"Keep trying, but you know what it's like. Constant interruptions."

"Okay, you got some stats for me?"

"Most of what you asked for. Took me nearly all the night though, mate. You owe me for this, big time."

Joey glanced automatically at the wall clock, which confirmed the time in Australia was eight a.m.

"I managed a couple of hours FOB this afternoon, but I had a bit of a session before that, so I really appreciate your input. The data I'm looking for could be crucial for both of us. What I need most of all is to put together a timeline covering multiple weather incidents in different parts of the world. My gut instincts tell me there's a connection between them we haven't yet made, but if we can link 'em up, we might be some way to working out a plan of action—that's as much as I can tell you. I'm involved in something with a classified tag I didn't even know existed."

"Sending the email as we speak...okay?"

"Got it, Rob. How are you coping with the floods?"

"The waters are going down. We can start mopping-up ops soon—maybe even today. The hospitals are coping, and I've not heard of any fatalities yet."

"That's a plus in itself. How about New Zealand? Some of my friends have relatives in Christchurch. They haven't been able to get in touch yet."

"The earthquakes have caused a lot of damage, but once again, there doesn't seem to have been any loss of life. Our local fire chief says he's come across a bushranger who also has relatives in New Zealand. He's been in touch with them, and the damage is substantial but not life-threatening."

"I'm more interested in the wider picture, Rob. I'm looking at the timeline of the tsunami which struck Japan just after the NZ quakes. About thirty hours later, by the looks of it?"

"Yeah, that's about right. Is the timing significant?"

"Could be the most important single factor. I'm starting to get an overall picture, and I'm not happy with what I see developing. I need more corroboration from other global locations before I take it to...my superiors because they're going to ask me for suggestions."

"Joey, don't bullshit me. We've known each other too long for that. I accept that you're working on something hush-hush, but you've already said you're collating data worldwide, so it doesn't take too much imagination. This is serious, my friend. Very serious, *n'est-ce pas?*"

"Rob, I've said too much already. I have to speak to someone in authority before I say another word. Do you have any sort of security vetting in Oz? Have you personally ever been involved in any military projects? If they run a check, would they find any dusty ol' skeletons in the cupboard? And would you be interested in joining the team, maybe running one of your own if he's satisfied with your security clearance?"

"If that happens, I'll need to have some say on the make-up of the team."

"I'm sure that can be arranged, Rob."

* * *

"Brigadier, the data I've received so far from colleagues at other weather stations around the world is giving me cause for concern. The overall picture is changing, and I'm not talking about minor, temporary or seasonal fluctuations in weather patterns or a random spike in climatic differences."

"Don't dress it up in fancy language, Doctor. We'll be here all night if you do that. Keep it short and simple and we may have time to plan countermeasures."

"Point taken, Sir."

Joey paused to collect his handwritten notes and decide how to put across what he felt to be the main points in non-technical terms.

"Set on a timeline of events, everything to date has followed from one of two random points of origin that occurred within a few days of each other. One was the eruption of the volcano at Eyjafjallajökull in Iceland."

"And the second?"

"At the moment, I can't give an exact time and date on this, but I'm working on it. The second event was just before the earthquakes hit New Zealand, some thousand miles or more to the northwest and several thousand feet *down*.

"We've known for a long time about the natural fault on the bed of the Pacific where two tectonic plates bump and grind against each other.

"In simple terms, Brigadier, what we believe has happened is that these two unimaginable masses of bedrock have surpassed a stress level that has been building for thousands of years, and one of them has slipped over or under the other, easing the pressure build-up and setting in motion a ripple of energy, which has travelled for the most part southeast— think anticlockwise if that helps—until it reached the west coast of New Zealand."

"So, this ripple you talk about. Is it possible that over the distance involved, it could grow and become more powerful?"

"Exactly, Brigadier. I won't go into the scientific formulae, but in a nutshell, that's what I think has happened."

"You mentioned a possible tie-in with Japan. In the opposite direction?"

"Basic physics, Sir. Did you ever hear 'To every action there is—'"

"An equal and opposite reaction," Groth interrupted. "Yes, as it happens, I *do* remember that one. You're telling me that's what you think happened here? That the earthquakes in New Zealand and the tsunami in Japan have a common origin?"

"That's one *possible* interpretation of the facts available at the moment, Sir. Of course, it might not be the only one. In truth, it might not even be the *right* one, but it's all I have to offer until I find something to back it up."

"I'm not clear on how this…event, as you call it, can affect two countries in totally opposite directions."

"Sir, it's precisely *because* they're in opposite directions the two countries were both affected. The ripple heading northeast from the site of the underground shift was the *reaction*, if you like, and for that reason, it was significantly weaker than the one which hit New Zealand and then Australia, I'd guess, though I haven't done my homework on that yet."

"It was strong enough to destroy their nuclear plants. We'll be dealing with the aftermath for the foreseeable future, all the same." Groth grunted, seemingly more to himself than to Joey. After the briefest of pauses, he continued. "The eruption at this unpronounceable place in Iceland. When it happened, we were all concerned with the effects it would have on the skies above, the potential for pollution problems—whether it would cause non-nuclear fallout problems with ash on crops, that sort of thing. Are you telling me the eruption would have set up similar underground shock waves at the same time, heading south to affect the UK?"

"Unfortunately, yes, Brigadier. Weaker, of course, but still following the same basic laws of physics and measurable on our instruments."

The brigadier seemed to mull this over but only for a few seconds. Next time he spoke, there was a much more authoritative, steely edge to his voice.

"I need your suggestions for an action plan, based on how to tackle the worst-case scenario if everything goes pear-shaped. For the moment, you can forget the logistics of evacuating people from affected areas or other practical matters. There are contingency plans available that could always be adapted to suit a different non-military scenario. I'm far more interested in anything you scientists can come up with to counter the physical, geological problems that lie behind the problem we have to tackle."

"How soon can you vet the list of people I want on my team? Because if we're talking about action plans, I'm going to need all the help I can get."

"Doctor Hart, I'm prepared to go out on a limb on this one if it will save us some time. I trust your judgement. If you're prepared to vouch for each and every member of your team, you can call in the expert help you feel you need."

"Brigadier, that's much appreciated. I've already sent my list."

"Yes, I've seen it. A small, balanced group. People with specialist knowledge. I don't foresee any problems with background checks."

"We won't let you down, Sir. I'll get the team together. We'll give it our best shot."

For once, Joey just might have beaten Groth to the punch, as he signed off the landline call while hitting the call button on Skype.

"Dave? Pack a bag, I need your input on my team."

CHAPTER SIXTEEN

P ETE'S BEEN ON Skype while you were out, Dave." Brenda
intercepted her husband as he came through the door.
"He said they had a few bits and pieces of crockery smashed
but otherwise no real damage where they live. The quake
centred on the capital, about three hundred miles from
where they live."

"Remind me to contact him for an eyewitness report
when we get to Bidston Hill. I'm sure Joey will be able to
find a use for a first-hand account. Have you got everything
we might need for an extended stay? I can't say how long
we're going to be away, sweetheart."

Brenda brushed back her hair. "Joey said we needn't
think of any food, drinks or anything of that nature. The
building was equipped as an emergency HQ by the MOD,
years ago. Several changes of clothes, I reckon, and we
should probably stop somewhere and pick up all the most
recent newspapers, although even news is something we can
get from the internet."

The distinct sound of tyres on gravel announced a visitor.
Dave opened the door as Errol was about to knock. He was
toting a paper bag that threatened to burst at the seams.

"Anyone thirsty?" he drawled, tipping his hat to Brenda
in the old-fashioned style of a cartoon Southern gen'leman.

"Perfect timing," Dave answered with an equally
deliberate, over-the-top grand bow of welcome. Brenda was
already hunting for glasses.

"You're off somewhere, I see. Anywhere nice?"

Caught off guard, Dave couldn't help blushing. They hadn't known each other long.

"I don't want to lie to you, Errol, but I'm not sure how much I can say. You know Joey Hart, from the climate talks at the pub. He's asked us to help him out with something, and it's classified."

"Security measures were invented in the US, y'know. No need to apologise." He grinned as he peeled three cans from the bag and popped them open.

"Still, it might make me change my planned script. I had intended to say goodbye or something similar. We've finished our engagement in Southport and are going our separate ways for a few months—some of the guys are doing some solo recording.

"Fact is, I've the sum of my worldly goods—or the only things that *matter*—on the back seat o' my car, 'long with my horn. I'm at a loose end right now for the first time in years, and if Doctor Hart's needs a gofer or an errand boy, I'd be dee-lighted to oblige."

"I'll need to make a call."

The relief in Joey's voice when Dave made the call was unmistakable. "If you'll vouch for him, I don't have a problem with that. In fact, my immediate boss has given me carte blanche to pick a team, and I recall Errol talked a lot of sense that evening in the Ship. He's clearly an educated gent, and he can probably help us understand the American viewpoint. This is no longer a UK problem, Dave. It's going global. I'll fill you in when you get here."

* * *

"There's more gen arriving by the minute, but I'm getting the overall picture from a more accurate plotting of the timeline."

Joey turned to the whiteboard that covered most of one wall in the lab.

"Chronologically, the first event in the chain was the volcano in Iceland at the beginning of October last year."

"I remember that all the experts were more concerned with the ash, and the possibility it might cause plane crashes?" Brenda queried.

Joey nodded. "That's right. And the underground rumblings were deep. They spread slowly and in several different directions. They didn't affect any heavily populated regions and caused little damage, so they were recorded by some stations, but others were quite possibly missed if they were in remote, inaccessible areas.

"After a week or so, when the ash had settled and we *hadn't* seen planes fall out of the skies or the seas run red, everyone relaxed and there seemed little point in any further investigation of the rumbles and tremors we'd logged. The next significant data we have is the flooding in Oz, immediately followed by the earthquakes in New Zealand, early December. As far as we can tell, there was no connection whatsoever with the volcano in Iceland."

"*Ey-ya-fyatla-yuh-kutl.* Not an easy name, but I *think* that's how it's pronounced," Errol offered.

"We'd better get used to how it rolls off the tongue," Joey said wryly. "I've a feeling we'll be using it quite a lot in our planning sessions."

"Why d'you say that?" Brenda asked, sensing something in Joey's voice that Dave and Errol had missed.

"This one's hot off the presses," Joey said, holding up an almost transparent flimsy. It took Dave a couple of seconds to recognise it for what it was.

"My God. Do people still *use* faxes?"

"Don't knock it, Dave. Some of my colleagues in the boondocks can't get a good wi-fi signal. They use landline and fax—I've heard rumours that some outlying stations in Africa still use carrier pigeons, but that's probably an exaggeration."

"Hmm. Okay. Now, what's so vital about that piece of news you're holding?"

"Simply this. Within the last twenty-four hours, there's been more volcanic action on Iceland. Different location, but the name—Grimsvötn—is easier to pronounce."

"Too far away to show any ripple effect in the UK, Joey?"

"Unlikely, at this distance. Even a strong quake hasn't had time to show aftereffects yet. Why d'you ask, Dave?"

Dave had been watching the twenty-four-hour BBC screen as a filler activity while Joey was concentrating on the scientific data rolling in from a variety of sources.

"There's a news item from Southport, which isn't a million miles away."

He turned up the volume for the benefit of the whole group. The person being interviewed was a middle-aged female who appeared to be spokesperson for a local conservation group.

"...and we're concerned about the tremors which were felt in and around Southport last night. The whole process of fracking to release shale gas from the rock must weaken the coastline and will inevitably destroy the habitat and environment for a number of endangered species, not to mention the possibility of causing earthquakes and destruction of property."

"Pure garbage," Errol growled with a ferocity that surprised everyone. His usual, laid-back Southern drawl and easy slouch had disappeared. He quivered with repressed emotion as he strode to the TV monitor at the end of the room.

"They haven't a clue what they're talking about." He pointed an accusing finger at the screen.

"How can you be so certain?" Joey demanded.

Errol turned his back on the TV and inhaled deeply, taking a few moments to compose himself before he addressed his friends in a calmer manner.

"I told you I was able to indulge myself in my music because I'm lucky enough to come from old money. My family was in the right place at the right time, and they made their money from oil.

"But that doesn't mean I've lived an idle life. My father insisted I learn the ropes, something of the ins and outs of the oil business. I served my time for two years as a roughneck on the rigs in Arkansas and worked my way up purely on merit. I even worked under an assumed name to avoid any..." He faltered a moment, seeking the best word.

"Any special favours?" Brenda suggested. Errol flashed her a grateful glance.

"I love my father dearly," he said with a sombre note in his voice, "but one day, I'll inherit his chair in the boardroom, and I'll make a better fist of it if I understand how the industry works. So I can tell you now, fracking, as they call it, is a relatively simple procedure. The technique has been used safely all over the world forever—or so it seems—and has never caused any problems for the environment. This news item is nothing more than sensationalist crap, deliberate scaremongering."

"How does the process work, then?" Dave asked.

Errol acknowledged the question, grabbed a marker pen and swiftly sketched a diagram on the whiteboard.

"The depth of the drilling isn't important, except for the numbers involved. The deeper you go, the higher the pressure, but that's not the point. In simple layman's terms, a mix of chemicals is pumped down to the stratum being explored and forced into the rock under pressure. Other liquids are then pumped behind it, and the pressure is kept in place while the rock dissolves away.

"When the pressure is released, the paydirt—oil or gas—starts flowing back to the surface and is given a helping hand by mechanical pumps. Inevitably, there's a limited amount of settling but never enough to cause any serious amount of subsidence or other environmental problems. I repeat. Fracturing is an essential and inherently safe process. It has never been the cause of any significant environmental damage."

Errol looked around the room. The delivery of a semi-technical lecture had given him the chance to cool down, and he was no longer angry and agitated. "Any questions?"

There were none. Joey looked up from the notes he'd been making while Errol was talking.

"My figures seem to bear out what you've explained to us—and explained very well, I should add. I don't pretend any expertise in engineering, but simple maths is something I *can* follow, and I'm happy to say the numbers all add up."

He was about to carry on but was cut short by Brenda's mobile. She glanced at the screen.

"Dave, it's your brother."

"Ringing from New Zealand?" With a puzzled frown, Dave fished out his own mobile.

"You need to switch those off," Joey cautioned. "They interfere with the equipment."

Dave grimaced apologetically and long-pressed the power button. "Sorry, Joey. But my brother wouldn't call unless it was urgent."

"Make it a quick one."

Dave took the phone from Brenda. "Pete?" ... "Yeah, okay, shoot."

After a few moments, Dave shook his head.

"One moment, Pete. There are others present who'll understand your technobabble better than me. I'm going to—"

"Get him to call back on this number." Joey scribbled on his notepad and handed it to Dave, who hurriedly relayed the number and hung up. Moments later, the speakers emitted an electronic ping. Joey clicked his mouse and gestured for Dave to speak.

"Pete, can you hear me?"

"Loud and clear, bro."

"Good stuff. Okay, credentials, for the benefit of whoever's in the room with my brother and his wife. Pete Whelan, marine biologist, on secondment to the Bay of Plenty Wildlife Refuge for the WWF. I have news of something which is going on literally as I speak and is linked to earlier events in this neck of the woods."

"Please be brief," Joey cautioned. "This is a secure facility."

"Roger that," Pete said. "I knew Dave would be somewhere official by now, and it's vital I get this info to you. What you do with it is up to you, but I'm sure it's important. New Zealand is experiencing aftershocks following last week's tidal wave. The shocks are nowhere near as strong, but each one is lasting longer. That tells me they're much, much deeper underground.

"Now the bad news. A super-tanker has run aground on a reef just off the coast. It's carrying something in the region of thirty thousand tonnes of crude, and it's already lost a couple of thousand. It's all but broken in half. We're facing another Torrey Canyon scenario, and this wildlife centre has no chance. The ship's so close we can see it from the shoreline. Every available aircraft has been scrambled, but it's a losing battle."

"There isn't very much we can do to help from this range," Dave said. "How did they even manage to hit the reef? In calm, clear weather, it would be easy to avoid."

"They were tossed off course by the tidal wave or the tremors or whatever," Brenda suggested. "It must have hit New Zealand from that direction."

Her entirely non-scientific hunch or instinct seemed right, somehow. Despite being the last thing any of them had expected, it was the only logical interpretation of the facts.

"Let's go with that for the moment," Pete said. "How the ship got on the reef doesn't really matter. The real question is, how do we contain the oil spill?"

"And is there any chance of saving the wildlife centre?" Dave added.

Joey shook his head. "If they can see the ship, the horizon's only about seven or eight miles away. Any leak that close to the shoreline will be too late to contain. Thirty thousand tonnes of crude is going to wreak monumental damage—it's probably ashore already." He sighed and scrawled a few hieroglyphs on his notepad. "The wildlife centre will be one of the first casualties."

"Action?" Errol asked.

"Chain of command. This is hot news if anything ever was. Most likely, my immediate superior won't have heard the scuttlebutt yet."

* * *

Joey was right. Brigadier Groth hadn't heard of the impending disaster off the coast of New Zealand and was gracious enough to admit it.

"Thank you for the advance notice, Doctor Hart. I'll forward this information to the relevant offices. Have you received any videos or other photographic evidence? No, perhaps that would have been asking too much. Forward it as and when you receive anything." The burr of an open line sounded from the phone's speaker.

"He doesn't waste words." Errol was the only one present who hadn't been party to an exchange with Groth, who was evidently back to his usual self.

Joey chuckled. "You get used to it pretty quickly—"

"Incoming from Pete," Brenda interrupted, nodding at Joey's monitor. "He says he's got pictures and we should *all* see them."

The series of clips scrolling across the screen was a mix of amateur videos shot by local people on handheld cameras and mobile phones, interspersed with more professional footage, aerial photos from NZAF and Coastguard planes.

"The oil's just pouring out! No way that can be contained." Errol's years at the sharp end learning the oil trade from the grassroots upwards hadn't prepared him for the shocking images on the screen.

"We're dumping all the detergent we can lay our hands on." Pete's disembodied voice floated from the speakers. He kept himself off-camera while he spoke, presumably to avoid distraction from the scenes of desolation on the screen.

"What sort of weather's expected?" Joey's practical query about conditions, which would be vital in controlling the oil slick, refocused their attention on the scale of the problem.

"Doesn't look very promising. There's a storm warning been issued less than an hour ago—I've only just read the email—and we're expecting the wind to reach at least gale-force ten. Rain's right behind it, sweeping southeast from Japan. It's the start of the monsoon season in the Southern Hemisphere."

"That's all we need," Joey muttered. "Suggestions, anyone?"

"What's this 'detergent'?" Brenda asked. "I mean, I've heard of this before, but I've never thought to ask anyone about the whys and wherefores."

"I don't know too much about the chemistry involved," Errol answered, "but the detergent forms a barrier the oil can't seep through. Well, maybe it does, but it slows it down, helps to contain it in a small area. Relatively small."

In his head, Dave added a drawled *y'all* to the end of Errol's statement, but Errol wasn't hamming up the situation. He was very serious.

"Would it help to conscript some crop dusters?"

In the tense atmosphere of the observatory control room, they'd temporarily forgotten that Pete was eavesdropping on the conversation via Skype, and everyone jumped when he spoke.

"Can you contact someone who might be able to set something up, Pete?" Dave suggested.

"I can ask, but I can't see anyone with a plane refusing to lend a hand. They've got a vested interest in keeping this pollution from contaminating the land they farm."

"And I'll contact the military from this end," Joey said, reaching for the phone. "We must have some aircraft at bases within flying range."

Brigadier Groth listened in silence as Joey relayed Pete's suggestion. Noises in the background confirmed he wasn't alone wherever he was working.

"Good teamwork. I'll make sure the RAF and others are aware of the offer of civilian aircraft to assist in mopping-up operations. Send me your man's contact details, please. I'll assume he's no objection to the same level of security checks as you've already been through."

There was no inflection, nor even the hint of a question in this sentence. Groth was accustomed to giving orders; he wasn't in the business of making polite requests and as usual signed out without formalities.

* * *

Eddie steadied his cup with one hand and snatched his mobile with the other. "Dave? Not far from Chester now, on the old A55 bridge, near-as-damn-it the Welsh border." ... "Yeah, that one. Those tremors and signs you asked me to watch out for? I'm witnessing something right now. Listen to this."

The tremor shuddered its way north before their brief phone call was over, but it didn't appear to have caused any damage to the road surface or the surrounding drystone walls, the fields or the countryside. Eddie gulped his cooling coffee in a single swallow and headed back towards Liverpool as fast as the roads would allow. He was grateful for the motorway network and the chance to open up the throttle but also acutely aware that there was nowhere near the volume of vehicles he'd expected, even allowing for the relatively quiet time of day. Glancing at the map, he decided to take the slightly shorter route through the Birkenhead Tunnel. Much as it pained his avaricious soul to pay for the privilege, it was best to get his ass back home as quickly as possible.

CHAPTER SEVENTEEN

*T*HIS IS THE *BBC. The Meteorological Office issued the following gale warning to shipping at 0050 hours GMT."* The calm measured voice of the anonymous World Service presenter had the intended effect of steadying the nerve of every sailor and aircraft pilot listening to deal with the inclement weather due to be unleashed on them.

"The overall position at midnight GMT. A high pressure is developing..."

The technical details went over the heads of everyone in the Bidston Hill Observatory—everyone except Joey Hart and Pete Whelan, half a world away in New Zealand, where it was late morning.

"That storm's moving in fast. The origin looks to be over towards Japan, heading southeast."

Despite the furious speed of Joey's pencil across the pad, it was Pete who made the first comment. A few tense seconds dripped by before Joey threw down his pencil and nodded.

"I won't argue with that. Are you using a computer to calculate this data? I thought I was pretty quick with notebook and pencil, but..."

A short humourless laugh greeted this question.

"That'd be telling. No, as a matter of fact, I think on my feet and rely on my gut feelings. I'm generally out in the field where there aren't too many power outlets available, and decision-making can literally mean the difference between life and death. It's stood me in pretty good stead to date. I'm still alive an' kickin', and I intend to keep it that way. These figures the Met Office is quoting are probably already out of date, anyway, especially at the speed this weather's arriving."

"But if it's blowing southeast from Japan," Brenda interjected, "won't there be a risk of contamination from the nuclear plant that went up at the start of these problems?"

"Good question, Brenda," Joey replied. "I've been saying for years we ought to have staff members who aren't scientifically trained in on all our projects for when we science bods fly off into the realms of fantasy. And I mean that, Brenda, I really do."

"But do you have an answer?"

"My point exactly. You won't be put off with a non-answer. I like that, too. However, you can rest easy where nuclear contamination is concerned. Wind and weather aren't entirely irrelevant, but they're not a major factor when we're dealing with this sort of incident. Admittedly, it was touch and go, but a meltdown *was* avoided, and the area was quarantined. And we were prepared for the monsoon season, which starts regular as clockwork. We aren't totally unprepared to deal with the sort of weather problems and damage limitation precautions we go through in the Southern Hemisphere around this time every year."

"Pardon me, Joey, but who's this 'we'?" Dave asked. "Are you involved? Have you been down to Oz or NZ to advise and get involved personally?"

"I don't even possess a passport, Dave. But I received multiple phone calls asking for advice or assistance with some of the technical matters arising whenever we're dealing with severe weather."

"So what practical steps can be taken, right now?" Pete asked. "The tanker will break apart completely as soon as the storm hits, and I'd guess it's already too late to do more than limit the damage. The vessel's a Liberian-registered supertanker."

"That's a damn sight bigger than anything we could tie up at the Pier Head. That's gonna be a helluva lot of crude oil."

As they digested this and imagined the implications for the rapidly deteriorating scenario as it unfolded, the red phone on Joey's desk shrilled. He mouthed *Groth* before picking up the receiver. "Brigadier, any update you have for us will be very wel—"

Joey froze in mid-greeting. As he listened, his face showed concern mingled with a hint of incomprehension until, finally, he replaced the handset at the speed of a B-movie zombie and turned to the screen.

"Pete, this is one for you. RAF flights from two different and widely separated locations report whales forming into groups large enough to be identified on radar screens, all of them, without exception, swimming hard in seemingly random directions."

Pete clearly hadn't expected this curious detail, and his involuntary gasp of surprise was amplified by the speakers dotted around the room.

Joey continued. "It's as if they're taking the quickest way out of Dodge before something happens—something I think we can take for granted will *not* be good news for the rest of us."

"Uh-huh." Errol nodded. "Anything dangerous enough to faze *them* big daddies, I for one don't wanna know what it is." His pretence of casual indifference wasn't fooling anyone in the cramped office that had become their operations centre.

Joey had been scribbling furiously throughout this exchange, becoming increasingly agitated in the process. "We have another problem to deal with, but we *might* have got our noses in front. This latest report from Japanese airspace indicates the storm's heading southeast, mostly over open water where there are no major landmasses. But if we look at the wider picture...what if it tacks off in another direction?

Turkey, for example, is not too far from the path the storm's expected to take."

"Surely it's too late to do anything to *prevent* damage being done," Dave said.

"I agree. But if we relay this gen immediately, it's still possible." He reached for the phone as he spoke, pausing barely long enough to confirm that he was connected to Groth before launching into a condensed summary of the scenario developing in the Southern Hemisphere.

"Thank you, Doctor Hart. I'll ask the RAF to supply some photographic evidence. Perhaps they'll be able to get some shots of the whale exodus as well."

As usual, the line went dead without any formalities. Joey was accustomed to it by now. It wasn't bad manners, he reminded himself, just military efficiency, but he didn't have to like it.

Another phone shrilled with an incoming call. Dave fielded the call and listened for a few moments.

"Joey, it's Carlisle. We may have a problem much closer to home."

"Great. Just what we needed. Okay, let's hear the latest bad news together, shall we?"

Dave switched the call to loudspeaker.

"Go on, make my day. We're all on the speaker at this end, so no cussing."

"I'm not entirely sure if this is related, Joey."

"Wouldn't be the first time one of your gut feelings has pointed us in the right direction, so let's hear it."

"We're getting readings of seismic tremors on our screens— but they don't seem to be originating north of here, as you told us to expect. They're coming to us from the south, and fairly close at hand. And they aren't from the event further south. Those aren't expected for another six to eight hours, and it's not certain we'll be able to log them this far north. They might lose momentum altogether before they get here."

"Best guess?" Joey prompted. "I can hear you aren't giving me the full story."

"The graphs are showing tremors which originate somewhere close by—fifty miles from here is my best guess, eighty tops."

"And...? Come on, I know there's something else."

"Something I haven't seen before, and I don't like things I can't explain. The tremors are too *regular* to be interpreted as being caused by any weather or natural event I can think of. So, logically, that means—"

"It's manmade? Is that what you're saying? Which means we're looking for some underground activity."

"Mining's the only one that springs to mind, but I can't think of any mining being carried out in North Lancs or the Lake District. Not in my lifetime, anyway. Not on any commercial scale."

"Can I butt in here?" Errol had been sifting through the latest updates on the BBC News Channel. "There's another news item here about that environmental protest group at the fracking site near Southport. They're concerned about potential damage as a result of explorations for gas in shale layers about eight thousand feet down. The process is actually called fracturing."

"That sounds pretty destructive," Dave said.

"It really isn't. Basically, water's pumped into the shale under pressure and held in place. When the pressure is released, any gas flows back to the surface where it can be analysed to see if there's enough to make it worthwhile carrying on."

"So it's possible that the washed-out shale *could* result in some subsidence, landslip?"

Errol shrugged. "I'm no specialist, and the fine details of the geology involved is way over my head, but the short answer is, theoretically, yes. It *could* happen, but it's been SOP—standard operational procedure—since commercial oil and gas drilling first began, and I don't know of any major problems affecting the environment anywhere fracking has been performed, which includes just about every drilling operation in history, I would think. But don't quote me on that. Like I said, I'm no expert. I can only give you a rough idea of the basic procedures."

"And the regularity—the pulse of the seismic records?"

"I wouldn't be surprised if it's related to the pumping of gas and liquids out of the drill shaft after the pressure is released. Just a guess, but a prolonged and regular, rhythmic beat of this nature is *not* something you'd expect to find in nature."

Joey turned back to his man in Carlisle. "How long do you need to be sure what you're recording is confirmation of what's happening? Or that it's coming from an identifiable location in the Southport area?"

"I'm already sure of the point of origin. The graphs are easy to read if you know what to look for."

"Yeah, okay. We'll have to take your word on that. Can you email me the results and—no, forget that."

"Already sent."

"Damn. You haven't got security clearance. I'll have to do that, and this conversation never took place."

"Security clearance?"

"I've already said too much. The less you know, the better for *you*," Joey snapped and regretted it immediately. "Geez, I'm sorry. I'm under a lot of pressure here. There are things happening that are out of my control. If I get the green light, I'll fill you in as far as I can, but that decision's not up to me, okay?"

"Okay, Joey. I knew you worked for a government office of some sort. I hadn't realised it was one of the hush-hush departments."

Joey's inbox pinged, and he breathed a silent sigh of relief. "Thanks for taking it in the right spirit. I promise, as soon as I've made a few calls, I'll get back to you and tell you as much as I'm allowed. For now, you have to trust me when I say we're on the side of the angels. There's nothing dodgy going on, I promise."

As he toggled the end-call button, Groth's name flashed across his monitor. Joey thanked his stars he'd ended the previous call and could answer immediately. He didn't like to think of the consequences of keeping the brigadier waiting.

"Bidston Hill. I have an update for you, Sir, and I'm forwarding a file of fresh data from a listening post in Region Six which I believe is relevant to the present situation."

Brigadier Groth's voice sounded calm and relaxed as he responded. "Doctor Hart, if you have some new data already, you've made good progress. But I must ask you to follow protocol. Confirm the ID of any caller who contacts you *before* you give out any information. And I mean, *any* information—anything at all. This is a military matter, with the highest possible peacetime security classification. You've never had any involvement with the armed forces, have you?"

"That's correct, Sir."

"As I thought. You'll have to get into the habit of thinking of the security aspect of everything you say and do every day."

"Understood, Sir. Now, I'm sending you the files I received a few minutes ago. They may need some technical interpretation, but the situation is this…"

Joey muted the call while he forwarded the data to the brigadier and gave him time to read the files. Several minutes passed in silence before the brigadier spoke again.

"Any suggestions, Doctor Hart?"

"We haven't had a great deal of time to go through the figures in detail yet, but if we could change one factor— say, by stopping the pumping process at an agreed time and date—we'd have something to set the present figures against.

If we see an immediate change in the readings, we can prove the connection."

"And you're asking me to step outside my remit of authority, give orders to a company whose principal interest is to make profit for their shareholders and tell them to close down operations for an indefinite period so you can take some readings?"

"Without that data, Sir, I can't give you an informed opinion. But if you want evidence you can use to persuade others rather than relying on my gut feelings, I need those figures."

"You don't ask for much, do you? I'll see what I can do."

This time, Joey felt the anger and frustration in Brigadier Groth as the line went dead.

Within ten minutes, the phone rang once more. Brigadier Groth had recovered his composure and identified himself. Joey envisaged it was the brigadier's way of reminding them to observe protocol in all future phone calls but kept his opinions to himself, as in the space of those ten minutes, the brigadier had called in some heavy-duty favours.

"All activity at the drill site will cease at exactly 1000 hours. Can you have your monitoring equipment online by then?"

Dave had Carlisle on a second line and repeated the information. He listened for a moment, then nodded rather than interrupt.

"Region Six confirm that, Sir. The equipment is already monitoring what's happening at present, and there's no change from the readings you have in hand. They're steady."

"I'll assume that's a good sign. Keep me informed of any change in the patterns."

"Understood—"

It was probably because the brigadier only needed confirmation that they were ready to proceed, but for the first time, Joey had managed to get the final word in before the connection was broken.

"Right, it's over to you, Carlisle."

"Acknowledged. All I have to do is keep a close eye on a couple of screens and charts, watch for any differences before and after ten o'clock, allowing for the time it takes to reach us, of course, but the time lag's simple schoolboy maths. We're almost exactly a hundred miles from the drill site, and the tremors are registering maybe twenty minutes after they're generated."

"You make it sound so easy. Let's hope pausing operations will provide the effects you're looking for."

Joey pored over his copy of the first email, which showed the details collated from the original tremors. The clockwork regularity of the graphs was unmistakable. There was no question of them being the result of a manmade occurrence.

"Errol. The pumping out of the waste you mentioned as part of the fracturing operation. Is it a lengthy process?"

"Depends, Joey. The depth of the hole, the pressures involved, several other things all come into the picture. Generally, the pressure comes off straight away, and you get the main blow at once. How long it continues depends on how much gas you've found, I suppose. Like I said, I only picked up a few basic principles."

"Still, you know more than us, and if I can ask you—" Joey was interrupted by the callback from Carlisle.

"Go ahead, Region Six."

"The graph readings changed a few minutes after ten o'clock. I'm emailing you the first pages now, but there's no doubt about it. Is that what you expected?"

"Yes—and thanks. It won't solve the problem, but at least we know what we're dealing with. Stay close to the phone. We're going to be busy. I need to forward this Upstairs. If I can wrangle you a security clearance, it might save us some time to have you brought into the loop from now on."

Groth listened without comment to Joey's explanation of what the changes in the graph readings implied but sounded dubious when he asked for security clearance.

"There's no time to consult rules and regs on this. I'll have to take the responsibility myself. Doctor Hart, your colleague in Carlisle. I've read his CV, and he's well qualified for the job. How well do you know him? And for how long? Can he handle pressure?"

"We grew up together, Sir. He's a Scouser, same as me, and he's always come up with the goods. He won't crack, I'm sure of it."

"This is what we'll do, then. I'll contact him now with a quick reply to this email and inform him he has limited security clearance. I'll keep him abreast of future developments by phone or email, but my details will be withheld. It means he won't be able to contact me unless I start the conversation, but that way, I'm only bending protocol rather than directly breaching it. My ass is—theoretically, at least—covered. That will have to do for now. Stand by."

Typically, the line went dead.

"Stand by?" Dave repeated. "What's *that* supposed to mean?"

"It means stay by the phone. I can only think he intends to call us again, Dave, and very soon."

* * *

Less than ten minutes later, the phone on Joey's desk rang, eerily at the same time a piece of equipment in the far corner of the lab emitted a series of hums and whirrs. Running over to inspect it, Brenda saw lights flashing beneath its translucent dustsheet. A roll of continuous paper began to issue from one end, reviving ancient memories of her first job. Now she could identify it as a fax machine, possibly vintage mid-fifties and no doubt standard issue whenever Bidston Hill had last been given a makeover.

The chatter of the keys was deafeningly loud compared with the near-silent PSC used to print emails and other documents, although it ceased its racket as Brenda removed the protective cover. She tore off the printed section and looked over at Joey, who was already talking quietly into the receiver, presumably receiving further information and/or orders from Brigadier Groth. An expressive pair of eyebrows and a vague hand gesture indicated a vacant spot on his cluttered desk. Brenda dropped the note unread, face down, and withdrew a few steps, just in case there were security issues at stake.

Joey flashed her a smile and ended the call as swiftly as he could without seeming to question his senior officer's authority. "It's time for an update. Let's grab a coffee while we can."

Once they were all armed with cups of the strong, bitter brew and decamped to a comfortable group of armchairs set aside from the work area, he relayed what the brigadier had told him.

"It seems Groth has a degree of clout I never suspected. He's only gone straight to the top and scrambled three Seahawks from a carrier on manoeuvres in the region to overfly a sector of the South Pacific and get as much footage as possible—stills and video. Both can be useful for different purposes, and we need all the data we can collect.

"The fax was sent by our bucolic cousins in NZ, most of whom are relying on hand-me-down equipment. It wouldn't surprise me to find out it's stuff we cashiered from here last time *we* had a refit. Oh, and Brenda, while I think on, you don't need to worry. The brig has cleared all of us for however long we're here, but *if* something really sensitive comes in, it will arrive encrypted and read like gibberish until the correct code for the day is applied."

"Thanks for that, Joey. Can you tell us what was in the fax?"

"Well, the fact that they decided to send it over the wire, not in a phone call, is a hint of it being important *and* confidential."

He had quite deliberately folded the sheet without reading it. Now he opened it and read it through without comment. He managed to keep his face expressionless, but Dave suspected it had not been easy.

Joey raised his eyes, looked at each of them in turn and cleared his throat. "Okay, this is straight from the horse's mouth—though maybe the front line would be a better description. Anyway, here's what it says."

DTG: *1010110910z*

From: *Christchurch, South Island, New Zealand*

For: *Joey Hart, Bidston Hill, UK*

Cc: *Senior Officer ?? Ops Centre*

Security: *Condition Red*

Seismic event indicated by readings taken @ 0700, 0730, 0800 d.d.

Point of origin northern extremity of the Pacific Fault running roughly N/S from c.200m North of Tonga, through Samoa. Associated shock waves on direct course for landfall north/northwestern coastline New Zealand.

Severe damage unavoidable. Timescale: 8<10 hours. Evacuation impractical. Curfew imposed, all non-military transport/movement curtailed.

Awaiting advice/instructions. Message ends.

CHAPTER EIGHTEEN

"IT'S A BIGGIE, Rob. We'll get the full force of it smack on the nose, but it's going to hit Oz too, my guess about five to six hours after it rips through North Island."

"Thanks, Pete. We can't do a lot from here to help, but we can keep our monitors focused on the region and record what happens."

Pete Whelan's mobile lost its signal yet again. When he attempted to redial, the complete deadness of the line suggested this time it was terminal. *Or maybe someone's commandeered the networks*, he thought. He didn't approve of such nanny-state tactics, and he wasn't a Big Brother conspiracy theorist either, but in the exceptional circumstances of a national emergency, it would be understandable if someone had decided to clear the airlines for essential calls only.

The authorities in New Zealand had reacted swiftly to the minimal warning received of a potential tidal surge heading their way. Information had been posted on all available radio and TV channels for people to 'go home and stay there', and military law had been invoked, with immediate effect. The streets were rapidly clearing of people who had been caught further from home than their luckier neighbours. Pete suddenly found something to be grateful for. He couldn't imagine the scale of the carnage which would have ensued if the threatening wall of water had arrived in the middle of the New Zealand night with most of the country's population asleep in the beds.

* * *

Rob looked around the Met Office which had become the operations centre from which he and whatever staff he could muster would have to plan to safeguard Australia, first and foremost, along the eastern seaboard, where the worst effects of the tidal surge were expected to strike, and then prepare the rest of the country for mopping-up operations once the danger was past. It wasn't promising. Normally, he could count on about two dozen assistants at any one time, but security clearance and holiday arrangements had reduced that number to eight, including himself, and the room seemed cavernous and almost empty. He hoped for a few more bodies to ease the workload at the next shift change, when those currently on duty would discover that they would have to crash on day beds or recliners in a side room, as Condition Red meant that they couldn't leave the facility. He wondered if anyone had taken the trouble to point out that clause in their contracts. It wasn't a task he'd volunteer for.

If I can't use the phone, how do I know what's happening out there? he thought irritably. He'd been on duty for over twelve hours straight, and he was coming down from the last adrenaline high his glands could juice up. For the moment, however, there was nobody else to lead the team. Another night fuelled by strong coffee and willpower seemed inevitable.

His head was starting to pound, a combination of stress, responsibility and the feeling that every breath he drew had already been through his lungs and everyone else's half a dozen times—one of the disadvantages of living in a hermetically sealed environment. After a while, recycled air, however clean it is, tastes stale and dead.

He grabbed a couple of co-codamol tablets from his drawer to dull the worst effects of the headache that would disable him as soon as he let it and glared at the innocent bottled water on the corner of the desk. The last mouthful he'd sipped twenty minutes ago had tasted as if it, too, had been recycled—more than once, and quite possibly via a donkey's kidneys.

I need a break, was his next thought. Coffee, he decided, would at least have a taste. Anything had to be an improvement on the anodyne non-taste of bottled water.

The first gulp of coffee washed the tablets down. It should have scalded the roof of his mouth, but he was now on autopilot and had reached the stage of being able to ignore such mundane matters. Tired or not, he was determined to enjoy the rest of the cup and forced himself to concentrate on experiencing the radiant heat transmitted to his fingertips through the walls of the polystyrene cup.

The exercise of crossing the room to the urn also made a pleasant change from sitting tensed up next to a useless phone. He performed an impromptu jig designed to encourage the returning circulation before leaving the rest area. A TV monitor was showing the latest headlines.

Of course. If he couldn't actively *seek* updates, he could still surf the news channels. He just had to hope the information he was looking for would prove easy to spot. He was as near as made no difference out on his feet. *Dear God, I could sleep for a week.*

Two TV monitors on a side wall were transmitting different programmes. One was tuned to the Sky channel for Australian and Southern Hemisphere news, while the other reported what was happening in the rest of the world through the BBC News Channel. The sound had been muted, replaced by subtitles. The text unrolled across the screen several seconds behind the live events depicted and, to add insult to injury, were frequently inaccurate, garbled travesties of what was being said on-screen, although Rob noted that the spellings were better than usual.

Probably because the news clip was being repeated for the hundredth time, and someone had had the opportunity to proofread it, put it into readable English.

"A second earthquake has hit Christchurch overnight. On this occasion, the local authorities had plenty of time to prepare and react, and as a result, there were few injuries and no fatalities. The tremor was measured at just over two on the Richter scale, and property damage was minimal.

"Breaking news: reports of further tidal surges approaching New Zealand from the north, ETA ten to twelve hours. North Island residents are advised to secure any loose property outdoors, remain indoors and listen to the radio for further instructions. South Island residents may opt to follow the same precautions, but the level of threat is not as serious."

Rob glanced across to the *BBC News 24* screen. It was approaching the hour, and a brief outline of weather reports throughout Europe was about to give way to the latest international headlines. He grabbed a remote and toggled the mute button.

"...news headlines at seven o'clock. A storm of unprecedented proportions is heading through the South Pacific region. All the countries of Australasia are at risk, especially New Zealand."

Rob's tiredness fell from his shoulders like a discarded garment as a jolt of adrenaline hit home. A warning voice at the edge of his logic taunted him that he'd regret it later if he kicked into another period of intense activity without a rest. He ignored it and concentrated on the news report.

CHAPTER NINETEEN

W E COULD REALLY use some up-to-the-minute details of what's going on—especially around the UK," Joey groused as he drained another coffee cup without recording the fact that it was stone cold. The action was almost automatic. The hit of caffeine had long since ceased to have any significant effect.

"Surely, we should be trying to understand the bigger picture, worldwide?" Dave queried.

"He's got a point," Errol drawled in support. "Things are happening everywhere you care to look, so if there's a link, a common denominator, there has to be some sort of programme we can use to get ahead of the game, maybe predict where the next problem's likely to show up?"

"If only it were that simple, Errol," Joey said with a tired grin. "Weather forecasting's still not an exact science, despite all the improved equipment we have to assist us and all the stats recorded over the years. Did you know, statistics prove that fifty-two per cent of all UK weather reports are wrong?"

"I hadn't heard that one, but it doesn't surprise me," Dave remarked.

Joey rubbed at his temples. The long hours of unbroken concentration on the fine details of graphs, charts and reports were rapidly catching up with him.

"All the same, we have to learn to walk before we can run, and maybe it's not a bad idea to simplify the task by looking more closely at what's happening locally in a much smaller region. It's quite possible it will give us some pointers to help

us understand what's happening elsewhere in the world—
always assuming there's something to connect all these
worldwide weather anomalies and it isn't just coincidence.

"My instincts scream there *has* to be some connection,
somehow, but we've no hard, physical evidence to confirm
this. We can't allow ourselves the luxury of guesswork, either.
We get one chance and one chance *only* to get this right."

"What's happening locally, you say," Brenda mused.
"Dave, how long d'you reckon Eddie needs to arrive
back home?"

Joey and Errol looked at her blankly.

"The friend of ours who had his holiday in France
wrecked and did that detour through Wales?" Dave
reminded Joey, who nodded in recollection and listened as
Dave gave a potted summary of Eddie's woes, finishing with,
"Last we spoke, he was on the banks of the Dee, just about
to cross back into England. He's home by now, I imagine.
Shall I call him?"

"Can he keep his mouth shut?" Joey asked. "This is a
matter of national security, and Groth's paranoid. If I allow
an unscreened civvy in on what we're doing without his
approval, he'll string me up—or more likely, *all* of us."

Dave and Brenda exchanged the briefest of glances.

"Eddie is Dave's closest friend," Brenda said, "and
while I've always said there's something about him..."
She paused, then shook her head. "I won't speak ill of
anyone. It's probably just me, anyway. I'd happily *trust*
him in any situation, especially where sensitive issues are
concerned. After all, he's a banker. He's used to dealing with
confidential business."

"And he's one of the good guys," Dave added. "Not one
of the chancers we've heard so much about recently. In fact,
he told us the reason he took off on holiday was that he'd
been given the bullet—probably because he's *too* honest if

you ask me—and he wanted some time to think and plan. He's a bachelor, lives alone, never mentions any family, and now he's no job to report back to, either. Considering the state the country's in already, he's ideally placed to drop off the map for a while and nobody would be any the wiser—at least in the short term. And I'm certain of this much. The Eddie I've known all my life is perfectly capable of keeping schtum on any subject."

Joey nodded. "Thanks for that, both of you—and especially you, Brenda. It must be difficult to admit there's something of the night about a person and say in the same breath, 'But I *trust* him.' Believe me, that tells me a lot more about the man himself than you might think."

He glanced back at Dave. "This is what we'll do. I'm *not* going to ask Groth for permission to bring your friend in on this. I'll take the flak myself—if there is any. Yes, Dave. Call your friend. Find out where he is and what he's doing at this very moment. If he hasn't reached home yet, perhaps he could save time by coming straight here. He must have some clean clothes in the car if his hols were cut short, and we've got a laundry as well as a kitchen and plenty of beds. But in fairness, you'll have to make it clear to him that once he's here, he stays. That's the only drawback of the Condition Red security level."

* * *

Outside the door was a narrow gravel track ending at an observation point bounded by a safety barrier between the River Mersey and the grass sward that was perhaps the length of a cricket pitch. Curving away from the hill, it had the effect of distracting the attention of a casual passer-by away from the unremarkable and apparently unused entrance to the bunker.

Dave turned left, away from the river, and rounded the corner which led to the staff car park. Eddie had just arrived.

He had his back to Dave and was removing his luggage from the car. Dave hailed him as he approached.

"Have any trouble following our directions?"

"Easy enough. I don't trust satnav. I prefer to rely on my instincts to find my way around."

"I've a feeling this government facility isn't listed on maps anyway, Eddie, and certainly not what lies below ground."

"Sounds very mysterious, Dave. You about to put a blindfold on me before you guide me through some sort of secret passage?"

"No need for that. The place looks like it hasn't been used for years."

Eddie said nothing when they rounded the corner and Joey waved them inside. He glanced all around to make sure they weren't being observed.

Back in the op centre, Brenda had a fresh pot of coffee waiting.

"I gather Dave's explained why you're with us for the duration?"

Eddie nodded. "I imagine he's also told you there's nobody waiting for me at home—and no guarantee I'll be able to continue to pay the mortgage unless another job comes up for grabs pretty soon." He shrugged. "Maybe I can do something useful here."

"What we need more than anything else is a first-hand account of the conditions outside this weather station. There are limits to what we can work out from reading instruments, no matter how sensitive or accurate. Or, as Dave cynically puts it, as expensive as those we have to work with. You might not be a geologist or a trained met. expert, but even the smallest details of things you've noticed as you drove home could give us vital clues as to what's happening right now, help us understand the situation developing, maybe even guess what might happen next."

Eddie sat back in his chair and sipped thoughtfully at his coffee. His brow furrowed as he focused on a completely random point somewhere in mid-air, recalling salient moments from the long haul north, perhaps, or maybe a page from one of the maps now scattered on his dashboard and passenger seat.

He refocused and roused himself.

"It's like I said. There were times while I was driving through France when I felt exactly like Charlie Brown in the *Peanuts* cartoons—like it was personal, and the rain was falling on me and me alone." He camped up a grotesque over-the-top sulky lower lip, then grinned as he continued. "It also gave me a new theory about why we call 'em Frogs. There's bugger all else could survive in their climate."

For a split second, Brenda wondered if she ought to consider this politically inadvisable comment as a racial slur. She still had reservations about Eddie which she couldn't quite define, but Dave's eyes sparkled, and Joey chuckled; the moment had passed. Perhaps she was being too hard on him. *Ease off, give him a chance. We've got to get along as a team in a sealed bunker for the foreseeable future. The last thing you need right now is to create unnecessary stress and discord.*

"The French aren't exactly trying to win any popularity contests recently, anyway," Dave offered, and even Brenda found herself nodding in wholehearted agreement.

Eddie opened a shoulder bag he'd held on to when he stashed the rest of his luggage in a convenient bedroom. "I collected a full range of newspapers on the way home— I didn't know how long you've been isolated from what's happening in the outside world. There's a few French dailies, and I've got every UK national published today."

"That's useful," Dave said. "The BBC News Channel has become a tad institutionalised in recent years. Sometimes

I get the feeling they've become a Government mouthpiece of sorts. That should probably be spelt lowercase. It doesn't seem to matter which party has a majority."

Brenda stirred. "Please, let's not get into yah-boo politics. That's all they seem to write about in the newspapers, and it bores me stiff."

"Point taken, sweetheart," Dave said. He knew how his wife felt about this subject. "We can leaf through the papers we have and pick out anything we can find which sheds some light on the climate, the weather and such like. Any articles which wander off-topic into opinions or political point-scoring can be binned. Agreed?"

"We've enough on our plates without going looking for more," Joey said, reaching for the paper on top of the pile, which happened to be a *Daily Mail*. Dave grinned.

"We could probably bin the whole of *that* paper, with the possible exception of the horse racing results, but never mind. Let's see what the *Telegraph* has to offer."

Brenda was quite happy to be involved in filtering out useful articles and up-to-date information and picked up one of the French papers. She had studied French at university and still read French fashion magazines from time to time to keep her language skills up to the mark.

There were a modest number of articles that satisfied the agreed criteria. These were deposited in a metal in-tray, and after being checked a second time by a different pair of eyes, the remainders of each newspaper were cleared to one side.

Brenda was restless. Something was missing from the Big Picture they were trying to piece together.

"Would it be worth putting all these events in some sort of order. A timeline, perhaps? The reports seem to be coming from every possible direction. There might be no connection between them at all."

"That shouldn't be a problem," Joey said. "Everything we've logged so far is time-dated. Give me a minute." He punched a few keystrokes and sat back to let the computer do the hard work of cross-referencing the data on file.

The first listing on the screen included a couple of items none of them had considered, which were not amongst those they'd plucked from the newspapers.

"This one's a fair bit outside the time frame we're working with," Dave said.

"I remember it, though. I was Stateside at the time," Errol drawled. "It made a helluva mess, and the lawsuits look like bankrupting a couple major players."

The reference was to a pipeline disaster off the coast of Haiti in April 2010.

"It can only be something in the archives downloaded by someone or other at an earlier date. I never even considered the possibility of researching our in-house historical data, but there's probably a lot of gen there we can access if we need it."

Joey's eyes gleamed at the thought, but he scrolled on to avoid the possibility of being sidetracked. "Seems the jury's still out on whether it was human error which caused the pipelines to rupture or a tragic natural disaster. The Northern Hemisphere has just been through the warmest winter since records began—over one hundred and forty years ago."

"I remember seeing daffodils poking *through* the snow in Calderstones Park in January," Brenda chipped in. "Now *that* was weird."

"The next item, however, is one we *did* log ourselves. Thank you, Brenda, for clipping this account of the storms that chased Eddie all the way through France."

"And from the other direction," Dave added. "Up north, not just one but *two* eruptions from the same volcano in Iceland which hasn't caused any problems for...?"

"Hundreds of years, Dave. They even thought they could harness its power and put it to some use."

"Instead of which, we had a month or so of total disruption of all air traffic throughout Europe."

Joey nodded. "Let's look at the problems further afield. The last few months have been one catastrophe after another in the Southern Hemisphere. Storms and flooding in Australia. Two severe quakes in New Zealand soon after. And the worst of 'em all, the tsunami which hit the east coast of Japan and took out a nuclear plant. We may never know how many people were killed and made homeless."

A sad silence settled on the room. None of them had been personally affected by the tragic events in Japan, but the sheer scale of the devastation had been mind-boggling, and they wouldn't have been normal human beings if they'd reacted in any other manner.

Joey reached into a drawer on his desk and pulled out a handful of blank templates. Dave recognised them as large-scale Mercator projections, with the familiar shapes of the major landmasses of the world spread in the usual 2D representation, which he always thought looked slightly distorted or stretched.

Joey peeled one off the pile and laid it out. It was big enough to use as a wall chart, covering most of his desk. Using a metre ruler and a freshly sharpened pencil, he began plotting lines on the map, taking coordinates from one or other of his scribbled notes.

"I'm looking at the readings we have from the Southern Hemisphere events," he explained to nobody in particular, as if thinking aloud while he worked. "These vectors aren't exact—nobody could navigate the Pacific Ocean from them— but they ought to give us a good general sense of where and when the tides and other underground disturbances have struck. Most important is some guidance of the direction of travel, where they started from, where they finished up."

"Are you looking for a common cause, a pattern of some sort?" Eddie asked.

Joey shrugged. "As if we could be *that* lucky. In an ideal research-lab world, that's what I'd be looking for. In the real world, however, that just don't happen. There may be something interesting, though. Look at this."

He bent closer and enhanced two of the first lines he'd drawn with two different coloured felt markers. They crossed on a vacant stretch of open water with nothing obvious in the immediate vicinity.

"Forget about the times for the moment. They're more of a distraction than a help. But look at the distance travelled from that point to where they reach the coastlines, northeast in Japan and southwest at New Zealand. What if some powerful force originating somewhere out there were to be the cause of both tsunami *and* earthquakes?"

Errol padded across and studied the map.

"I'm not a navigator nor a weather expert, but I can tell you, that's a lonely stretch of ocean. The only speck of land big enough to put up anything bigger than a tent is Guam. I did some exploratory drilling out that-a-way several years ago, but we didn't stay there too long."

"Why's that? Superstitious sailors, here be dragons, or maybe mermaids with seductive smiles luring you?"

"Sorry to disappoint, but it was boring old practical considerations. It's the deepest part of the seas, anywhere. The extraction of any oil reserves we might have found would have been too difficult and expensive to make it worthwhile. It would never have been an economic feasibility."

"Depth. Errol, that's something I haven't even thought about in my calcs."

Joey was suddenly busy again, manipulating three or four different calculators and scribbling hieroglyphics nobody else could have interpreted as he worked.

"Dave, there are some maps in that end cabinet over there. Find me a world map—one that's labelled 'topographical'—so I can cross-reference the depths of the oceans. We may be on to something here."

There was nothing practical for any of them to do at that moment or for however long it might take Joey to translate the data into a series of vector lines on the world map projection.

Brenda wandered around, collecting mugs and plates. Dave took the opportunity to start a fresh brew of NATO-issue coffee. Errol caressed his cheroot case and replaced it in his inner pocket with a pang of regret. He wasn't going to smoke in a closed environment, where the air supply had to be cleansed and recirculated. To distract himself, he glanced at the nearest TV monitor, showing the twenty-four-hour BBC News Channel. A 'Breaking News' banner marched across the bottom of the screen and grabbed his attention immediately.

Two oil rigs 150 miles offshore from Aberdeen evacuated while gas leaks are investigated. An aerial shot of what appeared to be a calm, orderly evacuation process accompanied the report. Errol looked around, decided not to disturb Joey, and caught Dave's eye.

"Come and look at this. I might be getting paranoid, but this could be relevant."

Dave brought two coffees with him, passing one to Errol as he sat down.

"Aberdeen? North Sea rigs?"

"I haven't been on that particular rig in the Elgin field, but I've spent some time on a couple of others. They're all dealing with similar downhole conditions, and they tend to be set up in much the same manner. It all depends on the cause of the gas leak—if it's confirmed that there *is* a gas leak, of course—and how they decide to deal with it. If it's a mechanical failure or down to human error, there are, or certainly *ought* to be, established procedures. On the other hand, if the leak is the result of an unexpected fault in the seabed..."

Dave didn't need to be an expert geologist to work out the implications of Errol's incomplete sentence. As they looked at each other, a phone rang. Dave was closest and picked it up. Conscious of security restrictions, he waited for the caller to speak first.

"Aberdeen. Doctor Hart—"

"One moment, I'll fetch him."

Joey wasn't so deeply engrossed in his calculations and reacted immediately on hearing his name.

"Caller won't identify himself, but he asked for you and says you gave him this number."

"Yes, I know who that will be, and I've a shrewd idea of why he doesn't want to give his name to anyone he doesn't know. Listen, I'm not being rude, but give me a few minutes alone. Errol, you can smoke in any dorm where there's no bedding on the bunk frames. You don't need to go outside."

* * *

Half an hour later, the red internal phone on the restroom wall shrilled. Dave had been expecting the call but still leapt out of his seat like a startled rabbit. Errol had been in an adjacent room, chain-smoking cheroots, but burst through the door as Dave collected himself and answered it.

"Okay. On our way."

He replaced the handset and relayed the message.

"Joey's got some fresh news, and it's not good. We'd better go and find out."

Joey was still plotting vectors on a map and added one more line before pushing the chart to one side and giving them his full attention.

"My source in Aberdeen is one of our leading geologists. He's not prone to wild conjecture, and he knows what he's talking about. There aren't many details as yet about the gas leak reported on the news, other than that it's located one hundred and fifty miles offshore, everyone's been evacuated and there were no casualties. Nobody can be sure until they've had a chance to investigate the rig, but they're drilling three thousand feet down and that's going to take some time.

"My colleague has run the available figures through a set of hoops of his own devising and says he is all but certain that the cause of the leak is a shift in the bedrock, or rather the layers of rock under the sea. He reckons they've been disturbed by a tremor passing from north to south at a depth of perhaps five thousand feet below the seabed, where you'd need to have equipment already installed to record any seismic activity."

"And since they aren't drilling that deep…" Errol interposed.

"Correct." Joey nodded. "We had nothing set that deep yet and therefore no chance of knowing in advance this was coming our way."

"What has your contact been able to tell you? Anything?"

"From the depth and the lapsed-time readings, the shock wave wasn't particularly strong and continued to move south. It's passed us by now and will probably run out of steam before it reaches the European coastline. Look at the map a moment, all of you."

Joey turned to the chart he'd been working on as they arrived. It showed the familiar outlines of the Americas, Europe and the rest of the Northern Hemisphere, not the schematic of the Southern Hemisphere he'd been working on when they left.

"I haven't had time to correlate all the data we've got on the events which have been reported so far, but there's a pattern developing. First of all, we've got the shock waves from two separate incidents rippling from the same source— the volcano in Iceland. I've marked them in two different colours, and you can see the shock waves follow the same general direction. The second eruption was less powerful, and as you'd expect, the effects don't reach as far south."

A green line terminated at a six-figure number.

"Grid reference," Joey said in answer to the unspoken question in Dave's eyes. "This is totally different. I've used the minimal preliminary gen I got from Aberdeen to sketch a profile of what's happening at the oil rig mentioned on the news. There's a degree of guesswork involved here, but my gut says it will prove to be close enough to what's happening for us to be able to use it."

A red line started from a point in open sea and ran roughly south-southeast, ending at another grid-referenced point in open water some distance short of the European coastline. Errol was reasonably sure an extension of the red line would have made landfall in Germany.

Joey reached for a metre rule and placed it carefully on the map.

"I'm adding a back extension," he explained as he marked a neat line of red dots along the edge of the ruler, running northwest from the marked oil rig. He continued until he reached a major landmass.

"The seismic event which caused the earthquake in the North Sea this morning had its origin in Iceland. It seems the problems caused by the volcano at Eyjafjallajökull could be returning, doubled and in spades. Now, look at this."

Joey flipped the map so everyone could see it. He remained seated, looking at it from the north. "These are the vectors from the two eruptions in Iceland." He placed his metre rule on two parallel lines very close together. "I've drawn them in two different colours to make them easier to see. For the moment, you can forget the dates. They're not important to what I'm sketching out here.

"Now, over here..." He referred to a different cluster of readings. "I must admit, these are probably not as accurate as the others. I had bugger all data to work with, for starters, and a lot of it is more guesswork than hard, established fact. All the same, it's what I expect to see from the oil rig gas leak we heard about in the Elgin field."

"How reliable do they need to be?" Dave asked.

"My source in Aberdeen is one of the world's leading experts. That's all I can tell you, but he's not a scaremonger, and he *never* makes mistakes."

"Good enough for me," Errol said. "I've been at a blowout, and it's not funny."

"This doesn't feel like a blowout, Errol. According to Aberdeen, the smart money should be on the problem being caused by downhole conditions. They're drilling some four, maybe five thousand feet below the seabed. He doesn't think there's any question of human error or equipment failure involved, so that means there's only one other possibility."

"A fault in the rock formation itself?" Dave guessed.

"Almost certainly," Joey confirmed. "Think of it as a layer cake with different strata of every conceivable kind of rock on top of each other—different types of rock with different stresses, strengths and characteristics. Every time the type of rock changes, there's a potential weak point which can collapse or fracture—"

Errol interrupted, "And then some son of a gun with a drill bit chomps straight through it like Pac-man, and the whole shebang goes sky high."

Regardless of the serious nature of the problem, they all smiled at the apt analogy.

"That's why every driller I ever met was paranoid about drill speeds, exact depth readings, downhole temps and pressures and a million other variables. After all those years on the rigs, I'm now beginning to understand why drillers feel the way they do."

"These lines," Brenda said, "are they likely to meet up with the others—the ones you've drawn travelling away from Iceland? And if they do, will anything bad—I mean, *really* bad—follow?"

She spoke hesitantly, clearly unsure if her question was valid or an unimportant distraction. To her surprise, Doctor Hart beamed at her like a pulp fiction caricature of a university don whose star pupil had uttered the Ultimate Question required to discover the real meaning of life, the universe and everything.

"Every research group should include someone like you, Brenda. Someone who will ask the one practical question which *should be* blindingly obvious. I've tried to make a guess at what *could* happen—call it a worst-case scenario if you like—but it's based on random scraps of information. It could be totally useless."

He unrolled a transparent sheet and laid it on top of the map, aligning it against a couple of pre-marked points.

"This is one of several things which could possibly happen if these seismic events either repeat or increase in severity."

He paused, giving them all a chance to study the extra vectors shown on the overlay. These were dotted-line extensions of the colour-coded paths mapped out on the sheet below. They crossed the shoreline of mainland Europe, noticeably closer together than they had been, and continued to converge.

Eddie was the first to look up.

"I think we can see they're going to meet up somewhere, eventually, but it seems not in Europe. Is that right?"

Joey nodded and replaced the Northern Hemisphere map with the one of the Southern Hemisphere he'd been working on earlier.

"I don't set too much faith in coincidences," he said, smoothing out some non-existent wrinkles in the sheet, "and I was *very* careful to ensure that the data I transferred from the other sheet matches exactly with the coordinates on this one. The point where the shock waves heading south from these two events are likely to come together is a certain lonely stretch of the Pacific we've already discussed."

The vector lines came together at a point in mid-ocean. The nearest landfall was barely visible, but Errol named it without hesitation.

"Guam? You're sure? Doc, I'll take my chances on the world blowing up this very day before I'd even think of going back to that hellhole."

"Easy, Errol. The only people who might be sent to the coal face, as it were, would be mining and geology experts, and that's if anyone goes there at all. But it's not Guam we're interested in. It's what lies at about twelve thousand feet beneath the waves, the deepest recorded seabed anywhere in the world. The Mariana Trench."

* * *

The French president had been chumming along with the German chancellor for several months. During this time, they had blatantly—some would say, shamelessly—taken advantage of their positions as leaders of the two biggest economies in Europe to formulate and trump through policies designed to strengthen the failing Euro, which both countries had adopted as their trading currency with the rest of the world.

Political lampoonists had sharpened their claws and lashed out gleefully. The president's diminutive frame had inevitably raised taunts comparing him unfavourably with Napoleon Bonaparte's supposed lack of authoritative inches. The German chancellor had been compared with a more recent political figure, but she was so much more than the Iron Lady of Britain in the 1980s. Muhammed Ali in the same ring as the butterfly he famously claimed to be was a fairer comparison.

Once these two fiscal heavyweights had wrested control of EU funding, it was only a question of time before large-scale projects in both countries became the beneficiaries of frequent and substantial awards from Central European Funding. The opinions of the remaining twenty-five countries which had signed the Treaty of Versailles were simply ignored. The combination of German hauteur and Gallic insolence proved to be an impenetrable defence. France reverted once again to her traditional role as the 'Foe from the South', and there were still many British residents who had very painful, personal memories of the most recent conflict involving the efficient German Wehrmacht.

There were even those who looked elsewhere with fearful concern, half-expecting an unholy three-way alliance with an increasingly vociferous Scotland, where a burgeoning nationalist movement had forced through concession upon concession over a decade or more and was now demanding full independence from a far-distant London-centric government.

Every country in Europe, it seemed, was hunkering down with growing mistrust against every other nation, trusting nobody. And nobody, it seemed, believed in the brooding menace of the gathering storm.

CHAPTER TWENTY

T HE RED PHONE on the corner of Joey's desk burred twice.
"Brigadier Groth. Sitrep, please."

"Good morning, Brigadier. I have some figures based on updated data we have received from a reliable source."

"Is your source security cleared?"

"I'm not at liberty to name my—"

"Doctor Hart, if your informant has security clearance, you can be certain that his name will be on a *very* short list, which is on the desk in front of me as we speak. I can also assure you that I don't have a higher authority to refer to. All security clearance is my responsibility. Your informant?"

"He is based in Aberdeen. There are three others in the room with me whose names you know, but they only have limited security clearance."

"For the moment, I'll accept his codename."

"Angus."

There was a brief pause. Joey managed to make himself understood with a series of desperate hand signals. His team retreated to the far end of the room, allowing him some privacy on the phone.

"He seems to be doing more listening than talking," Eddie murmured.

Dave grinned. "Par for the course when the brigadier's on the other end."

"And he'll probably sign off in a hurry. He usually does," Brenda added.

The surprised expression on Joey's face and the way he glared at the receiver before replacing it told the onlookers that Groth had followed the usual procedure. Joey waved at them to return to the desk.

"It was touch and go, but I don't think Groth's going to have me shot at dawn for breaching security. My informant is on his list—for the moment, I'll continue to refer to him as Angus—so he's accepted that the information I received from him can be used, but I got a rollicking for not telling him first."

"Was he asking for information or giving it out?" Errol wanted to know.

Joey grimaced. "He has a way of getting more out of you than he gives away, but he fed me some interesting scraps, so I suppose that's something I ought to be grateful for. And I also got the green light to use anything else I get from Angus without having to ask for permission. That will save time, and time could be crucial if we have to deal with a situation at any of the potential trouble spots."

"How many of them are there, Joey?" Eddie was still playing catch-up. "I mean, we've got data from Iceland, the North Sea and this one in the middle of the Pacific." He flapped a hand in the direction of the chart lying on the table.

Joey brought him up to speed in a few words. "At first, we thought we were looking at two or three separate events. They're so far apart, we still can't be certain there *is* a connection, but I'm beginning to think a link isn't totally out of the question.

"The Pacific location is central and precisely the worst possible location to affect seismic events all around the Southern Hemisphere. Before you arrived, Eddie, we'd had reports of earthquakes in New Zealand, flooding and bush fires in Australia, and a tsunami in Japan which destroyed a nuclear power plant. It's almost impossible to guess how much collateral damage that's going to cause."

The blood drained from Eddie's face as he listened to Joey's terse assessment of the current state of play. He'd heard and read of all these things but hadn't yet had time to sit and reflect on the overall picture or even consider the possibility that there might be a connection between the events.

"How does this brigadier fit in? And does what he told you just now help or hinder our work here?"

"The brigadier and I have never met face-to-face, but I've worked with him on training exercises for a good few years. As far as security goes, his remit is absolute, and there isn't a court of appeal. What he says goes. And just in case anyone thinks maybe I can't count, I stuck my neck out asking you to join us, Eddie. I'll have to come clean with Groth next time he rings, but I decided it was better politics to avoid the complication of informing him of the current headcount. You're as vital to this team as anyone else, but Groth has enough on his plate, and there's no point in me adding to it."

"Bottom line, Joey." Errol tapped the map. "You were about to give us one possible interpretation of all these... these vectors? Was that the word? Does what you and Napoleon chatted about have any bearing? Does it change your guesswork any?"

"I'll have to re-calculate to answer your second question properly, Errol. I need some quality time with my computers for that. But the situation I see, based on what data I've had available until now, is this."

He took both charts and pinned them onto a blank whiteboard in their respective positions, showing the major landmasses and waters of the world.

"We have two seismic shocks—one stronger than the other—following almost an identical path originating from Iceland, travelling roughly south-southeast. From the north, we also have a weakish tremor heading almost due south. Providing these forces aren't deflected by something too solid for them to crush aside, and I can't offhand imagine anything *that* strong, these vectors should have them coming together at the point I've pencilled in—and for the record, you're right, Errol. The nearest land of any consequence is the island of Guam."

"You seemed more interested in the fact that the region has some extremely deep water, I think?"

"Spot on again, Eddie. The Mariana Trench has been measured to over twelve thousand feet deep—deeper than anywhere else on the planet."

"And this is important because…?"

Joey shook his head. "At the moment, I'm not sure. But until or unless I can gather more data and we can estimate the scale of the problem and how fast it's approaching us, it's going to be well-nigh impossible to work out any effective countermeasures."

Errol leant forward to catch Joey's attention. "What do we know about the Mariana Trench? You said you had a gut feeling it could be important. Go with it."

Joey nodded and set up a Google search. "It's the deepest part of any sector of seabed which has been recorded to date." He paraphrased the information which flowed across the screen, editing out the technical jargon to make it relevant for non-specialist ears.

"Depths of over four thousand metres—that's twelve thousand feet or two thousand fathoms in old money—have been confirmed, but mapping at such depths is always going to be a bit hit and miss. And here's something interesting. Apparently, some new life forms have been discovered.

"What can possibly survive at that depth? The water pressure must be tremendous."

"Nature's amazing, Dave. Somehow, things always find a way of adapting to their environment, no matter how harsh it is. The organisms discovered appear to be some form of primitive shellfish—I can only guess that the shell forms part of their natural defences against the pressure.

"The trench runs roughly northwest-to-southeast for a distance of…well, various estimates—a polite way of saying guesswork—between fifty and two hundred miles. And don't ask me to convert that into kilometres. The theory is it marks where two of the Earth's tectonic plates overlap. They've been coming together, chipping bits off each other's leading edges for millions of years, until one of them became too fragile and collapsed…"

A startled look came into Doctor Hart's eyes as he continued his résumé of the data scrolling across the screen. Instinctively, he reached for a notebook and the nearest calculator.

Dave completed the sentence Joey had started. "…which would set up a reaction in the surrounding bedrock."

"Of the infamous equal-and-opposite variety," Errol contributed. The logic was irrefutable.

"On a geological scale, the sort of collapse we're theorising could have taken started two, three thousand years ago, and it would only just be starting to show the effects now. But the calculations are straightforward. Rocket science, it ain't." Joey flourished his calculator as if it were Excalibur. The figures which filled the screen were meaningless to his captive audience, but they evidently meant something to him. He pounced on the red phone which had no dialling buttons and snatched the receiver. He wasn't waiting long.

"Brigadier Groth. Permission to use speakerphone at this end, Sir."

A nod, a wink and a thumbs-up, Joey hit a squelch button and replaced the handset on its cradle.

Groth's clipped military syllables marched out of the speakers. "Sitrep, Doctor?"

"This is a qualified guess, Sir, and needs to be verified from an independent source of some sort, but I feel it's worth investigating. Contacts in Australasia are probably best placed to supply this."

"Go ahead."

"I've mapped some records I have of seismic events in different parts of the world." Joey gave a concise report of his findings, clipping his words in unconscious imitation of the unseen brigadier at the end of the line, finishing with, "I haven't yet come up with any hard, scientific *proof* of this, Brigadier, but my gut feeling tells me the Mariana Trench will prove significant. We need to know what's happening in the South Pacific zone."

"I'm in touch with New Zealand on another line. I'll contact Australia when we end this call. Stand by."

The hum of a vacant line was magnified through the speaker unit as Groth, true to form, ended the call abruptly.

"Damn. I'd just about manned myself up to tell him you've joined the happy crew, Eddie. I'll probably get a right roasting next time I speak to him."

A stutter of *ping* tones announced a flurry of incoming email messages. Joey sprang into action and read swiftly through each of them.

"Groth's kicking ass elsewhere, by the looks of things. With any luck, he won't have me transported to the colonies for dropping the ball and not telling him we have one extra man on our team.

"Here's New Zealand, first to react. He said he already had a line open to them. There's an update from Australia too, but that looks like a general-state-of-play statement. They aren't giving me any updated figures to work with. I'll make a start by crunching the numbers New Zealand have sent—they appear to have been taken less than half an hour ago."

He seemed oblivious to the fact that he was talking to himself as he fell into a chair. His fingers danced across the keyboard seemingly with a life of their own. He certainly wasn't looking at the computer screen.

After several minutes of entering long strings of data, Joey looked around the room, crossed his fingers and hit *enter*. Columns of figures disappeared and were replaced by a revolving screensaver. As he stretched for the red phone, it shrilled. Groth had beaten him to the punch.

"Sitrep, please."

"I'm processing the latest info from Australasia as we speak. NZ's input seems more detailed than Australia's. Stand by."

Graphs and charts flickered across the computer screen in rapid succession, while on a side table a printer began to run. The continuous roll of paper ran to at least nine or ten A4 pages of single-spaced text. Joey scanned the opening page without detaching it from the roll.

"Results are just starting to come back. I can give you bullet points, but I'll have to study them."

"Bullet points will do nicely for now."

"I tried loading the data sequentially, by date of occurrence. Then I set it up as if they'd all originated from the Mariana Trench and rippled away in a northerly or southerly direction. As I expected, I got readings of shock waves pulsing along the ocean bed at regular, predictable intervals."

"Doctor, why do I think I can hear a 'but' at the end of that little speech?"

"Some of the waves don't follow the pattern I expected of them," Joey admitted. "They're still regularly spaced but weaker than...I'll call it the main beat for now, until I think of something better. There's the same time difference between them. They appear on the graphs almost as if they're an echo of some sort."

"Could they *be* an echo?" Errol asked. "From rolling over some hollow cavern beneath the seabed? We drilled into quite a few of them when we were testing in that sector."

"Hmm, possible, but it doesn't *feel* quite right. But look at the timeline. The echo effect isn't there at the start. It kicks in later."

"And it still has the same pulse as the stronger peaks," Dave noted. "There has to be a connection. It *must* be the same shock waves."

"Perhaps it's like radar," Eddie speculated. "Not an echo but a reflection? If the shock wave comes up against something it can't flatten or work around." He'd been frustrated, unable to make any meaningful or helpful comments due to his very basic layman's understanding of the technical issues involved.

"That sounds plausible."

"It does, Doctor Hart," Groth interrupted, his voice brittle with suspicion, "but I don't recognise the voice. Who's the speaker? Do you have an unauthorised extra person present?"

Joey rolled his eyes and used fingers and a thumb to put an imaginary pistol at his head.

"Brigadier, I haven't had a chance to inform you yet, but I had to make a spur-of-the-moment decision. In the circumstances, I don't think there's any security risk, and Dave will vouch for his friend's integrity."

In as few words as possible, Joey explained how Eddie had joined the team. Groth waited a few seconds before replying, and when he did, the tone of his voice suggested that Joey was not going to be shot at dawn.

"For the moment, Doctor, I believe you've used your initiative and opted for the best practical solution to a difficult situation. Mr. Holmes—that's H-O-L-M-E-S, I take it?—can remain with you as part of the group. Email me his date of birth, national insurance number and any other details he can provide. I'll run a full security check. Until that comes back clear, he's to be accompanied at all times and cannot be allowed to work on any task which I flag as classified. Is this acceptable? I assume you've got the speaker activated. I'll need confirmations from both of you."

"Agreed."

Both spoke at the same time.

Joey felt he'd used his get-out-of-jail-free card with the brigadier and sought to improve his chances of survival. "Sir, if the tremors *are* a rebound, so to speak, from the first shock wave meeting the bedrock of Australia, it would most likely ricochet in a northeasterly direction. That would explain it affecting the region around Christchurch, New Zealand, approaching from the south."

"Agreed, Doctor, but we need some corroboration. Would it fit with the timeline, the sequence of events so far?"

"It's sketchy, but yes. There's nothing I've spotted that would make it impossible, but that isn't the evidence you—we—need to work out what countermeasures to put in place. We only get one shot at this."

"So it has to be right. Point taken, Doctor Hart."

The brigadier paused. Joey was almost certain he could hear him take a deep breath before continuing.

"Have you looked further north? How would the theory of the tremors originating from the Mariana Trench affect the problems along the east coast of Japan or—even further away—could it possibly have a bearing on the earthquakes in Haiti? Depending on where you stand, I'm guessing that might be a little too far away, and if we're looking for cause and effect, too early in time?"

"Not really, Sir. For two or more seismic events to originate in or near the same spot, I'd say the odds are in our favour. And if we take the trench as the centre of all the shocks—or more correctly the *epicentre* of whatever's going on—then yes, the tremors could well be spreading in every direction at once, like ripples in a pond."

"So, events in Haiti and Japan could also be part of the overall picture. Thank you, Doctor. I'll leave you to study the available data as thoroughly as you always do, but on this occasion, please remember that time is *not* on our side."

The monotone hum of an empty line replaced Groth's final warning.

Joey looked at the handset, shrugged, and replaced it. "No time like the present. Better get on with it, I suppose."

* * *

"I need the most recent data you can send me, Rob. What you've sent so far, I can work with, but I need to check these figures, see if there have been any significant changes."

"I'm getting up-to-the-minute reports now. I gather your brigadier has been kicking some serious ass. What's your top priority?"

"I have a gut feeling that the source of all the quakes and tidal problems being recorded in your neck of the woods could be the Mariana Trench..." Joey summarised for Rob Jones his theory about the ripple and echo shocks rumbling deep beneath the seabed. "...and it's possible that the tsunami which destroyed the nuclear plant at Fukuyama also originated from the northern end of the trench. We're going to have some serious repercussions there, no doubt about it."

"We could do with some readings from that part of the Pacific, but I don't know of any ships out there. We get all our gen from unmanned weather stations or from GPS satellites. How 'bout your general? Has he got the clout to chivvy someone, twist a few arms?"

"Brigadier, you mean. I've never actually met the man, only talked to him on the phone, but I can ask. He seems able to get things sorted. There's one final item, some data I've just emailed to you."

"Just reading it, Joey." Rob still sounded casual, unflappable, typically laid-back Australian. "Save me time. How do the results of seismic events in GB and various parts of Europe have any bearing on Oz and New Zealand?"

"My calcs say the aftershock is heading for the same sector of the South Pacific, straight for the Mariana Trench. It could be the infamous final straw, Rob."

"The one that broke the...yowzah. You think that's a possibility, Joey?"

"As far as effective planning goes, we need a worst-case scenario to look at. The way I see it, this is one of several possible worst cases, but nowhere near the horror of a total meltdown in and around Fukuyama."

"What if you're proved right? What if the trench *is* the underlying root of the problem?"

"One thing at a time, Rob. If that happens, we'll find a way of dealing with it. But I'm convinced the trench is somehow involved in the problems we're having. Possibly the solution will also have a close connection to the trench."

"Okay, Joey. Listen, you must be rushed off your feet, and I know you've got none of your regular staff on duty, so I'll do the chasing around by phone from this end. There's some I can blag into giving me info they'd never dream of giving a Pom, God damn their scrawny red necks."

CHAPTER TWENTY-ONE

D AVE ROLLED OVER and managed to open one eye. It felt as if his eyelid was coated with coarse-grained sandpaper scraping the sensitive surface of his cornea. The computer across the room, which Joey had set up for Dave and Brenda to use, emitted another series of beeps. Who the hell would be calling him in the middle of the night? He paused and checked his watch before accepting the voice call, noting the time, 3:17.

"Mmm, yeah? Hello?"

"Dave, it's Pete. Haven't you been following the news?"

Dave suddenly found himself on his feet, a jolt of adrenaline scouring the last vestiges of sleep from his system.

"*Au contraire*, dear bruv. I've been worried sick about you since the quake in Christchurch."

"That's quakes, Dave. We've had another major shock, not counting the aftershocks."

"All the same, I couldn't ring to find out how you were coping, but I can give you a quick heads-up, and that's probably more than I *ought* to be telling you. We're under something called Condition Red security restrictions, which is only one step from being on an all-out-war footing. If the CO finds out I've spoken to anyone—even you—he'll have my guts for garters."

"No worries, bro. He won't find out anything from me."

"Anyway, Pete, as long as you're okay, you can pay me back."

"How so?"

"We're isolated, and nobody is allowed in or out. We're using every scrap of data we can find about the weather and the problems it's throwing into the mix in your part of the world. Our problem is time lag. Everything we're getting is a report on something which has already happened. The best we've had is an update less than three hours after the event, but it's usually more like ten to twelve hours before it trickles down to us. You're fairly high up in the natural sciences arena. Is there anyone you can lean on?"

* * *

After the call, Dave left Brenda sleeping and headed for the ops room. Joey was still there surrounded by the tools of his trade.

"Don't you ever take a break?"

"Not until I have another met officer or geologist to relieve me, and he'll also have to be able to read my scribbles." Joey grunted, without looking up. "What's got you out of bed?"

"Pete rang me." Joey's head snapped up. "I think you should hear what he has to say."

Joey's facial expression was difficult to read, but Dave thought he saw the light of anger die away from his eyes. After a couple of seconds, which seemed to last forever, he nodded and moved aside so Dave could reach the computer and return the call.

"Pete, I'm with Doctor Hart." Remembering they hadn't had time for formal introductions the last time Pete had called, Dave added, "Doctor Joey Hart, meteorologist and team leader. He's also a geologist and has alphabet soup after his name."

"Doctor Hart of Liverpool Uni? The author of most of the readable books about weather and climate change which have been written in the last twenty years?"

Joey had the grace to flush and offered a tired smile. "Nice to know someone other than me has read them—otherwise it would have been a total waste of my time."

"And we have a mutual friend in Australia, I believe," Pete said. "Doctor Rob Jones at the Met Office?"

"Yeah, Rob and I go way back..."

Dave's appreciation of Joey leapt several notches. To hold the position he had at the uni, of course, he had to know his subject, but until now, Dave hadn't realised that he'd also earned his stripes as an expert in his chosen field. He tried to tune back into the Skype conversation, but Joey and Pete had progressed rapidly on to technical matters which were beyond his understanding.

"Okay," Joey said, "this is what I need from you, Doctor Whelan. Data on any more tidal problems in your region as soon as you get it. We're looking for anomalies, unexpected readings, anything out of the ordinary. I know that's a bit vague, but you must have some geologists and other weather experts you can, in your brother's words, lean on." Joey gave Dave a sideways glance, his remark confirming he was monitoring all communication.

"I'll call you, or more likely, Dave will, at 0800 our time. That's 0700 Zulu, we're on Daylight Saving now. I make that 1900 for you, okay? Our CO is a man of habit. He's not due to ring me until an hour later, and if I've got some fresh ammo to surprise him with, it'll make my job of telling him there's someone else joining the team that much easier. You should also have a potted bio and your personal details to hand when we speak. He's going to demand a security check. There won't be any way to avoid that."

"Wilco, Doc. I have no problems with the security angle, I wouldn't expect anything less. If my reprobate kid brother can pass for a human being, I'm sure your nameless CO will find my stats and info acceptable. Dave says you push yourself too hard. I suggest we all get some sack time and speak again four hours from now."

* * *

"Pete? For Christ's sake, I said I'd call—"

"You also said you wanted updates as soon as I had something."

The tension in Pete's voice as he interrupted his brother spoke volumes. Dave snapped fully awake and glanced at the time. He'd collapsed back into bed less than two hours ago, and now Brenda was showing signs of waking. He kissed her cheek and padded out of the room, stretching the phone cord as far as it would go, so he could concentrate on whatever Pete had to add to the picture.

"This is happening as we speak. Tremors recorded at Richter eight point five, Indian Ocean, about three hundred miles east of Sumatra. A tsunami warning has been issued—I'm sending an email with the prelim data we have so far."

"I understand why you jumped the gun. You're excused. Pete, I'm going to get Joey out of bed—if he ever *went* to bed. Try to get what you can on this quake, and I'll call you back as planned, two hours from now."

* * *

Brenda passed around coffees as Dave placed the call.

"I hope Groth's not been working through the night," Joey muttered, immediately sipping the hot liquid. "I could really do with any advantage Pete's info might give me...Pete."

"Good morning, Doctor Hart." Pete's voice floated out of the computer speakers.

"Tell me you've got something concrete I can use."

"I have. Lots of remote sensors were installed on the QT after the last big quake in the area five years back. State-of-the-art stuff, too, some of it still at the testing stage, but that info is classified, so be careful who you tell. It all seems to be holding up, no malfunctions reported, and I'm sending you some data now."

The email inbox pinged: Joey went to another terminal and began reading.

"The epicentre's coppers short of three hundred miles east of Formosa. First indications place it twenty miles below the seabed."

"Twenty—that's two-zero *miles* deep?" Dave queried. "That sounds incredible. You're sure?"

"Not so surprising," Joey commented. "I've worked with forces buried at similar depths before. In a way, I'm relieved to hear it. At such depths, the tremors themselves are too deep to cause structural damage when they reach landfall, and we can discount any possibility of a tsunami or other tidal dangers. Ocean swells are only caused by much shallower disturbances."

"That's what my boffins tell me too, Doctor," Pete confirmed. "So I guess that's one bit of good news for your boss."

"At the moment, we'll take any crumbs that fall from the table," Dave replied. "But I think it's best I shut up and let Joey do the talking."

Joey had two charts laid out side by side: one was the familiar projection map of the world's main landmasses; the other resembled a schematic of rounded arcs, reminding Dave of the layers of an onion chopped in half. This seemed to be far more interesting to Joey, and after a few seconds, Dave guessed it was some sort of schematic cross-section of the planet's interior, showing the composition of the layers of different types of rock at different depths.

Joey glanced at his notepad, then took a ruler and added one last line on the projection map. All the other lines were solid and in a variety of colours. This one, drawn in red, was a series of evenly spaced red dots and appeared to originate from somewhere in the Northern Hemisphere.

"Pete, I'll email you something in a moment. Let me just explain what it is first. It'll save me having to go through it a second time with my team. You'll need to use a bit of imagination until you get the graphic to look at, but I think it's pretty straightforward."

If Joey was aware of the incongruity of his statement applied to the unpredictable, dangerous forces of nature at play, he didn't show it.

"First, the world map. What I've drawn here represents the confirmed seismic events of any significance reported so far. They're a matter of historical record, so they're all solid lines. Different colours—my own choice—to show different strengths. With me so far?"

A series of nods from the 'team' confirmed they all were.

"Good. Pete, this is where I need you to think carefully. I've added one final piece of data, based on info you won't have at your fingertips because it's related to several different events in the Northern Hemisphere. I haven't received much in the way of confirmation or verification yet, so I've made a provisional vector by showing it as a dotted red line. It begins from the South Coast of the UK near Dover and runs on a bearing of one hundred and seventy degrees."

"Heading my way, then." Pete didn't sound too surprised. "How strong is it?"

"Insufficient data for more than a blind guess. But there's nothing wrong with your imagination." Joey paused for a moment, then continued more seriously, "This is really a cobbled-together result from multiple separate Northern Hemisphere events which all took place within a few days of each other at different locations. However, by the time they reach the Channel, they're converging so closely that I decided it would make no significant difference to the direction and strength of the line to combine them into a single vector."

"What's a vector?" Brenda murmured to Dave. He hesitated, unwilling to disturb the flow of data between the two specialists. Joey heard her and nodded to acknowledge the question.

"A vector. Something which has two or more main parts or components. In this case, power and direction."

"Thanks, Joey." Dave had already worked this out but was grateful for a simple definition.

"The graphics are on their way, Pete." Joey hit *enter* on his keyboard as he spoke. "And to save a few seconds, I can tell you the heading extends through the European landmass and meets up with the Southern Hemisphere readings right in the centre of the Mariana Trench. I'm not a great fan of coincidences at the best of times, but in this case, I'm convinced we ought to be concentrating our research on what we know about the trench."

He glanced at his watch. "We've a max. one hour before Groth is on the line, and he's going to haul my ass over the coals if I haven't got some hard facts to lay out, and preferably some suggestions for how to deal with the problem. See what you can get for me, Pete. I can only find sketchy details on file up here, but I know your oceanographic department did a lot of the fieldwork."

"I'm on it. I've got your graphics. I'll try to get something back to you before you have to face the music. Bye for now."

CHAPTER TWENTY-TWO

J OEY FLINCHED AND stared at the clock as the phone shrilled.

"Damn you, Groth, you said ten o'cl…" He was already reaching for the handset when he realised the incoming call was not on the direct connection from the brigadier's office. A flashing light redirected his attention to a different outside line. The handset was an ancient dialling model; no pushbuttons, no mini-screen to identify the caller.

"Hello?"

"Joey, has your boss whipped your ass yet?"

"Angus! No, you've beaten him to the punch—just. He's due to call in the next ten minutes, so we haven't much time. Word of warning, though. For security reasons, I can *only* use your codename. There are people here with me who haven't been cleared yet. That's something I hope my boss can sort out when he rings."

"Understood. I may have something for you—I've already emailed you details of another incident, which is literally taking place as we speak. I don't think the tremor heading south from the seismic events in Iceland and the North Sea could have reached Northern Italy yet, so this is almost certainly a separate incident."

"Did you say *Italy*?"

"You heard me right, Joey. Initial reports say it's about a six, epicentre Modena and Bologna, extensive structural damage to ancient historical sites."

"Angus, you might just have saved my life. I'm going to cut you short, but any more details you can email will be useful."

Joey barely had time to replace the handset before Groth's direct line sounded off. Rolling his eyes in not-quite-feigned terror, he wiped imaginary beads of sweat from his forehead as he picked up.

"Sitrep, Doctor Hart?"

"Sir, my scientific source, codename Angus, has reported an incident which he believes is further evidence of a general pattern. The full effects may not be known for some time, however. The incident is in progress as we speak, and the data needs to be analysed." Joey closed his eyes and prayed for a split second before continuing. "Just after four this morning, local time, an earthquake measuring six on the Richter scale caused severe structural damage in Bologna, Modena and other parts of Northern Italy."

Joey summarised the information from Angus while scanning emails and scribbling notes. Groth remained silent, and Joey was grateful. He doubted he could have kept a fourth ball in the air if the brigadier had interrupted with questions.

"Doctor Hart, is it possible the minor tremor heading south could have acted as a catalyst of sorts, provoking the more serious incident in Italy?"

"I wouldn't say that's impossible, Brigadier, but it's unlikely. I'd need up-to-the-minute data to investigate that, and something's telling me we don't have time on our side."

"Agreed. Now tell me this. Can you predict how far the effects of this latest incident may spread, or in which direction?"

"Once I can analyse reports of any aftershocks, that may be possible. First indications from the data I've already received suggest it's likely to follow the line of least resistance—

in other words, west through the Med and into open waters, south or southwest."

He paused, as Errol bent over the map and placed a finger on a specific point that was already highlighted.

"Doctor Hart. Are we still connected?"

"Yes, Sir. One of my team has several years' experience in offshore drilling. He's worked in the South Pacific, and from the recordings I have in front of me, I have to agree with him. With its present speed and direction, the shock wave from this incident is heading directly towards the Mariana Trench, the deepest crevasse in the Pacific seabed. The earlier events in the Southern Hemisphere—Japan, New Zealand, Australia—may also have been initiated by disturbances in the same region."

Errol nodded his agreement. "When you look at the time elapsed since the first incident, this could be a return wave of sorts, bouncing back after meeting the resistance of solid bedrock when it reached the Italian mainland."

"If that's your drilling expert speaking, Doctor Hart, perhaps we'd better stop and listen to what he has to say. It sounds reasonable to me. Can you investigate the theory with the data you have, or do you need more?"

"Errol tells me the phenomenon is pretty common in the offshore drilling world, but now I know what to look for, it should be easy to confirm."

"Errol. Doctor Hart, perhaps you ought to pass me his details. I don't doubt your judgement, but I really *do* need to run basic security checks on everyone connected with the developing situation."

"Quickest and easiest if I let him speak to you directly, Sir. I believe he has something to contribute to the discussion too."

Joey stood and allowed Errol to take his place.

"I gather you'd prefer to clear the formalities first, Brigadier. Errol Dwight at your service. My details..." Errol reeled off his social security and passport numbers, date of birth and anything else the brigadier requested.

"Thank you, Mr. Dwight. In view of the pressure of time, I'm going to assume there are no security problems in your background. Doctor Hart tells me you have something from your drilling experience which may be relevant?"

"Yessir. I've drilled in a sector close to the Mariana Trench. It's not easy drilling at such extreme depths. Without getting too technical, most of the problems are related to the temperatures and pressures involved."

"That much I can appreciate, Mr. Dwight, even as a layman without any specialist knowledge or experience. Carry on."

"When work has finished on a drill hole, it has to be capped or sealed. Sometimes this is a temporary seal—if the operator plans to return for further investigation or exploitation later. Sometimes you draw a blank and seal the hole permanently. In such a case, the hole is usually filled with materials that closely resemble the types of rock and minerals which occur naturally in the region, to avoid cross-contamination.

"There are also situations where there's a risk of a blowout or another environmental disaster. Then you pump down whatever you have on hand—the heavier, the better— and hold it back until the pressure drops. Filling up an open formation such as this isn't as straightforward as filling up a pipe, but the principle's the same. We just don't know the dimensions of the hole or how much material we're going to need."

"Hmm. I'll take your word on that, for the moment, but I'm sure most people would consider the two variables you mention vital data for a successful operation."

"No question about that, Sir. But if we can get some approximate figures..."

Joey had been scribbling again. Now, as a short pause developed, he seized the opportunity.

"The tremor passing through mainland Europe has turned to the west after the incident in Italy. As we predicted, it's taking the line of least resistance, off along the Med, heading for open water—it's easier to flow through water instead of rock," he added, by way of explanation. "That means it's heading directly towards the Mariana Trench."

"Is this good news or bad?" Groth's voice was completely dispassionate.

"Think of it as an underwater avalanche of rocks, mineral deposits and other assorted solid matter. On its present course, it will tip itself *into* the trench. If there's enough material being swept along, it will certainly backfill a fair percentage of the fissure's total size and make our clean-up operation significantly easier."

"Is there anything we can do to control the direction of this avalanche as you call it? Or the speed at which it's moving?"

"Sir, the total mass of this moving body is unimaginable. We'd probably have to invent some multi-gigatonne unit to describe it. Control of any sort would be impossible. We must be grateful it's moving in exactly the right direction. And as for the velocity..."

There was the briefest of pauses while Joey crunched a few more numbers, which were totally beyond a layman's comprehension.

"Latest available data says it will take about three days to reach the northern end of the trench—maybe a further two days to reach the southern end."

"Doctor Hart, the volume of material being carried in this avalanche. Would it be sufficient to fill the trench?"

"We don't have a definite measure of the size of the trench, Sir, but even without that information, I can tell you it wouldn't even come close. The length and the width of the fissure confirms this, regardless of how deep it reaches."

"There's another drilling process which might be worth considering." Errol's Southern drawl was back, but he sounded far less confident this time around. He looked to Joey for permission to continue, but Brigadier Groth's voice cut in.

"Go ahead, Mr. Dwight. Anything you can contribute based on your professional training will be useful."

"There may be another way to backfill the trench, but it's something I have no *personal* experience with. I can only tell you the theory behind it. There are most definitely risks involved—it's something of a last-ditch solution when all other options have failed.

"When a hole has to be capped in a hurry—if there's a risk of a blowout, for example—explosives have been used to collapse tons of rubble from the walls."

"Thank you, Mr. Dwight. I'm familiar with the idea of using controlled explosions in mining and demolition work."

"That's correct, Sir. Like I say, I have no personal experience of using this technique, but you can certainly find more information on the internet, including the names of people able to tell you more about it than I can."

"We'd need a considerable amount of explosive to attempt this solution, I imagine?"

"No doubt about that, Sir."

"Thank you, Mr. Dwight. I may have sufficient contacts in the military world to make this possible, but three to five days before the avalanche passes the trench altogether is a far bigger problem than acquiring the explosives. I'll speak to some people I know. Doctor Hart, please ensure this phone is manned at all times."

For once, Groth's abrupt sign-off technique seemed both natural and logical. He had a lot of phoning around to do; that much would have been obvious to anyone.

Brenda voiced the obvious question. "How big a fish *is* this brigadier? I always thought the TA consisted mostly of part-timers who sign up as volunteers."

"Even volunteers and weekend warriors need effective, trained leaders, darling," Dave answered. "There will always be full-time career opportunities for an officer with Groth's qualities."

Joey nodded in agreement. "He's been a brigadier in the TA for longer than I've known him, and in that time, he's declined three offers of promotion that *I* know about—says he didn't sign up to 'fly a desk', and he'd rather remain in an active role. So he's well-connected. For that reason alone, I'm guessing he's about to do some serious arm-twisting and calling in of favours."

* * *

Almost two hours passed before the phone rang. Joey looked around the group and shrugged. He made a theatrical performance of crossing himself before picking up the receiver on its second ring.

"Doctor Hart speaking."

"You may leave this on speakerphone if you wish. I've had your colleagues' security checked. The information I have will affect you all."

"Understood, Brigadier. Go ahead."

"All your instructions will continue to come directly from me, and me alone. However, this is now an international operation, and I will be relaying orders from a higher authority.

"The option of sealing the Mariana Trench by using shaped charges, as suggested by Mr. Dwight, has been approved in principle. Every country that has signed the NATO treaty will contribute the most powerful weapons at their disposal. A request has been issued to other non-NATO powers known to have a stockpile of conventional *and* nuclear weapons to reciprocate. The window for setting things in motion is tight, but anything which can be flown to the site will be delivered. Your team are not on the need-to-know priority list, but for your information, I can add that this *will* include some tactical nuclear weapons for maximum effect in a confined space and at a depth that should ensure there are no grounds to fear any radiation leakage or danger to human life after the event."

"How about the sea life?" Dave interrupted. "Sealing off a major feature like the Mariana Trench is bound to affect marine ecology. This is the deepest recorded sector of *all* the seas and oceans on the planet. We already know of some unique plants, fish and invertebrates which aren't found anywhere else in the world."

"I appreciate your concern, Mr. Whelan, but unless we can close off this trench in less than four days, all the volcanic actions and other natural disasters currently venting through the fragile crust of the planet will only intensify, and we may be left with the very real possibility of the rock in space we call home being blown apart by internal pressure. We have no choice."

"But *nuclear* weapons?"

"What sort of power did you think we have at the *nucleus* of our planet?" Groth snapped, then took an audible breath to regain his normal composure. "It keeps vast lakes of melted rocks at such high temperatures, they erupt as boiling liquids. Army demolition experts assure me that there's minimal chance of contamination. We have the equipment to pour on layer after layer of concrete if we have to, but the consensus is that the rockfall alone will be more than enough to protect all land life and almost all sea life. Radiation will be reflected downwards and simply add to the fires at the planet's core."

"Nice one, Errol," Joey said. "You had that one sussed—without the uni background or the scrambled egg on your collar 'n' cuffs."

"Like I said, ma paw put me to work when I was still in diapers."

"No need for the comedy act, Errol. Don't belittle yourself." Dave slung an arm around the musician's broad shoulders. "You went with a gut feeling, and you were right."

"Gentlemen, can we concentrate on what's needed right now? We're desperately short of time."

"Apologies, Sir," Joey said with a grimace at his comrades.

"You're still my eyes and ears for the operation, Doctor. In an ideal world, I'd come and join you, but I can't leave my command centre in someone else's hands."

"We've got access to the latest radio telescope, Sir, but you probably knew that already."

"I also do my homework, Doctor, so yes, I'm aware you're well equipped for the task in hand, and I know I can count on you. If you turn to your main screen now, I'm patching you in to a real-time link. What you see is happening as we speak—with a maximum eight-second lapse."

Joey turned to the screen, as did the rest of the group.

"These are the Wolf-class rapid-response vessels which have already been despatched by the Royal Navy. They're fully loaded and expected on the scene within twelve hours. They were taking part in an exercise which you don't *need to know* anything about. They were already in the Southern Hemisphere and easy to re-deploy. They'll be the first to arrive."

Eight sleek warships appeared in a tight formation. Each pushed a hue bow wave, indicating that they were travelling flat out.

"The US has released some larger and slower vessels carrying larger weapons, but they also have further to travel. France has committed to respond—they should be on the scene soon after the UK vanguard and before the Americans. They will be carrying conventional weapons only. You are essentially the traffic cop on point duty. Your responsibility will be to guide each vessel in and out and ensure there are no collisions. I don't have to tell you how disastrous *that* could be.

"All commands will be issued in English. I haven't time to provide linguists with the necessary security clearance, but we don't anticipate any problems there."

"Information, Sir," Dave interrupted. "Brenda is native-fluent in French. We have some back-up if need be."

"Duly noted." Groth acknowledged. "The vessels will be instructed to prime their payloads once they are above the trench, then drop them and depart immediately. The weapons will be detonated by an electronic charge, not by pressure depth. This leaves ultimate control in our hands and gives the final vessels time to steam away from the danger zone before the button is pressed. Once the first few bombs are activated, the chain reaction they initiate will complete the process.

"I can't say yet how many non-NATO pact countries will respond positively, but you'll have your hands full controlling the shipping lanes. It's going to get crowded out there before we're finished, so I suggest you all get what rest you can in the meantime. The ships on your screen are about six, maybe seven hours from reaching the trench. Good luck."

The phone line went dead. On-screen, the British ships continued to spear through the featureless waves of an anonymous sector of what was presumably the South Pacific. They appeared to be coming from somewhere southwest of their present location. Dave suspected they'd been on manoeuvres in the vicinity of the Falklands, sabre-rattling to remind Argentina to respect the wishes of the islands' residents.

"The brigadier's right," Dave said. "We all need a rest—especially you, Joey. You haven't left this room since we arrived. Now, sod off and lie down before you fall down. We can't afford to have you collapse on the job. Without you, none of us have got a clue how any of this equipment works."

Joey wasn't going to give up without a fight, of course, but Dave knew him well enough to talk him round, make him see sense.

"The phone will be manned anyway, Joey. I can sleep anywhere—just ask Brenda. Now, no more arguments. I'm taking the first shift. If it makes you feel any better, I promise I'll wake you if it rings. But you've got to get some proper sleep."

* * *

The phone remained stubbornly silent through the remainder of the afternoon and evening, but Dave wasn't surprised by that. It was too early to expect anything of significance to show on the overall operations map. The main screen continued to show the convoy of eight Wolf destroyers arrowing through an empty sector of open sea, their wakes demonstrating a single-minded intention to arrive at their destination as swiftly as possible.

At one point, it occurred to Dave that the resolution and clarity on the screen were exceptional. It was being relayed via an orbiting satellite who-knew-how-many miles above the scene but could just as easily have been taken from a low-flying spotter plane equipped with the latest in tele lenses. *Probably top-class military equipment*, he thought to himself, *and more than likely still being tested—by us, amongst others.*

He had to think hard before reconciling that it was now night where he was, so looking at a full daylight scene at the other end of the world was to be expected. He was aware of information being plotted on other screens around the room, but either they showed graphs and charts, or they were clearly marked 'radar'.

He could tell they were being updated automatically from an outside source. He could also see there were considerably more dots on each screen than there had been. They were in different colours and all converging steadily on a rendezvous point further along the British convoy's projected course. He'd had no radar training and was therefore not in a position to interpret the figures, but he understood what Groth had meant when he spoke of this particular sector of the world's largest ocean becoming 'crowded' before the operation reached its climax.

CHAPTER TWENTY-THREE

I'M GLAD TO see you—" Joey checked the ID photocard pinned to the soldier's breast pocket. "—Sergeant Jackson. We're a random group of amateurs trying to cope with a situation that needs trained pros. I take it you're the senior officer?"

"That's right, Doctor Hart. And from what the brig told me at our briefing, you've all done a remarkable job."

"We've done our best," Joey replied humbly. "The brigadier has been a great help, even at the far end of a phone line. There are plenty of rooms available for you and your team. D'you need a few minutes to settle in and unpack, or...?"

Joey paused as the sergeant raised his hand and turned to point at two squaddies, then at the stack of luggage and equipment stashed in the corridor.

"They'll sort out my kit as well as their own. The sooner I get to the ops room the better. Lead on, Doctor. Let's see what's happening. The Insats team will join us as soon as they've billeted."

Eddie ended a phone call as Joey entered the control room. He scribbled a few more words on a notepad—presumably the last phrase of the message he'd been taking—and waved it above his head. "Looks like another UK incident."

"The US cavalry's arrived, Eddie." Joey gestured to the man next to him. "Sergeant Jackson's in charge now. The others will be with us as soon as they've stashed their gear. What's the score?"

"This one's from mid-Wales. Small town not far from Aberystwyth. They've had about a fortnight's rainfall in the last twenty-four hours, and the walls of the dam at the head of a local reservoir have been breached. The RAF is evacuating people." He brought the note across the room as he read from it. "The weather station at Valley on Anglesey rang it in. Someone who asked for you by name when he called—Martin Dring?"

"Yeah. We go way back. He's no scaremonger and knows more than most people about weather patterns."

Joey studied the note and handed it to Sergeant Jackson, who scanned it indifferently.

"My colleague reckons there's a connection with the last tremor travelling south, most likely point of origin somewhere in Cumbria," Joey explained, mindful that the newly arrived military leader probably wasn't qualified to interpret the densely packed columns and rows of figures on the printout Eddie had in his other hand. Nevertheless, Jackson gave it a cursory look-over when Joey passed it his way.

"D'you mean there might be a connection between these earth tremors and the recent bad weather?"

"It's a theory," Joey confirmed. "So far, we've no idea how we might test it, but..." He shrugged and started scribbling some figures on a scratchpad. "Is the weather still as bad? I've almost forgotten what outside looks like."

Eddie grumbled to no-one in particular, "I'm going stir-crazy here."

Jackson handed the paperwork to Joey with a nod of thanks. "You'd better file these somewhere. I'm sure you can use the data more efficiently than I could. Now, show me the radar screens. That's something I *can* make sense of."

* * *

"The NATO flotilla has mustered and is approaching the drop zone from the north in close formation. ETA at present speed approximately two hours."

"Acknowledged, Sergeant. Task Force Two approaching from the south and west. They ought to be further away from the drop zone. What's your assessment of their progress?" Groth's clear, clipped diction was without emotion, businesslike, a calming influence to ease the tension developing with each minute that passed.

"The timing of when the last few vessels dump their payload may get a bit tight, Sir, but on paper, there's time enough for maximum coverage. We have a window of three, perhaps four hours before depth pressure will make the explosive charges unstable. We may be able to delay remote detonation an extra hour, but not much more. With empty holds and steaming at full speed, they should be at least fifty nautical miles from ground zero. It's tight, but as long as there are no mishaps, they should be able to ride the wave."

"Is radiation likely to be a factor?"

Sergeant Jackson winced and stared at the map for several long seconds.

"We're in unknown territory here, Sir," he said, gravely. "All the testing of nuclear warheads under controlled conditions over the last sixty years and more have been just that. Tests. I don't have to remind you what happened when a single device was detonated at Hiroshima."

"I accept that—reluctantly. And the total tonnage of conventional weapons involved is also unprecedented."

A trace of emotion crept into Groth's voice, which even the artificial timbre of the PA speakers couldn't disguise.

"We have limited choice—in truth, none whatsoever. The trench *has* to be sealed, and permanently. We get one shot at this. We *have* to get it right, first time."

Jackson wiped his brow and straightened up as if the brigadier had suddenly entered the room.

"The nuclear warheads will be buried beneath conventional weapons. The megatonnes—gigatonnes—of rock displaced by the blast will be far greater than the estimated capacity of the trench. Any radiation released by the blast is expected to be contained *beneath* target depth where it will combine with the molten core of the planet. That, Sir, is the conclusion of the scientists who attempted a risk assessment for this scenario."

"Sergeant, your team—which specifically includes *all* civilian personnel—will continue to be the eyes and ears of the operation. Get all vessels out of the area as swiftly and as far away as possible. Instruct all ships to head west and disperse into open waters."

"All the world leaders have been alerted and summoned to London. They will be briefed, and remote detonation will be carried out from a location somewhere in the UK."

"Your first responsibility is to direct all shipping away from ground zero post-haste. Your second objective— which is also vital—will be to buy us as much time as you possibly can before the executive decision to detonate has to be taken."

"Understood, Brigadier."

"And may God have mercy on us all."

Sergeant Jackson was stunned into silence. Before he could draw the breath needed to respond, the opportunity passed as, true to form, Groth ended his call without the formality of a signing-off protocol. To the civilian members of the team who had become accustomed to the brigadier's *modus operandi,* the familiar hum of an open telephone line seemed louder than ever before.

* * *

"Orders from High Command, Sir."

The scene on the bridge of *HMS Liverpool* was being replicated almost simultaneously on the bridge of every other warship in the NATO flotilla as they reached a sector of the sea directly above the northern limit of the Mariana Trench.

The instructions were clear. The fleet was to realign into two columns two nautical miles apart. After releasing their payloads, the right-hand column was ordered to pull slightly ahead of their partner to allow room to manoeuvre before turning hard to starboard and steaming away from the trench at full speed.

"It sounds simple," grunted *Liverpool*'s captain, "but it's going to be very, very tight. There's no room whatsoever for error. It's like *Come Dancing on Ice* but with a formation team of sixty-thousand-tonne warships. Still, orders is orders. We just have to trust that the traffic cops back in Blighty keep their eye on the ball and keep us all a safe distance apart as we turn."

Similar discussions were echoing around the command consoles of every vessel in the convoy as the ships paired off and positioned themselves above the target. Radio silence was imposed, but with typical naval resourcefulness, each ship remained in constant contact with its running mate using mirrors to semaphore Morse messages so they could fine-tune their speeds and relative distances from each other.

* * *

At Bidston Hill, the Insats military team had paired off with the original civilian amateurs and familiarised themselves with the intended procedures by carrying out dummy runs up to the point of issuing the final order to release their weapons.

"The crucial move—and the one we *have* to make sure happens on time—is going to be the 'hard a-starboard' *after* they've dumped their payload."

"I can plot out the angles for you, Sergeant," Joey said, "but we're going to need input from someone who knows how much space a vessel that size needs to change course, especially at speed, and safely."

"The brigadier has all that data at his fingertips. I'm sure he'll have a team of experts on hand to advise him, as he's no personal experience of naval operations. All we need to do is keep him updated with what we see happening on radar. He will decide the best time to hit the Big Red Button based on what we tell him."

Joey looked around the room. Three of the professional soldiers sat by three computer screens, partnered with Eddie, Dave and Errol. One screen provided a bird's eye view of a flotilla of ships; the remaining two showed radar screens on which the approaching fleets converged from the north and the south.

"Even I can see that the northern group is a lot closer than the other one," Joey said. "As long as they can drop their cargo and scarper, they can be well on their way before the second wave arrives from the south."

"The theory's all very well, Doctor Hart, but it might only take one breakdown—or worse, a collision. If either of the ships involved is still carrying its load, the consequences don't bear thinking about."

"So Groth wasn't exaggerating when he said our role as 'traffic cops' is vital. Am I glad you army guys came to make sure it all runs smoothly." Joey sat with Jackson at a central desk, which had been cleared of all papers and anything else that wasn't nailed in place in order to serve as clearing house for data from the screen consoles and instructions from outside.

"You were doing a terrific job before we arrived," Sergeant Jackson countered. "Don't be so modest about it. You saw for yourself—your team members didn't need a great deal of coaching. They cottoned on straight away.

You must have been following the recommended army data-processing practices already."

Brenda appeared at the door, pushing a trolley laden with a stainless steel urn of impressive dimensions, cups, plates and all the standard accessories. A crew change followed her through the doors and relieved the three soldiers sitting at the radar screens.

"This team is fully rested. They'll take the night watch on their own. I'll rotate my personnel as fairly as I can if we're here for a couple of days, but the night watch will undertake solo shifts. We're used to long work spells, and it wouldn't be fair to subject civilians to such intense concentration for six hours at a time—possibly more."

Automatically, Joey glanced at his watch. Being indoors and with no window to give him a glimpse of the outside world, he hadn't realised the swift passage of time. His brain rebelled. He couldn't prevent a yawn of painful, jaw-cracking dimensions. Sergeant Jackson rounded on him immediately.

"You're all in, too. And you didn't tell me when we arrived how long you've been on your feet."

"Too bloody long." Joey was suddenly too tired to protest or muster the mental alertness to lie convincingly.

The NCO stood and assumed a waspish, enunciated command voice that could have penetrated the foot-thick walls of a lead-lined nuclear shelter. He named the failures and sexual foibles of Joey's immediate family tree over three or four generations, then told him explicitly and at length exactly what he intended to do to Joey if he caught him out of bed at any time in the next eight hours.

"There's still at least two hours before the first ships of Task Force One arrive at ground zero. This is a good time for all personnel *not* bound by army regs to get what rest they can. Tomorrow's going to be a *very* long day."

* * *

"Task Force Two, sitrep."

The southern contingent's instructions were being relayed from Australia, but the point of origin and where every operational decision was now being taken was an undisclosed base in England.

"Making twenty knots, sea calm, visibility good. All vessels holding station one nautical mile from designated partners. Over."

"Understood, Two Leader. Can you estimate distance to target or approximate ETA?"

"In these seas, three hours at current speed."

"Stand by."

A British voice replaced that of the Australian commander-in-chief in the captain's cabin.

"Task Force Two, the CC in Adelaide will continue to monitor transmissions. They may even offer information and suggestions, but all future orders will come from the UK. We can save time by speaking to *both* fleets simultaneously."

"Roger that, London."

"My name is Brigadier Groth, and I didn't say I was in London. Confirm receipt of the revised chain of command. Over."

"Understood."

"Command Officer, Task Force One. Confirmation please."

"Understood, Brigadier."

"Task Force One, you are re-classified as Wolf Pack One until this operation is complete. Similarly, Task Force Two, you are now Wolf Pack Two. All operational orders will come direct from me. Where possible, emails will follow to confirm your orders, but do not, repeat do *not* wait for them before initiating any action. Confirm."

"Understood, Brigadier."

"Accepted. Wolf Pack Two, reduce speed to eighteen knots. If you continue at your present speed, you may be too early arriving on station. Wolf Pack One needs the biggest possible window of opportunity to swing west and steam away. You will be performing a similar manoeuvre once you have released your weapons, and we don't want any collisions."

* * *

"Who is this guy? And when did the rank brigadier get included in the senior ranks of movers and shakers?"

The connection with Bidston Hill was still open, but Groth had curtailed the transmission outlining the revised orders in his usual abrupt manner. The CO at the ops centre in Adelaide wasn't prepared for this, and he certainly wasn't amused.

Sergeant Jackson took pity on him. Hoping that Groth wasn't listening, he offered an explanation.

"What can I say? The brigadier is old school. My understanding is, he has opted to retain the rank brigadier for personal reasons. It ought to be obvious to anyone that his real authority is considerably higher. And I never said that. Just thinking it is probably a breach of the Official Secrets Act."

"Understood."

"Wolf Pack Two, I'm closing this link. Wolf Pack One are in position. Follow amended orders and stand by for updates."

Sergeant Jackson's sign-off technique was less abrupt than Brigadier Groth's but just as effective.

CHAPTER TWENTY-FOUR

S OMETHING THAT'S BEEN bothering me…"
Eddie was sitting with his assigned squaddie, glued
to their allocated screen. The young man's military sweater
lacked a nametag, either embroidered or pinned to his chest,
nor had he offered a name, but Eddie decided it was best not
to enquire.

"Go ahead." His accent placed him immediately as
a non-Scouser, but he seemed friendly.

"We're getting all this information from all over the world,
but as far as I'm aware, nothing's being reported on the BBC,
CNN, Sky or any of the other news agencies. I thought we
were living in a world of instant communications."

"You should ask the sarge. He'll know where the need-to-
know line's been drawn."

Perhaps Sergeant Jackson had sensed his presence was
required. As the squaddie finished speaking, he stood at
Eddie's elbow.

"Good question, Eddie. I'll tell you as much as the
brigadier has given me permission to say." He paused
a moment before adding, "Ever heard of a 'D' notice, issued
in times of national emergency?"

"Some sort of censorship? I don't mean to sound
negative, but…"

"It comes under that broad definition, I suppose. But
it's done for the best interests of the country. All the media
channels—perhaps I should say, all the *responsible* media
channels—have been asked to refrain from publicising

certain items of news until further notice. It's preventing mass panic, but it's not going to last forever."

Eddie glanced at his watch. "In less than two hours, that time frame's going to become an academic question, isn't it?"

"Which is the main reason we've got to make sure we get this right. If you look back at the screens, you'll see how close we are to the drop zone. Can I get you a coffee or something? We're going to get busy pretty soon."

* * *

HMS Liverpool had maintained position as lead ship, fronting the ruler-straight right-hand column of the flotilla. Her wake would become the guide for every vessel turning west after releasing their deadly cargo.

A marker buoy filled with red dye was tossed over the stern to mark the approximate beginning of the trench. The release of *Liverpool*'s contribution to the total payload was achieved swiftly and efficiently, and she was soon on her way, waiting only for her partner from the head of the left-hand column to make the slightly longer turn on the outside lane before firing up her diesels to full speed ahead. Side by side, a mile or so apart, the two ships leapt forward like greyhounds from a trap, setting the pace for the remainder of the fleet.

With constant advice and assistance from Bidston Hill, each pair of ships in Wolf Pack One sailed slightly further south than their predecessor before depositing their payload and turning as tightly as possible westward. As darkness fell, the natural phosphorescence of the previous vessel's wake became a reliable guide for the lengthy tail wagging behind the sea dog.

"It's working," Brenda breathed, watching the computer screen over her husband's shoulder. The screen showed the last three pairs of ships heading south. The rest of

Wolf Pack One was already on its westerly escape route, apart from two pairs of ships still in the process of turning away from ground zero.

Wolf Pack Two was clearly visible at the southern edge of the screen.

Sergeant Jackson's hand strayed towards the red direct line, but it rang before he touched it.

"Sitrep please, Sergeant."

"Wolf Pack One is finishing its run as we speak, Brigadier. Wolf Pack Two has reached the southern marker and has been cruising significantly below full speed for over an hour to allow Wolf Pack One optimum conditions to alter course."

"Thank you, Sergeant. Can you confirm the lead pair are already above the trench proper?"

"Affirmative, Sir."

"For now, the timing is working in our favour. However, if any unexpected complications arise or if you spot any inconsistencies on your screens, I'll be here waiting for your call."

"Roger that, Sir. We won't let you down."

"I wouldn't have left you and your team running the ops room if I didn't have full confidence in your ability, Sergeant. Once all the weaponry is in place, it will be up to me to detonate the largest explosion in history. I can only suggest you pray to whatever god you acknowledge. We're going to need all the help we can get, wherever it comes from."

"With you on that, Sir. This is Bidston Hill, listening out."

There was a brief hiss of clear line static, then silence.

Sergeant Jackson looked around the room.

"Did I just get the last word in on a call from the brig? That has to be a world first."

CHAPTER TWENTY-FIVE

"Hard a-port."

"Hard a-port. Aye, Sir."

Mirroring the actions of its opposite number, the lead ship of the left-hand column in Wolf Pack Two peeled away westwards after releasing its payload close to the mid-point of the Mariana Trench. There was a full moon, which made the phosphorescent wake of Wolf Pack One's tail-end Charlie easy to pick out.

***

Barely five minutes later, the red phone on Joey's desk trilled.

"Doctor Hart, is there a way we can tell how accurate the northern fleet's deposits have been? I realise this is probably a long way outside your particular field of expertise."

"The radar screens are showing the relative positions of the ships in the region, Sir. They aren't showing what's happening beneath the surface."

"Surely all we need is a camera?" Brenda seemed unaware of having spoken her thoughts aloud. Immediately, she flushed a deep crimson, but it was too late to recall her words.

Errol was first to react. "It's something I'd want if I was in charge of an explorative offshore drilling project. Can we get someone from Wolf Pack Two to drop something over the side? They *must* have some sort of surveillance equipment on board."

"That's easy enough to check." There was an edge of enthusiasm in Groth's voice which had been either absent or extremely well hidden in every phone conversation to date. When he continued a few seconds later, he had regained control.

"Stand by."

There was a faint hiss, suggesting that the direct line had been left open. Nobody dared speak. The three squaddies on duty continued to scrutinise the radar screens for any hint of problems involving Wolf Pack Two. An expectant silence settled on the ops centre as they waited for Groth to complete his enquiries. They weren't kept waiting long.

"The next pair of vessels to deposit their payload will also release several submersible cameras. They won't survive the blast, of course, and very few of them will function at that depth. In truth, I'm not expecting them to transmit anything useful once they get beyond six thousand feet, but they should give us some idea of how accurate our aim has been."

* * *

"*All* of them, Captain? Every camera?"

"Yes, Number Two. All of them."

"Some are prototypes, state of the art. They cost millions to develop. Who is this Limey officer?"

"The security codes are correct, that's all that matters. I doubt even the Admiral of the Royal Australian Navy has a need-to-know clearance for the CO's identity. My guess, for what it's worth—a large percentage of the cameras will fail before they reach target depth, but the information must be crucial to the success of the operation. It's up to us to get it for them, by hook or by crook."

"Aye, aye, Captain." Number Two replaced his cap and snapped a formal salute. "I'll make the necessary arrangements." He wheeled and marched off the bridge.

His body language displayed his unmistakable disapproval, but years of navy discipline won the day.

* * *

"Cameras offloaded, each dressed with ballast to sink them quickly, perhaps keep them upright. We managed to muster about a hundred cameras. I can confirm that my running mate has delivered a similar number a mile east of my position."

"Acknowledged, Captain. Make speed to regain your position in the convoy. It's vital you get as far as possible from ground zero before detonation. I cannot promise you more than about two hours after the last vessel has dropped its load."

"Understood, Sir."

"Good luck, Captain. I only wish I could promise you a wider safety margin."

"We'll do our best, Sir. Over and out."

Bidston Hill had eavesdropped on the exchange between Groth and the unidentified Wolf Pack Two captain. It wasn't intentional on their part, but Groth had apparently decided to keep them in the loop for reasons of his own.

"Sergeant, Doctor Hart, is the whole team present in the ops room?"

Sergeant Jackson glanced at Joey, silently begging permission before opening the mic. Joey nodded, grateful to allow the NCO to speak for them all.

"Affirmative, Brigadier. Awaiting instructions."

"While we have a few moments, I'd like to thank you all for everything you've already achieved—and particularly the groundwork carried out by the civilians before the military personnel arrived.

"I have to remind you that now, more than ever, you are the eyes and ears of the whole operation. I will be *completely* dependent on the quality of the information you gather, and the speed at which you relay it. I have no doubt you can do it. I only wish I could be there with you in person. When this is over, I look forward to shaking you all by the hand.

"Reactivate your link with the Zodiac satellite programme on Screens Two and Three. Monitor the radar scan on Screen One. Expect images from one or more underwater cameras very soon."

The briefest of nods from Sergeant Jackson, and the relevant screens dissolved before reforming. Screen Two cleared to display open sea. Halfway to the horizon, two warships were steaming towards the camera. Screen Three remained blank, apart from an occasional flash suggesting it was still live but temporarily inactive.

Joey guessed Screen Three would be the first to display any images from the submerged cameras and congratulated himself a few moments later when he was proved right.

Every eye in the ops room had been glued to the three screens while these adjustments were made. Not a word was spoken, but there was a frisson of anticipation in the air, rather than fear, dread or any other negative emotion.

The image on Screen Three resolved into a submarine scene, but Joey couldn't force his eyes into focus to interpret the blurred, water-softened images he was seeing as the camera sank and tumbled end over end.

The first reaction came from Groth, whose sharp intake of breath was clearly heard, magnified by the powerful speakers of the PA system.

"Sergeant, is there any way of adjusting the ballast on the cameras, stabilise the images we're receiving?"

"I suggest you put the question to one of the captains on the ships, Sir. It's not something I've ever dealt with."

"They both have enough on their plates, getting a safe distance from the detonation. We can assume they're both listening in. Contact me directly as soon as possible if you have any suggestions. For the moment, we'll watch and hope the images improve."

The screen darkened as the camera sank deeper and the last remnants of the dawn's early light failed to penetrate the fathoms of the deepest sector of the South Pacific. The wild, frantic oscillations of the camera slowed; an inbuilt lighting system activated. Both factors produced a significant improvement, and it became possible to read the text on the images being relayed by the lens.

"Tell me the depth of these images, Sergeant."

"On-screen data says this camera has just passed five thousand feet, Sir."

"Close to half target depth and still functioning. I could really use images from some of the other cameras, especially if any of them are deeper, closer to the trench."

"This is the CO of 256, Wolf Pack Two. Permission to speak?"

"Go ahead, 256."

"I have someone seconded to my crew for this trip solely for the purpose of testing the cameras we've deposited over the target. That's all I'm allowed to say about him or the equipment, but I trust you'll understand that the cameras themselves are *not* standard issue and the data they record and transmit will be more than adequate."

"Understood, Commander. As your Ultimate CO, I assure you, you may speak freely. There are eight people other than myself listening at this end, and I can vouch for all of them. If you have security clearance for everyone on your bridge, we can continue."

"Affirmative, Sir. I'm alone with my Number Two."

"This is Wolf Pack 322, confirming I share the bridge with my Number Two. He has the same security clearance as me."

"Your sitrep, 322."

"My special attaché has stated that some of the experimental equipment is expected to deliver ultra-high-resolution images, even in extreme environmental conditions. The disadvantage, however, is their lightweight nature. They are likely to take *longer* to reach target depth than cameras of a comparable size. It's also possible they may drift off course for the same reason."

"Is it possible to speak to him directly?"

The CO hesitated. "He is...reluctant to disclose his identity, Sir. He's SBS, and technically, I don't have the authority to issue a direct order."

"Hmm. Special Boat Services. Well, he certainly passes the security clearance checks, and he will have compelling reasons for keeping his identity concealed. The name he's sailing under won't be the one on his birth certificate, but I'm sure that won't surprise you."

Sergeant Jackson's voice spliced neatly into the exchange. "Images are arriving from beyond the nine-thousand-foot mark, Sir. They confirm that the payload is on target. I repeat, we are hitting our target."

"Sergeant, are you sure? How clear are the images? Can you email me copies? Not because I doubt you." Groth hastened to add, "But this is crucial information, the most important data so far. I need to analyse them, consult with a few people before I complete the detonation. We only get one shot at this."

"Video already on its way, Sir. Emailing the stills as soon as I have a hand free—thank you, Corporal. Stills forwarded, Sir."

"Received, Sergeant. Stand by for further instructions."

This time, there was no hiss of static. As far as signing off was concerned, Groth was back to his old habits.

CHAPTER TWENTY-SIX

I DON'T UNDERSTAND HOW the news channels aren't carrying even a rumour of what's going on out there."

The tension in the ops room at Bidston Hill was becoming oppressive, and Brenda was frustrated. She needed something to occupy her mind, but there was nothing to relieve the monotony of waiting and watching the three computer screens.

"Think of it this way," Sergeant Jackson said. "It tells us that the 'D' notice is still serving its purpose. The usual suspects in the news media will have worked out something major is going down, but they will also have been ordered to sit on it until further notice. The last thing we need is civilians running around like headless chickens. In fact, running around of any kind is probably the worst thing to do right now. There's never been an explosion of this size, and we can't begin to guess what the consequences will be, or even which parts of the world could be most affected."

"*Never*, Sarge?" Errol sounded outraged. "You mean we're about to blow up part of the planet without knowing what could happen?"

"I'm just following orders, Mr. Dwight. The decisions are made elsewhere." There was no trace of emotion in Sergeant Jackson's words, but it was clear he was relieved he was not directly responsible for the ultimate, agonising decision to unleash a power of untried size and unknowable consequences.

Errol still wasn't satisfied. "I've never drilled at that depth, but there are always problems when you go really deep. Basic physics, y'know? Every action has an equal and opposite *re*action. If you cap the pressure all in one place, it's going to seek an alternative outlet."

"Your maths is sound, Errol," Joey said peaceably, "but there's a lot more to it than that." He was about to add a few words of explanation but was interrupted by Groth's disembodied voice from the speakers.

"Doctor Hart, your team may be in a secure facility, but you could be heard by anyone who happened to be listening alongside me."

"Sorry, Sir," Jackson responded quickly on the team's behalf.

"Accepted Sergeant. Although as it happens, I'm on my own, so no harm done. But let's keep security in mind. Pretty soon, we'll have to lift the 'D' notice. While we want to avoid mass panic, we still have a duty to the public. We can't set off an explosion of this magnitude without warning people. But you've also earned the right to know what we hope to achieve. This is the bottom line—if all goes according to plan.

"Mr. Dwight, the action-reaction you mention works to our advantage. The stockpile of weapons has been laid down as evenly as possible. Put simply, it becomes what's called a *shaped* charge—in other words, we can control the direction of the main force of the blast.

"Our boffins tell me that force will be directed downwards, towards the hollow centre of the planet, effectively stoking up the volcanic activity which supports life. If all goes as predicted, there should be nothing more than temporary, minimal effects on the climate and day-to-day life."

"What happens if it *doesn't* go to plan?" Joey asked.

"Then we have *real* problems, Doctor, but no worse than the problems we face already if we do nothing."

"Understood, Brigadier. I'd hate to be in your position, having to press that button. For what it's worth, we're all sure you'll make the right decision when the time comes."

"Thank you, Doctor Hart, and I mean that, sincerely."

With the stress and pressures Groth had endured over the past few days, it was no longer a surprise to hear the underlying emotions in his voice. The line went dead before Joey could work out if they were now into the fourth day of the emergency which most of the world knew nothing about.

The movement of traffic on the three radar screens had slowed to a crawl. A red dot flashed angrily in the southeast corner of Screen Three, roughly in the centre of the Mariana Trench: ground zero. Concentric circles were overlaid on the screen. Dave wandered up close and discovered they were set at ten nautical miles apart. Every ship had passed the second marker, and there were only a few pairs of vessels still showing on Screen Three. Two more disappeared westward and onto Screen Two as Dave watched, while Screen One resembled an untidy car park, crowded with images of vessels breaking away from the strict formation they had observed up to that point, dispersing into open water under the orders of their individual captains and commanders.

"Sitrep at 0700 Zulu." Jackson's status report startled Dave out of his observations, and he returned to his seat. "No vessels showing in the immediate vicinity of ground zero. Closest convoy vessel has passed the thirty-sea-mile beacon. Over."

"Acknowledged, Sergeant. First stage of Exodus is now complete. We are slightly ahead of estimated time, which is good. Can you confirm there is still adequate distance between vessels, especially those which have passed the sixty-sea-mile mark?"

"Affirmative. The scatter on Screen One indicates distances between vessels have increased. The only vessels in that sector are attached to the convoy."

"That was anticipated, Sergeant. I gave the necessary orders to all the major civilian lines several hours ago, but thank you for the information.

"I will now issue a general command, which I need you to monitor. Each craft will be required to calculate their exact position and realign with their stern posts facing the trench. They will continue to make all possible speed on that heading unless they encounter a landmass, in which case they will be instructed to remain in open water for their own safety. Your role will be to monitor their positions relative to each other and any landmasses in that sector. There *will* be some sort of tidal surge, but at that distance from the trench, it is not expected to be a serious threat. A full-blown tidal wave or tsunami is not anticipated on this occasion."

"Question, Sir. Vessels entering the outer quadrant..." For the team's benefit, Jackson indicated Screen One. "Will they also be ordered to disperse individually or continue in formation?"

"They will continue in formation. The fanning of the lead vessels onto new headings should mean there is adequate space for those following to fall in and assume the positions the lead ships have vacated."

"Acknowledged, Sir. We'll continue to monitor the situation and keep you informed. Listening out."

The hands of the clock seemed reluctant to drag themselves around the dial. The fleet continued to disappear from the centre screen until every vessel was on the theoretically safer westernmost screen.

"That's everyone accounted for," Dave remarked with cautious relief, "but will eighty-odd miles from the trench be far enough for them to ride the surge?"

Joey hadn't stopped scribbling for hours, and Dave had the impression it was as much about having something to occupy his mind and his hands as running essential calculations, which could have been done on one of the many computers in the room. Dave wasn't even certain his comment had been heard, but after a few seconds, Joey paused, frowned at his notes, and allowed himself the smallest of 'maybe' nods.

"There's no existing data I can use to make any predictions. No comparable explosions close to the magnitude we expect from this one. I'd have to go back to prehistory to find anything even close to it, as far as sheer power is concerned."

Errol nodded and hummed in thought. "I recall reading somewhere that Wales and New Zealand were connected at one time, until a major eruption occurred."

"No way!" Brenda protested. "That's *got* to be an old wives' tale."

Joey turned to one of the idle computers, tapped a few keys and scanned the results on-screen. "The theory's been around for a while, and I recognise some of the authors of these papers. Don't forget, we're talking in terms of hundreds of millions of years. If we treat evolution as a twenty-four-hour clock, in historical terms, *Homo sapiens* only swung down from the trees at about ten to midnight."

"I guess we all learn something new every day." Errol drawled. His lazy, laid-back style had the effect of easing the growing tension in the room.

The clock hands inched forward a few more endless minutes while they studied this pub quiz trivia. The radar dispersal pattern continued to expand. There was no apparent pattern to the scattering of dots representing the individual vessels, but Dave realised that the individual captains would be setting the courses they considered safest.

Eight-thirty GMT somehow slid past without anyone noticing. Dave was about to comment on this, but the direct line beat him to the punch, shrilling into life as the wall clock begrudgingly recorded 0833.

"Sitrep, Sergeant."

"All vessels are now in Sector Three. Estimated minimum distance from ground zero in excess of eighty nautical miles."

"Acknowledged. Stand by."

A faint hint of static suggested Groth was thinking on his feet, preparing to make the biggest decision of his professional career—and the final decision of his life if he guessed wrong.

"Here are your revised orders, based on the latest updates of information.

"Detonation of the stockpile will remain on hold unless conditions at ground zero deteriorate. This will give every vessel the widest window of opportunity to reach a safe distance and prepare for the inevitable tidal surge. It's vital you monitor the event constantly and provide us with up-to-the-minute reports of your observations."

"We'll do everything we can from our end, Sir."

"I have every confidence. Stand by."

Eddie looked from Dave to Joey, then back at the nearest screen. There was something that had been bothering him. Now, suddenly, he realised what it was. He rounded on Sergeant Jackson and pointed at the empty seascape.

"How accurate are the charts our vessels are using? When were they last updated? And would they show every island, including any which are too small to support a human colony of any consequence but could still be hazardous for a ship fighting to survive a tidal surge?"

"There are rocks and eyots all over the globe which haven't yet been mapped," Joey pointed out.

Jackson nodded. "I concur with Doctor Hart. This sector of the Pacific is not on any main shipping routes, so it's not as thoroughly surveyed as other parts."

Eddie exploded. "It would only take *one* insignificant reef to sink a ship. Old maps were full of notes such as 'Here Be Monsters' and the like, and I never believed that tales of whirlpools and giant whales, mermaids, the Sargasso Sea or even the Bermuda Triangle don't have some foundation in fact. Something must have happened to get all these stories started in the first place."

"Your point is taken, Eddie. It *is* Eddie, isn't it?" Groth had evidently heard everything and invited himself into the conversation. He sounded less official, more relaxed—even faintly amused. "It's a fair comment, even if we ignore the fairy tale and superstition element of tales told in taverns by the Ancient Mariner. Current status..."

He didn't say 'sitrep' this time, Dave thought, wondering if this hinted at a partial melt of Groth's hitherto precise, clinical military language.

After the briefest of pauses Groth carried on.

"I have a series of real-time satellite images, enhanced to the max. As you note, there are a number of isolated rocks and small islands out there, but I don't believe they pose any immediate danger to our ships.

"On balance, I've decided to initiate the detonation. Once the decision was made to set the charge, we were committed to taking this final step sooner or later. We've been extremely fortunate to postpone the action for far longer than I dared hope, even to being able to choose the timing of it ourselves. Gentlemen—and madam—that moment has arrived.

"The main purpose of this call, which is being recorded, is to provide you with documented evidence which exonerates you from any blame or fault, in the event that this attempt fails to solve the problem and enough people survive to launch an enquiry or other legal proceedings. I am placing it formally on record that no criticism can be raised against my team of civil and military personnel, who acted entirely according to orders issued by me, and me alone.

"I've signed and dated a hard copy of this statement, and on a separate sheet I have recorded the names and personal details of each of you, so there can be no doubt for any court—military, criminal or civil.

"When I close this link, I will activate the detonation. My final orders to you all. Do not attempt to call me. I will remain offline until further notice. I don't know how long it might be before we see the results of our efforts or the extent of the repercussions. What I do know is it's been my privilege to work with you. The best of luck to you all."

The call ended with a loud *click* before anyone could respond. This time, the silence was on the cusp of assuming a full, palpable, physical presence. Every eye swivelled automatically to the computer screens. Of the three, only Screen One still showed any detail: a red dot, pulsing silently over the location designated *ground zero*.

Perhaps a minute elapsed before the pulse of light suddenly ceased. Although they had expected something of this nature to follow Groth's decision to take the irrevocable step, they all flinched as if anticipating an immediate reaction to the event several thousand miles south of their secure location.

A darker shadow appeared and spread northwest and southeast from the point on the screen where the ground-zero beacon had been, following the by-now-familiar shape of the Mariana Trench. Dave's tense muscles threatened to lock painfully, and he forced himself to relax. His heart was racing, blood pounding a loud tattoo against his temples as adrenaline flooded his nervous system. A quick glance around the room confirmed he wasn't suffering alone.

Sluggishly, concentric rings populated the screen. Ground zero was high in the northern quadrant of the screen, and the ripples—as Dave's non-technical mind decided to call them—moving north left the field of the screen almost at once, leaving arcs of up to three-quarters of a circle spreading quickly south, apparently not so rapidly east or west.

"So far, so good," Sergeant Jackson breathed. "That's what I'd expected to see as the result of a directional, shaped charge. It's out of our hands now. All we can do is watch— and pray, if you think there's anything to be gained from it."

Dave felt Brenda's fingers lace through his own. They both attended church regularly, but Dave had rarely felt the need to ask the Man Above for any special consideration for himself or his family. *Still*, he thought, *it can't do any harm*. Returning the discreet pressure of Brenda's fingers, he gazed into her eyes and with his free hand sketched a swift sign of the cross. The habitual, formulaic *Paters* and *Aves*, he sensed, would be inappropriate at this juncture. A more personal approach was required.

The advice of a long-forgotten SJ from his school days chimed in his inner ear, "*Speak to God as you would an old friend you haven't seen for years. You'll find He's always prepared to listen.*" He had to trust there was some merit in this homespun Jesuit philosophy.

The clock on the wall confirmed Groth had bought them over an hour's delay before pushing the 'destruct' button. With that thought in mind, Dave sent up an urgent plea that it would not prove a futile gesture made in desperation, doomed to failure.

CHAPTER TWENTY-SEVEN

THE ARCS SHOWING the thrust of the wave generated by the blast at ground zero continued to pulse south and east across Screen One without a sound, a silent movie that seemed unreal. Dave turned to Sergeant Jackson: something occurred to him which he realised he ought to have queried long ago.

"Sergeant, we managed to evacuate all the vessels involved in the setting of the charges. We're looking at blank screens, so we know we've achieved that. But what about *other* traffic? Shouldn't there be some evidence of ordinary shipping using the South Pacific? Container ships, cargo vessels, cruise liners? Two-thirds of the planet is covered by oceans. Surely there's some traffic out there. Won't they be in danger? It can't have been possible to impose a total ban on all shipping movement, not in the time we had available."

Sergeant Jackson caught the eye of the nearest of his military group and nodded towards the large conference table, which had been pushed to one side and now doubled as a convenient coffee bar. With no on-screen activity and Groth's explicitly imposed radio silence, there wasn't a lot to be gained from continuing to monitor the three screens as carefully as they had up to receiving their last set of instructions. The Insats group stood as a unit and moved to sit around the table. Sergeant Jackson indicated that the civilian element of the group should join them. He was the last to sit on one of the padded armchairs and waited for everyone who wanted a refill to top up their coffee mugs.

"You all heard Dave's question about other shipping, and I'm not going to lie to you. You're all intelligent human beings. Yes, there will be casualties. That much is inevitable. A surprising amount of shipping *was* directed away from the region. That much I do know, but we could do no better than restrict collateral damage to an absolute minimum. I'm not happy about it, but I was obliged to follow orders and observe the standard protocols and procedures. Everything was done on a need-to-know basis, and as far as we're concerned, that's still the case.

"The BBC seem to have kept a tight rein on their newshounds. I can't say how other elements of the media have been muzzled, but up to—" he glanced at his watch "—about three hours ago, the BBC was still playing the three monkeys' game—'See no evil…' and so on. Perhaps we should tune in to the World Service and see if they decided to tell Joe Public about the detonation *before* these massive waves crash down on shorelines all over the world. Look, it's almost the hour. Let's do it now."

Anything would have been an improvement on the deathly silence that had developed in the ops centre before Sergeant Jackson called this semi-formal meeting. Scant seconds after he re-tuned the radio to the correct wavelength, the familiar strains of the World Service's *Lily Bolero* warned them the news was imminent.

"*BBC World Service. Here is the news at eleven hundred GMT.*

"*There is a red weather warning in effect across the UK. Flood warnings have been issued in ninety-four regions. The entire east coast will be worst affected. Landslides and flash floods have been reported in several places between Newcastle and Berwick. Secure your property as best you can and make sure you have basic supplies to hand—blankets, bottled water, first-aid kit, preserved food which needs little or no preparation or cooking. Until further notice, all TV and Radio stations will only be broadcasting public information programmes."*

Sergeant Jackson muted the TV and glanced around the ops centre. He'd been the first to roll up his sleeves and drag furniture around, creating a comfort zone of low coffee tables and upholstered armchairs as far as possible from the business end of the room. Now he picked up his coffee mug and nodded silently in that direction. He padded off, and everyone else followed automatically.

"We don't know how long we're going to be here. We might as well be as comfortable as possible for the duration. It seems a case of 'so far, so good' as far as public reaction is concerned."

The radio remained stubbornly silent, and they'd run out of mundane, repetitive maintenance tasks to fill the day. There was a limit to the number of times a floor or other surface could be washed or polished, or stock cupboards inventoried.

"Maybe people are still shell-shocked by the speed of events," Dave suggested.

"That's a possibility, but it would be useful if we had an idea of which way the public is going to jump when the reaction sets in."

Joey shook his head. "I'd be grateful for some reliable info about what's happening outside. I really need some facts to work with—something which hasn't been processed by the Beeb so there's nothing left in what gets broadcast which might frighten your grandma."

"Well, let's just remember we know a damn sight more than almost everyone else, and the brig. will have extremely good grounds for his decision to have full control of radio traffic. After all, we're still on the highest possible level of security."

"I'm sure you're right in that, Sarge," Dave said. Somehow, the informality of the group had not revealed

Sergeant Jackson's first name, and he seemed to prefer to be addressed by rank.

The sergeant looked up at Dave but checked before replying. His attention had been snagged by the three squaddies, who sat together in one corner. They all wore a discreet wings emblem on their jackets, which they never took off, no matter how hot and sticky the closed environment of the bunker became at times. They hadn't given their names, so the civilians had dubbed them Tom, Dick and Harry. Dave didn't need a sixth sense to tell him their identities were classified. However, he assumed it was standard operating procedure for all serving members of the SAS and let it slide. If it became important later, they would no doubt choose to reveal their real names.

They were embroiled in a lively, private conversation that involved more hand gestures than words. In fact, the few sounds Dave could hear resembled grunts and animal noises rather than distinct words. As Sergeant Jackson stood to approach them, the group split. Harry remained where he was on an ancient leather settee, while Tom murmured a few words in the sergeant's ear, and Dick headed for the airlock-style locked door which gave onto the corridor. Tom's whisper produced a short, decisive nod from Sergeant Jackson, which was apparently the response he'd expected. Tom straightened up and stood to attention, then turned on his heel and marched across the room to join Dick at the door. Sergeant Jackson waited until the door slammed hollowly behind them before enlightening the civilian element of the group about the sudden development.

"There may be a way we can obtain the uncensored 'word on the street' you're asking for, Doc."

"I can hear a 'but' coming, Sarge. Something's bothering you?"

"The buck stops with me on security, and the brig has opted to disable our outgoing calls facility for reasons he considers valid. I have to follow the orders I'm given, but without up-to-date information about what's happening around us, there's little I can do to deal with a local emergency situation. However, the disabled landline was installed within the past decade, an update on an older system. The bunker itself is much older—you should see the dates printed on some of the tinned food in the storeroom."

Jackson allowed himself the ghost of a grin before continuing. "Those two—" he nodded towards the door "—have some special skills, especially Tom. He's forgotten more about telecoms than most people ever learn. There's a good chance he can trace the wiring from the earlier system, which he reckons is still buried out there. Disconnected and inactive but serviceable.

"If the wiring's still there, they'll find it. And once they've checked it through, we'll be able to make outgoing calls without Groth or anyone else being any the wiser."

Joey nodded. "I understand why you have reservations about flouting Groth's security orders, but surely you've got some leeway? Things can happen."

"He'd expect me to wait for him to contact me. As far as he's concerned, we're completely out of touch. Officially, we have no idea what's happening locally or nationally."

"Wait a moment," Brenda interrupted with a puzzled look on her face. "If this phone line's been updated, surely everyone else has also been too?" She paused a moment and added sarcastically, "So who ya gonna call? Ghostbusters?"

Brenda's tongue-in-cheek tagline provoked a few silent grins. Laughter had been in short supply recently. Despite the flippant tone of the delivery, Brenda wasn't jesting. She stared defiantly at everyone, demanding an answer.

Sergeant Jackson held up his hands in a token of sincere surrender. "Okay, I could have phrased that better. 'In for a penny, in for a pound', as they say. I've stuck my neck out this far. I suppose Groth can only have me shot at dawn once."

He crossed the room and rooted briefly in the document case he treated as a mobile office. It had never been out of his sight and rarely more than an arm's length away. He kept it securely locked.

When he found what he wanted, Dave thought it was an early model of a mobile phone: an enormous *Starsky & Hutch* number which truly deserved to be a museum piece.

As if reading Dave's mind, Jackson said, "It's older than you think. It's not a mobile—it isn't even a phone. But I can assure you it still works as well as the day it was made."

"Which was?" Errol inquired.

Jackson reversed the solid brick he was holding and allowed Errol to read the manufacturer's stamp on the base.

"Nineteen sixty-five. This, my friend, is a short-wave radio. Standard US and British Army issue before technology developed mobile phones. The older style phone line Dick is searching for will be compatible with this dinosaur, and I can use it to send a message that will remain under the radar to anyone using the current digital wiring."

"Just one problem I can see, Sarge," Eddie cut in. "You'll need someone *on the outside* with another short-wave radio—"

"Who will need to be listening for a transmission from *me*," Sergeant Jackson completed the sentence. "And I believe I have a way around that."

* * *

"We have to be clear about this."

Jackson was on his feet and pacing nervously around the comfort area of the ops room. Every time he turned, he studiously avoided glancing towards the work area, as if it bothered his conscience to be reminded of the official reason for their presence in the secure Cheshire bunker.

He cleared his throat and continued.

"What I'm planning to do is most *definitely* off-limits however you care to read the regs defining security levels. The last information we received stated we were on Condition Red, which is *never* used in exercises, only in active warfare. The buck stops with me on this one, but if anyone feels uncomfortable about it, this is the last-chance saloon. I can't—and *won't*—do it without full commitment from all of you.

"You need to know what I have in mind, and you have to understand what could happen if things don't go as planned. My short-wave radio is the key. And, as Eddie rightly pointed out, it's only useful if there's someone out there, expecting a call. I have an older brother, retired from active service. He has the partner to this, and they're tied to a very tight waveband some distance from the standard range of military wavelengths.

"Believe it or not, tomorrow's Friday. We've been isolated here for almost a full week—four full days since detonation. But more important is the fact that I *always* call him on a Friday. No excuses, no exceptions. It's a military thing, I suppose, but he's what you'd call an 'old school' soldier. Even if there's a general embargo in place on private phone calls—which, for all we know, is quite possible if the situation has deteriorated—he will still expect me to find a way around it."

"Dick and Harry have unearthed a line and identified it as the disused analogue phone connection. When my brother doesn't get a call from me, his first reaction will be to try my landline, and when he can't get through, he'll know there's a problem. I'll use the short-wave to alert him. Once I know he's listening, we'll cobble a connection on the old line. As this is officially redundant, it'll be untraceable, or at least, nobody will be monitoring it, which amounts to the same difference."

"Wait a minute, Sarge," Eddie interjected. "Are we depending on your brother's reactions to a missed phone call?"

"You mean him expecting me to find another way of contacting him? Eddie, I know my brother. He's the type who polishes his boots 'til they don't just shine, they sparkle. He's also a creature of habit and still spends Friday evenings servicing his kit. That includes checking the battery on his CB radio, and by early evening, he'll be impatient for my weekly call."

He looked at his watch.

"It's almost one o'clock. Dick and I have a couple of hours to Gerry-rig some sort of link via the old cable. There's guaranteed an ancient handset forgotten somewhere in a supply room or broom cupboard. I suggest everyone else get some R and R—Joey, I only hope the scuttlebutt you're asking for doesn't prove to be a combination of wild exaggeration and total bullshit."

* * *

Di-dah-dah-dah. Di-dah-dah-dah.

At just after 1800 hours, Sergeant Jackson sent his prearranged signal—two letter Js, tapped out using the Morse key on the side of his short-wave radio. Within seconds, the signal was answered.

Di-di-di-dah. Di-di-di-dah.

"Letter V, twice. That's the correct response. It's safe to assume it's from my brother and that he can talk freely. I expect him to send a test question—something nobody other than me could answer. It'll come in Morse, of course. He'll want to prove he's still that little bit faster than me tapping out a message."

The handset began spitting long and short beeps. Jackson's lips moved silently as he grabbed pen and pad, memorising the pattern of the first few letters while his fingers played catch-up with the opening line. Within thirty seconds, he'd filled a full A4 page with groups of dots and dashes which only an experienced telegraphist could have translated as quickly as Jackson did.

"*Q, what colour Max's eyes?* See, told you he'd send a test for me."

Jackson smirked in amusement as he tapped a response. His fingers seemed to function automatically. When he was done, he looked up and explained, "Max was a dog we had as kids. He came to us from a rescue shelter, and he'd lost one of his eyes in an accident *before* we took him in. I've sent him a suitable response."

"While telling us the backstory at the same time?" Brenda said, notably impressed. "How d'you manage that?"

Sergeant Jackson shrugged. "Morse is like riding a bike, I guess. It becomes automatic as breathing after a while... 'scuse a moment, I'm getting big bro's answer."

His pencil flew across the page once more. Looking over the sergeant's shoulder, Dave could see that he was writing words, not dots and dashes, transcribing the message as he heard it with no doubt, no hesitation.

He stopped writing and looked at the rest of the group.

"*Propose continue to use radio for contact. My phone line updated within two years, includes broadband. Digital cable, not possible to receive calls from analogue line. Over.*"

"These radios have a range which will make it possible for me to contact my brother at his home address for at least twenty-four hours between charges. That should be more than adequate. I can rely on him to keep his handset in full working order. I remind you all, as the ranking officer—the *only* officer present—this counts as an executive decision, and the buck stops with me.

"In the circumstances, I'm going to use the radio, and because I don't expect anyone to be listening for radio transmissions, I'll speak to him rather than use Morse—

it's quicker. Plus, since we won't be using a landline, we've a very good chance of getting the info Doctor Hart is asking for without alerting Groth or anybody else to this breach of security. Dick, Harry—sorry your little sortie looking for a phone line seems to have been a waste of time. Questions?"

"Sortie. Does that mean you went outside? Can you give us a local weather report?" Dave wanted to know. The two squaddies hadn't yet had time to wash since their return, and their combats were damp and muddy.

"We disabled the alarm and had a swift look a few feet either side of the entrance, checking which direction the cable we located runs. It was heaving down, visibility no more than fifty foot in any direction, and there's a thick fog low on the Mersey." Harry spoke slowly, as if a sadistic dentist was extracting each word with pliers of cartoon proportions and without anaesthetic.

Dick nodded agreement. He seemed more willing to contribute, adding, "No wind to speak of, and the fog's got that 'orrible sulphur stink to it I remember when we was growin' up. All the fac'tree chimlees belched stuff out all day an' all night, proper pea-souper fogs we useter call 'em."

Dick's rapid-fire Scouse accent was as sharp a contrast as could be imagined, especially set against Harry's slow, thoughtful West Country burr. Joey's eyes gleamed at these first-hand, non-technical and uncensored assessments of local weather conditions and demanded more details. Sergeant Jackson briefly withdrew to the far end of the work area so he could discuss the information he wanted from his brother. Dave and Eddie drained their coffees. Brenda appeared from nowhere in particular with a fresh pot and refilled everyone's mugs.

Within ten minutes, Joey and Sergeant Jackson had both extracted as much information as they could about the weather conditions in the immediate environment and from somewhat further afield.

"I could kick myself for not checking the barometer for local readings," Joey muttered, furious at what he regarded as a highly unprofessional error. "This was built first and foremost as a weather station."

"No harm done, Doc. We've all been under duress for several days, and we couldn't have *used* this info before we had something to set against it, to compare weather conditions, look for patterns and other hints at what changes—if any— last week's detonation might have caused."

"And while we're at it," Errol added, "let's remember this is all theory, anyway. We'll need a lot more hard *evidence* that there really is a connection." He looked around and turned on one of his most persuasive grins. "Hey, if the door alarm's been disabled, can I please, *please* step outside and puff on a cigarillo? I haven't had a smoke in four days."

* * *

"Seems I haven't lost the basic skills of logging weather details from the simple tools we have on hand. Wind speed gauges, a barometer, even the humble thermometer for air temperature readings." Joey laid aside his pencil and tidied the stack of notes he'd made. He shuffled through them, rearranging a few sheets, then spread them out again in a specific order.

"I'm looking for some sort of pattern," he said, pre-empting the question that was on everyone's mind in one form or another. "I'd have to compare these figures with records for July and August over the last few years, and the info is all there on the internet, which, of course, is useless right now. However, I can tell you straight away, the wind speed's *way* off the scale. Force nine, gusting to ten isn't normal for this time of year."

He picked up a phial of liquid and held it against an overhead strip light to study it. It wasn't completely clear, and it contained some sediment.

"This concerns me, though. The Mersey's been getting cleaner and healthier year on year for a long time, but the pH of this sample is dangerously acidic. I daren't think about what's settling out at the bottom of the tube. I hope whoever collected it scrubbed up afterwards?"

Dick nodded but glanced anxiously at his hands, palms and backs.

"I wore gloves, and tossed 'em straight into a bin, but there's no harm in an extra trip to the 'eads," he said, catapulting himself from his seat and heading for the bathroom.

"Doc, I think you should hear this."

Eddie had been sitting closest to the radio tuned to the World Service.

"*...an estimated four hundred tonnes of cliff fell on a popular campsite in Dorset. At least one person is known to have died, crushed inside a caravan which took a direct hit. There was no warning, and it is thought that the cliff may have been loosened by non-stop heavy rain over the past two weeks. Rescue teams are still searching for other possible casualties.*"

Joey's pencil flew over the page, leaving a trail of hieroglyphics that meant nothing to anyone but him.

"The timescale's about right, and the heavy rain will certainly be a factor, but if they don't include the likelihood of aftershocks in their calculations, we could be in serious trouble. Damn you, Groth. This is exactly why we need to be able to make calls. We can see the news as it happens."

Right on cue, the phone interrupted his rant.

"Brigadier, I must insist you restore our outgoing calls facil—"

"*Insist*, Doctor? May I remind you that under Condition Red, the whole country is effectively in lockdown and subject to Military Law?"

"I appreciate that, Sir, but I've just heard the breaking news, and—"

"Doctor Hart, the BBC are also operating under licence. The news they're reporting—I assume you're referring to the incident in Dorset?—occurred five hours ago. I rang you as soon as it went public in case the time difference is a significant factor in your calculations."

"Thank you, Brigadier. My apologies if I seem a little abrupt. However, I hope you'll trust us enough to allow us an outside line—even a single direct line to your location would be enough if we chance upon something which might not seem important to..." he hesitated, seeking a diplomatic word or phrase.

"Non-scientists?" Groth suggested. In those few syllables, he conveyed a degree of sympathy for Doctor Hart's plea. "That was the other reason for this call, Doctor. I never thought of your team as a security risk, but there are protocols which must be observed. The British Army is still reluctant to think on its feet without putting everything under a spotlight and hauling it before a panel of officers—I'm as guilty of that as any of my superiors. That said, I am authorised to reinstate your phone line, and I'm happy to do that. As soon as we finish this call, you'll find it's already live."

"Brigadier, we've also collected some local data, which we've had a chance to analyse. Some of it gives me serious cause for concern."

"How did you obtain this data?"

"We had cause to inspect the area immediately outside the bunker. We used full HazMat suits and incinerated them at once on re-entry. Monitoring gauges indicate no change to our environment inside the base."

"Thank you, Doctor. What concerns you about the new data you collected?"

Joey praised all the gods that Brigadier Groth was cutting them some slack. He'd been expecting a reprimand for acting without obtaining permission, but it seemed as if they'd escaped censure. He was on solid ground now. In simple, non-technical terms, he described the alarmingly high acidity readings in the water sample taken from the Mersey and the abnormal wind strength on the anemometer.

"I'll forward these figures for analysis," Groth commented. "Has this data given you any ideas, suggestions for a possible course of action?"

"We haven't had time to discuss that yet, Sir. We only obtained the readings within the past hour. But the cliff damage on the south coast is as great a worry. From my analysis, I'd say it's highly likely that it's the result of aftershocks from the detonation in the Mariana Trench rather than local weather conditions."

He listed his preliminary findings based on the few facts he'd been able to verify from the samples they'd taken.

"Good work, Doctor. I'll inform you at once if anyone on our research team has anything useful to add."

The burr of an empty line confirmed the resumption of Groth's habitual telephone habits.

Sergeant Jackson was first to react. "None of you—with the possible exception of my colleagues—know the brig as well as I do, but I can tell you this. He's impressed with what you've offered him based on very little data. He never even chewed us out for leaving the bunker."

"Which reminds me," Joey said. "We *did* incinerate the suits, didn't we? And has anyone checked stock levels in case we have to go outside again?"

"Sorted, and that's to *both* questions," Dick confirmed. Nobody had noticed his return from the bathroom. Dave glanced at the squaddie's hands, which had been subjected to a merciless scrubbing and were now a painful shade of red.

Dave wondered if Dick would feel embarrassed or upset if he offered some sympathy but was spared the choice when one of the redundant monitors lit up with an incoming Skype call. Dave looked to Joey for permission to answer.

"Go ahead."

"Pete."

"Hey, bro. Are you all hanging in there?" The call from New Zealand couldn't have come from much further away, but it was as clear as if it had been made from the next room.

The brothers briefly exchanged pleasantries and confirmed all was as well as could be expected on both sides, then Dave got down to business.

"What you got for me? I assume you've spotted some weather data on your state-of-the-art computer systems?"

"Jealousy will get you everywhere, our kid. Not my fault your government's flat broke and won't pay your leccy bills."

"Okay, you've had your dig. Now, let's hear it."

Pete's voice changed. He became businesslike, professional. "So far, we've been monitoring tides, tremors, earthquakes—essentially, subterranean problems."

"We're doing the same here," Joey said, which wasn't strictly true, given the lack of access to equipment outside of the op centre, but he was already making good headway. "We've had precious little info to guide us, but we had to start somewhere. You sound as if you've found something?"

"Maybe, Joey, but there's no direct link, as such."

"Go ahead anyway."

"It's forty-eight hours now since we tried to seal the trench. Here in the Southern Hemisphere, we've seen a definite temperature increase—up a full two degrees compared with the average for this time of year. And on the back of that, there are fires blazing out of control in Greece, Spain, Italy... not to mention the bush fires we've had in Oz for the last few weeks. I have a gut feeling there's a connection."

"Hmm. I have someone who might be able to check your figures from a different angle."

"There's more. I've kept this to last, not because it's only just dropped on my desk but because it scares the crap out of me."

Joey's grip tightened until the pencil he was holding creaked under the pressure. His fingertips turned white as the blood supply was effectively choked off from one heartbeat to the next.

"I'm not gonna like this, am I? You've never been one for wild rumour and scaremongering. Go on, break it to me gently."

"I've got what appears to be solid data and evidence, tables and figures which back this up. I'll forward them for you to look at and pass on. In short, a group of scientists have published the results of a survey, and the total loss of ice mass at the South Pole has trebled in the past ten years, equivalent to two thousand gigatonnes."

"In a decade? And nobody noticed until now?"

Joey didn't doubt Dave's brother's words for a second, but this bald statement took his breath away.

"It wasn't so much that nobody noticed. The Antarctic doesn't have the same observable, year-on-year decline as the Arctic. Indeed, the variability of the annual minimum and maximum of Antarctic ice coverage is becoming increasingly extreme, which may also be a factor in recent climatic events."

"Pete, I need those figures asap. I have to forward them to our research team."

"Email's on its way—I'll clear the line. Keep me in the loop as much as you're allowed."

"Will do. I wish I could say thanks, but I can't see anything to cheer about."

"Good luck, Doctor Hart. Something tells me we'll need as much as we can get."

As Pete's call ended, the red direct line buzzed. Joey managed to lift the receiver a few nanoseconds before the second ring. "Receiving, Brigadier."

"I've had the last data you forwarded analysed, Doctor Hart. Continue to monitor the water quality in the river. I want hourly samples. There is no immediate risk to the public, but there will be no access to the foreshore until further notice.

"The south coast has been designated an emergency zone, and everyone living less than three miles from the coast will be evacuated to temporary accommodation in army camps, church halls, schools and any other available buildings. This is purely for your information. It won't have any direct influence here in the North West."

"Acknowledged, Brigadier. We have more data for you from further afield, received since we last spoke."

"Is it a reliable source, Doctor?"

"I don't know what criteria the army would use, Brigadier, but the information comes from a team of scientists reporting directly to the government of New Zealand. Their report is the result of a five-year project."

"How did you come by this data?"

"Doctor Peter Whelan, Sir. The technical data is in a separate email. Permission to summarise the content of the findings?"

"Granted, Doctor Hart."

"Thank you. Essentially, the scientific forum that has researched this topic over the past decade has established that the permanent ice at the southern pole has depleted significantly in the past ten years." He repeated the bare bones of the report in the same simple, non-technical terms Pete had used. Groth listened without interrupting.

"Your email arrived while you were speaking. I'll forward it to our technical support team and flag it urgent. Is there any possibility this meltdown could have been caused by the volcanic activity in the Mariana Trench?"

"It isn't something which has happened overnight, Sir. The survey covers ten years of research. On the other hand, we don't know how long the volcanic activity in the trench has been developing. But if you want my gut feeling...?"

"It's as valid as any other we have on the table at the moment."

"Depending on how deep the point of origin may be, the temperatures and pressures underground could have been rising steadily for ten, fifteen, twenty years before reaching the fissure on the seabed known as the Mariana Trench.

"It's certainly possible that a subterranean temperature increase could have influenced the temperatures *south* of the trench for many years undetected. It would be worth your team corresponding directly with the New Zealand scientists to look for any evidence which may confirm this theory. It might not lead us directly to a solution, but if we can be certain of the cause, at least we'll know what we're dealing with."

"That sounds very sensible, Doctor Hart. I'll speak to my team and suggest they liaise with their counterparts in New Zealand. You are to continue to monitor local weather conditions. Along with John Lennon Airport, your instruments are probably the most accurate in the North West. I'll also expect your assessment of the data you've forwarded for my team as soon as you've had a chance to study it."

"Understood, Sir. I'll have a prelim ready for you this evening."

"I'll call you at 1800 hours. Groth out."

Joey stared at the handset for a moment before replacing it. Was the brigadier feeling the stress? This was the first time he'd signed off a call instead of leaving him listening to an empty ring tone.

214

CHAPTER TWENTY-EIGHT

THIS EQUIPMENT ISN'T what you'd call state-of-the-art, but it's easy to use."

Brenda had linked a bank of phones to a central desk. Everyone else was now sitting in pairs at desks while she ran through what they needed to know to operate the telephone network.

"You'll have noticed that these phones are fitted with dials, not a keypad. Some were still in their original packing. They've never been used. Those which had been unpacked are in as near mint condition as makes no difference, and according to the *Installation Handbook*, they're a government standard issue."

"Is there a publication date on the handbook?" Errol wanted to know.

Brenda flicked open the front cover and scanned the copyright page. "This is a reprint from 1955. First published by HMSO in 1944."

She laid the manual to one side and waited until she had everyone's full attention.

"They will have been delivered in time to see some service in the final months of World War Two, and they were designed to be easy for non-specialists to use. I came across them when I worked with the TA as a signals op, and I found it easy to learn. I'm sure it'll be just as easy for you."

"I've only ever seen these dial models on old black-and-white movies," Errol remarked.

"But they work," Dave said. He picked up his handset and held it aloft. Everyone could hear the steady dial tone. He nodded and replaced it.

"We can now make outgoing calls, so I'm going to make a few calls from the main switchboard to other observatories around the UK. When they start replying, I'll relay them to one of you, and you'll copy down the data they send. I expect a slow start, but it's bound to get hectic after a while, so we'll have to be on our toes once the info starts coming in."

"Sounds like this is my last opportunity to have a smoke," Errol said with an exaggerated martyr's grimace.

"I don't smoke, but I'll join you for a breath of fresh air." Dave pushed back his chair and followed Errol to the exit door.

* * *

Opening the solid, hermetically sealed door which isolated the bunker from the outside world proved to be far more difficult than either Dave or Errol had expected it to be. The grooves in the floor and the roof were clear of any obstructions and adequately greased, but sliding the door to one side required a lot more muscle than they'd needed to apply on earlier occasions.

"D'you think there's something jammed against it?" Dave panted.

"If there is, it's something large and heavy," Errol grunted, "But I think I felt it move that time...here we go."

The door began to slide to the left. By the time six inches of free space was showing, they were both drenched from shoulder to knee by a solid sheet of torrential rain driven straight off the river by a vicious wind. Even through the layers of clothing they wore, the raindrops were striking them hard enough to cause actual, physical pain.

Dave was closer to the part-open door and staggered under the full brunt of nature's unexpected blind fury.

Errol was slightly behind him and not as badly exposed, but all thoughts of slipping out for a smoke disappeared in an instant. Instinctively, both men took three or four paces back to escape the thorough soaking they had received and looked at each other, scarcely able to believe the evidence of their own eyes as they stood and dripped onto the concrete floor.

"I've joked about the weather in this godforsaken country o' yourn, but this is something else. I never dreamed it could be this bad."

Errol pulled a super-economy-class kerchief out of his fairly dry left pocket and commenced mopping-up operations on his hair and face. Dave had nothing of the sort to use for running repairs and turned to look at the limited slice of the outside world visible beyond the part-open door, hoping Errol might think to offer him a corner of the cloth before it reached the limit of its capacity to absorb moisture.

"I've lived here all my life—I've only been abroad on holiday once or twice—and I can assure you, I've never seen anything like this. Not even close. But at least the wind isn't directly behind it—or rather, it's not a direct headwind. Look. The rain's coming from an angle. It's only striking the first six inches or maybe a foot inside the gap."

"Guess we should be thankful for small favours then, Dave," Errol muttered, sounding anything but grateful as he tried unsuccessfully to squeeze some moisture out of his denim jeans. Catching the hopeful look in Dave's eye, he passed over the kerchief with an automatic but sincere apologetic shrug. There wasn't a lot of drying potential left in it, despite its impressive size.

"We have to risk another soaking." Dave sighed. Clearly, he didn't fancy the prospect. "If we go back and just say, 'Hey, guys, guess what? It's raining out there!' I don't think we'll win any popularity contests. We need to 'observe', not just 'look'. We've set up a whole bank of phones to collect data from around the country, and we need to report on local conditions when we go back in."

Errol tucked his tobacco tin into an inner pocket.

"I don't think I'll be using that on this trip, but if we've got to go out there and have a mosey 'round, I say we'd best grab us a pair of them dinky coveralls we used last time. They're stashed in this storeroom, aren't they?"

This time, they could leave the face masks open, making the HazMat suits slightly less claustrophobic, but they took a pair of protective goggles each to protect their eyes from the torrential downpour. Dave found a bucket, complete with snap-lid, and tossed a few tools into it.

"The doc will no doubt be grateful for a few soil and water samples," he said as they waddled their way back to the entry door. The pool of water around it had grown and spread rapidly but didn't seem to have any significant effect on the concrete flooring.

"Better bring a broom and sweep the worst of it out when we get back." Errol was surprised to discover how much he'd had to raise his voice to make himself heard over the hiss of the rain, magnified in the confined space of the narrow corridor.

Dave nodded his agreement and leant his shoulder against the corner of the door. "Come on, then. Let's see how bad the weather has become out there."

With both pushing, the door slid smoothly if reluctantly to the fully open position.

"We'd better check that before we go in again," Dave said. "If something's obstructing the tracks, we might not be able to open it at all next time we want to get out."

"Agreed. I saw a couple shovels in that storeroom, but if we want to get some samples before we go gardening, we need to work fast."

Dave had been concentrating on a possible explanation for the door being so difficult to open. Now he swung around to see what Errol had spotted. He almost dropped the bucket of tools in disbelief.

The rain was a solid, almost vertical sheet, with little or no wind driving it. No storm blasts, no hurricane cutting a predictable path of destruction from one point of the compass to another. This deluge was governed solely by the immutable and inevitable laws of gravity, and its menace was its sheer volume.

Visibility, if you could call it that, had been severely reduced. The car park Dave had used on arrival was a maximum of fifty metres to his left, but try as he might, he couldn't even make out a dark patch or an unnaturally straight line marking the boundary between the grass lawn and the tarmac surface.

A similar distance immediately in front of the door, he knew with absolute certainty that he ought to be able to see the safety rail separating the riverbank from the promenade. As he strained his eyes in a futile attempt to make out the smallest detail, the tiniest of white surf caps appeared towards the edge of his field of vision. Turning his head slightly to the left, he refocused on roughly where he thought he might have seen something. He was rewarded when a wave crested, creating another mini-surf tip, then fell back, kinetic energy expended. For a brief second, the unmistakable shape of a cast-iron guard rail post was revealed, then was covered again as another wave rushed to take the place of its predecessor.

With an approximate range to work from, Dave glanced to the right, upstream, and located more rail support posts by the telltale surf caps. Tracking left, downstream of the first sighting, proved inconclusive. Dave suspected the water might be deeper at that point, covering the height of the rails completely.

He grabbed Errol's elbow and had to bellow his words. "Can you see the top of the guard rails along the prom?" He pointed as he spoke to help Errol locate them. After a few seconds' hard stare, he nodded. "Even if a high tide's due at this time of day, it should *never* reach over the retaining wall and swamp the rails along the prom. That's a good ten foot higher than the highest tides recorded during *my* lifetime.

"We have to be practical." Dave forced himself to focus on their reason for being outside. "We haven't a lot of time. The river's burst its banks. I suspect most of this surface water is from the river rather than the rainfall, and it's already halfway up the hill. We have to get back inside and seal the door before the bunker's compromised. We'll just have to hope that the seal holds, and that we can find a way of exiting either through this door or another one—if there *is* another one—when the time comes. If you tramp down to the waterline and get a bucketful of water, I'll get the soil samples and record the air temp, barometric pressure and whatever else these instruments and gizmos will allow me to test in two minutes or so. But hurry. We can't hang around out here any longer than that."

Errol took the bucket, then squinted at the overpowering deluge which continued unabated outside the door. "If I want a sample of water from the river, I'll have to keep the lid, too. Hope you don't need it."

Dave shook his head and stumbled through the door with the spade in both hands, the smaller items stuffed in the Velcro-sealed pockets of his coverall.

At least I can find the door again, he thought as he drove the spade into the semi-liquefied soil at his feet and poured the sample into a container. Errol had vanished from sight two or three strides from the entrance.

Fighting his way back to the gaping hole, Dave struggled to his feet and checked the thermometer's readout: 30°C, which was a hell of a lot warmer than he'd expected considering the rain. He pulled the barometer from the suit pouch and looked at it dubiously. He wasn't sure if he needed to hold it over his head, shake it, tap the glass to see if the needles on the gauge reacted—he'd seen actors in films do this but had always doubted if this was actually necessary.

Mentally he shrugged. The needles were both firmly planted on 'Rain'—surprise, surprise—and a value of just over 800 *somethings* on the number scale around the perimeter of the glass. All he could do was report what he'd seen once Errol found his way back. Should he risk going outside again and looking for him? Or would that result in them both being lost?

He placed the soil sample and the weather instruments a safe distance from the entrance and stepped outside with the spade in his hands.

He began to beat on the metal door, trying to maintain a regular rhythm as he screamed the musician's name at the top of his voice.

"Err—ol. Err—ol."

He wasn't consciously counting how many times he called the name, striking the door with each syllable, but it wasn't long before a shadow loomed at his shoulder.

Words were unnecessary and almost certainly impossible in the circumstances. They turned and supported each other to fight the short distance to the open door, then turned to secure it. The silence which fell as the door thumped into the 'lock' position was shocking. Even in the comparatively short time they'd been outside, exposed to the elements, they'd both become inured to the noise all around them.

"I didn't realise we were soundproofed as well as everything else," Errol remarked, tugging at his earlobe in discomfort.

"The door's a good six inches thick, Errol. Joey did say it was designed to take a direct hit."

"Bombs are a lot bigger now than they were in 1945. But I take your point, and I don't suppose ol' Ma Nature's got that mean a streak in her."

"We didn't get around to sweeping this water out, but I don't fancy opening the door again. D'you reckon we can let that slide?"

"Best make the effort, Dave."

By the time they'd revisited the storeroom and found what they needed, most of the water must have seeped through invisible—to the naked eye—cracks and fissures in the concrete flooring, and some of the mud which had flowed in was beginning to stiffen, but they swept and mopped what they could off to the side walls where it would be less of a hazard. When they got back to the central command room with their samples, they were amazed to discover that the whole operation had taken less than an hour, and the results from around the country were only just beginning to trickle in.

Dave beckoned Joey to an empty table on one side of the room, where he laid out the samples for analysis. "I can't give you hard figures or anything solid to munch on, but the weather conditions outside are off the scale. I've never seen anything like it."

He gave a simple account of the conditions they'd encountered while collecting the samples. "I don't know if the CCTV scanners will show you how heavy the rain is, but it really was just like standing under a waterfall."

"We can take a look." Joey went over to one of the terminals and clicked a few keys. A window opened on-screen, showing nothing but white noise. Joey fiddled with a couple of dials, and the image became slightly less fuzzy but remained obstinately grey and grainy. After a moment, he slapped his forehead.

"Of course! Idiot that I am. That's the sharpest image we're going to get. It's not grainy at all. It's a high-resolution shot of the rain in close-up."

As soon as he knew what he was looking at, the picture resolved in Dave's eyes, like one of those sketches you could never guess what it was going to be until the artist adds the final brushstroke.

"The air temperature's a lot higher than I expected, Joey. How significant is that?"

Joey looked at the digital thermometer and frowned.

"Thirty degrees—in *this* muck? I'd have said impossible. That's more like tropical monsoon conditions. Heavy rain in the UK, you're lucky if the air temp reaches double figures at this time of year." He sighed and looked at the pot containing the soil sample. "I think I'll take a look at Errol's bucket of river water first. That should be easier to analyse, and it might tell us something of what's happening upstream. Remember the high spike in the acidity of that sample we collected yesterday? I can use that for a comparison."

The phone lines were buzzing with increasing frequency, and Brenda was busy routing them to the desks.

"North East. Reports of a major landslip, A5 closed in both directions north of Huddersfield."

"South West. More cliff damage reported, south coast near Taunton"

"Mid-Cheshire/Flint area. River Alyn has burst banks."
This call came to Eddie's desk and included a photograph. His hand immediately shot in the air, urgently flapping for Brenda's attention. "I recognise this. It's the bridge on the A494 where I stopped on my way home and rang you,

near-as-dammit on the England/Wales border. The river
was certainly high at the time, but I've never seen it this
high before."

Joey came across to study the photo. The central span
of the stone-built bridge had been swept away. Two cars,
probably from the car park of the pub in the background,
were on their sides, jammed against the remnants of the
safety walls on the Welsh side of the river.

"Plenty of mountains for it all to come down from—
the flat Cheshire plains are going to be swamped." He was
already reaching for the red phone on his desk when it
shrilled at him.

"Brigadier, I was just about to ring you with a sitrep."

"It may save time if I tell you what I already know from
other posts."

Groth sounded calm, dispassionate. Joey wondered how
many times the brigadier had been in similar circumstances,
coping with a potential catastrophe. He decided he didn't
want to know. When it concerned knowing how close to
disaster they might have been—and how frequently—
perhaps ignorance really was bliss. He picked up a pencil
and prepared to make notes.

Groth reeled off reports from many of the outposts
which had also reported to Bidston Hill. Nothing which had
happened in Scotland, North England as far as Birmingham,
or along the South Coast seemed to be missing, but there
was very little from Wales or the North West.

"We've managed to collect some samples for analysis,
which should give us an accurate assessment of local
conditions. I can have some preliminary results with you
in half an hour or so. We've been a bit stretched receiving
reports from all regions. I haven't had time to analyse them
yet, but there is one report from Wales that's of interest. One
of my team is familiar with the location and tells me the

water levels are much higher than usual. My calculations based on his estimates suggest the River Dee will burst the flood damage barriers within the next hour or so—may have done so already."

"Acknowledged, Doctor Hart. I'll mobilise extra troops to assist in strengthening the defences there. Continue to monitor all regions. For your information, all civilian traffic will cease at 1800 today, until further notice. A curfew will be imposed between 2100 and 0700. If you can spare a screen to cover a live feed from a static camera in Liverpool city centre, that would be useful."

Without waiting for a reply, Groth reverted to form and ended the transmission.

Dave was immediately suspicious. From the very beginning, he'd regarded Groth's abrupt, cavalier manner with phone calls as rudeness. There had been times when he'd wondered if there might be some ulterior, not quite honourable motive behind his apparent lack of courtesy.

The incoming phone calls had eased off somewhat, allowing one of the squaddies—Dave was reasonably sure it was Tom—the opportunity to leave his desk. He began to populate a large-scale wall map with red flags, showing where each report had come from. He paused with a flag in his hand and glanced from the printout to the map and back again.

"Dick, can you confirm the coordinates for log thirty-five? The figures I have place it a good distance from any roads."

Dick found and read back a six-figure reference, which tallied with the figures Tom had in front of him.

"They didn't come from a road post. I got them from the British Waterways office," Dick added. "There's been a breach in the walls on the Trent and Mersey Canal. It's flooded a local farmer's fields."

Tom nodded and placed a flag on the map. "That's going to cause problems. It's miles away from any road link, so we won't be able to get any heavy machines on site to repair that. Inform HQ. They'll need to mobilise something in a hurry."

Brenda reached for her phone on the central switchboard. "Joey, carry on with your number-crunching. I'm perfectly capable of making a phone call.

"Brigadier, this is Bidst...sorry, Juliet Bravo. We may have a problem. These are the coordinates."

"Stand by."

Brenda glanced at Dave, who shook his head, his annoyance showing on his face and in the stiffness of his shoulders. Within a minute, Groth was back on the line.

"Juliet Bravo, there's a REME platoon barracked in Crewe. They've sent a couple of men on scrambler bikes to have a look at the damage. They should be able to get there along the canal towpath. Doctor Hart? Are you listening?"

"Yes, Sir," Joey responded but continued to stare at his latest set of calculations with a deep frown on his forehead. "There isn't much we can do from here until we know the extent of the damage to the canal walls. And there's something about this latest set of figures."

He scribbled another set of hieroglyphics which only he could have read, let alone interpreted. "Remember what I said about water slopping around in a glass and developing into a wave moving with the Earth's spin?"

Dave nodded, but Joey seemed to be talking to himself, thinking aloud, so he didn't interrupt.

"The sheer weight of that unimaginable volume of water would be enough to affect the tilt of the Earth's axis. Sudden extremes of weather would be a natural result. We've just recorded an air temperature almost double what we'd expect in the UK at this time of year. The seas are turning acid, and the Arctic ice sheet has lost two hundred gigatonnes of mass in a decade—that's a heartbeat in world history."

"It's also a lot more water to slop around, as you put it," Errol remarked.

"My point exactly. We can only hope the explosion we engineered to seal the trench wasn't so strong we managed to destroy the world and every living thing on it."

CHAPTER TWENTY-NINE

"S COUTS REPORT THE Trent and Mersey Canal wall is breached about a mile and a half north of Northwich." Joey lifted the account from which he was reading as Dave deposited three more on the desk. "Several tons of rubble and mud blocking the waterway, farmland west of the canal totally flooded. The site can only be approached on foot, using the canal towpath."

The brigadier didn't miss a beat. "I'm committing a full platoon from the REME in Crewe, and as many scrambler/off-road bikes as can be commandeered. Those who can't get there on two wheels will have to approach on foot. All I can ask of you, Doctor Hart, is to monitor them and keep me informed of progress."

"I don't have anyone here who can, Sir."

"Set up a link. I sent you three of my own, remember? They *all* have special skills. I could even set it up remotely from this end if I had to. I believe you've designated them Tom, Dick and Harry. If they're comfortable with that, fine—but, gentlemen, if you decide to reveal your names, you won't be subject to discipline."

The three specials had accepted their nicknames with typical military gallows humour and had taken to wearing handwritten adhesive tags.

"We'll stick to the names we've got, for now," grinned Dick. "But I guess telecoms is *my* field. Sir, can you give me a short-wave radio link to the Sapper team?"

Telephone traffic was steady but not overwhelming for the following half hour, building a picture of the worst affected regions of the UK.

"Another earth tremor reported in Cumbria."

"Road closure due to landslip, Dorset."

"Fire service evacuating residents, sheltered accommodation in St. Helens."

A constant stream of incidents were logged, and a smaller-scale map of the UK was pinned up next to the local map. Joey wasn't directly involved and was able to concentrate on his notes and calculations. He was convinced there had to be some detail he was missing and leafed back through his earlier notes.

I need more time. That's the crucial factor: the timeline of all these incidents, in the right order.

He shuffled the individual reports of the first few incidents, then re-sorted them according to the time of the incident as opposed to the time it was reported. This resulted in several documents changing place. He came to one which was on computer printout paper with serrated edges and noticeably thinner than standard duplicating paper. He paused and studied it closely. It had a military feel to it, with the legend 'DTG:25081105a' centred at the top edge. He frowned and looked up. Dick was still testing the link to the team the brigadier had dispatched and even had video, which was providing a decent picture on the main screen, but there seemed to be a problem with the sound feed. Joey caught Tom's eye and beckoned him over.

"Is this a military term?" he asked, pointing to the mixture of letters and numbers which meant absolutely nothing to him.

Tom nodded. "Date and Time Group, 25th August at 1105a. The 'a' means British Summer Time—Alpha time— as opposed to Greenwich Mean Time, which is designated 'z', or Zulu. International ops are almost always recorded in 'Zulu' time. Not every country uses daylight saving measures, so it's a bit unusual to have a document which includes a reference to Alpha time."

"Thanks for that," Joey said. The explanation of time zone designations was unnecessary, but he appreciated Tom's efforts. "I can see why this is from a military source. Can you give me a hand? I need to find all the reports with a 'DTG' placing them, say, within the first half hour after detonation."

Ten minutes of scrutiny turned up twelve documents. Eight were reports from Europe and North Africa; the remaining four were all from locations south of the Mariana Trench. Joey felt the hair on the nape of his neck stiffen. He picked up the red phone receiver, instructing Tom as he placed the call.

"Try taking this selection in chronological order. If they're spreading at a constant speed from the same point of origin—the trench—we should be able to predict how long they'll take to reach other points where the reports will come in much later.

"Brigadier, we may be on to something."

For the first time, Joey felt he was arguing from a position of strength. He was, after all, *the* climatology and weather pattern expert.

"Thank you, Doctor, but I'd like a sitrep on the progress of the REME team first. Short-wave radio messages don't really give me an accurate picture."

"Understood. We have an excellent picture, and I believe audio is also patched in. Last headcount, there were approximately fifty, five-zero, men on site. It's hard to judge exactly what they're doing, but they're standing in organised groups close to the breach in the canal wall. I can only assume they're shoring up the walls to prevent further collapse.

I can see hoses being unrolled downstream of the damaged section but no sign of any pumps yet."

"Thank you, Doctor Hart. I've just been informed that the pumps have been driven as close as possible by road. They'll be manhandled from there. Now, your news, please. I hope it's positive?"

"Brigadier, I've taken the data I have to hand and tried something different. I've set it up as a ripple effect spreading outwards from the Mariana Trench. Now, because of the geographical location of the trench itself, the ripple spreads naturally in a northeast to southwest direction, so the combined vectors of speed and direction make it possible to predict where the effects are going to be felt. We may even be able to guess how strong they will be."

"Does it give us any clues for countermeasures?"

"I'm starting to get some ideas, but nothing definite. I'm short of data from mainland Europe. The UK is well covered, as is Southern Hemisphere by the teams in Oz and New Zealand. If you can get me some data from Spain, Italy and France, it would be useful. I need to establish a timeline.

"I'm looking back at the earliest incidents—the ones which occurred on detonation day. At the time, I thought a directional surge or wave might develop. Given the mass and volume of water involved, it could have grown in strength as it gathered momentum. That's how a tsunami forms.

"However, the reports of incidents *after* detonation day are far more significant. I'm convinced they're the direct cause of the extreme weather conditions we're experiencing north of the trench. The tidal surge which cut away large sections of the crumbly chalk cliffs along our southern coast is a case in point, and there's also the question of how the winds in the upper atmosphere may have been affected. Don't forget, it's the prevailing winds that carry rain-bearing cloud and create areas of high and low pressure. The only question in my mind is, how long will these disturbances in weather patterns continue? And, following from that, if they persist, how do we adapt and cope with them?"

"Understood, Doctor. I'll concentrate on incident reports from mainland Europe and forward anything I receive. Any suggestions you might have regarding countermeasures would be appreciated."

"Understood, Brigadier. Juliet Bravo, listening out."

* * *

"How's it going, Doc? Need a hand?"

"I wish there was something I could farm out, Eddie, but this is all specialist stuff, weather data and the like."

"Fair enough. I'm at a bit of a loose end. Everyone bar me seems to have some special skill they can offer, but all I seem to do is answer the phone and make coffee."

"Making coffee's as important as those other things, Ed, but you can certainly help me catalogue these reports. I need to input them into a spreadsheet so I can easily order them by time, location, speed and distance."

By the time the stack of reports had been flipped through for what felt like the hundredth time, Joey's hands were grey with printer ink. He rose and crossed the room to sluice the worst of it away and splashed his face to freshen up. Gazing blearily at the water spiralling down the drain, a sudden thought struck him, and he hurried back to his desk. He re-read the first few reports then went directly to the final three, the latest to be reported.

"These mention a weather system originating in the Arctic region, travelling south. Brenda, contact all our observers in Scotland, Norway, Iceland—the further north, the better. I'm looking for any suggestion of tremors, tidal surges, gale-force winds. We could be seeing a bounce-back effect. If the shock wave slaps against something solid, like an ice cliff, it's going to come back on itself, but it's likely to lose a lot of its energy and move more slowly, making it difficult to detect unless we're actively looking for it."

Brenda made a couple of short, businesslike calls. Joey launched into another round of theoretical calculations, and the rest of the team were kept busy fielding the calls now coming in from mainland Europe. These included serious landslides and flooding in southern Spain as well as the Netherlands, where the coastal defences were being overwhelmed.

By the time Groth's direct line flashed, Joey had received four reports from northern outposts in Iceland, Norway and Scotland. Not a great deal, but it was a start, and it confirmed what he'd suspected and feared.

"Brigadier, I think we're looking at a new development. The shock wave appears to be reversing back along its northern path."

"Does this suggest any possible course of action, Doctor Hart?"

"The ripple as the wave recoils will be losing power and momentum as it returns, rather than grow as it did on the first outward surge. But there's something else to consider.

"Until now, we've been recording the effects of an immense body of water—two-thirds of the whole planet—swirling around the deepest of our ocean beds.

"Now, there's something called the Coriolis effect, which is why water down a drain *tends* to flow clockwise in the Northern Hemisphere and anticlockwise in the Southern Hemisphere. There are other variables involved, of course, and it is my theory that a slight wobble to the smooth spinning of the planet may have resulted from the size of the detonation used to seal off the Mariana Trench. It wouldn't take very much to cause a dramatic change to weather patterns worldwide, but I'm confident the effect is temporary rather than permanent. Our best option is to continue with the holding operations we've already set in motion, reacting to each incident with whatever we have and can mobilise.

"Every situation will have to be approached according to its own needs, but this is a worldwide weather problem and a logistics problem of global dimensions. It needs to be tackled in an appropriate fashion, with total commitment from all the world's leaders. I don't see any part of the planet being unaffected, and the solution has got to come from a unified effort from every country, without exception."

Several seconds of silence followed. Joey had to assume that the brigadier was taking this new information on board.

"We're going to need some unprecedented levels of cooperation between governments for this to work."

Even listening to this brief sentence, Joey sensed the brigadier had already worked out a possible solution.

"One question, Doctor. If this rebound wave *is* going to die off in the manner you describe, how long do you think it will be before we know for sure one way or the other? I need as much time as I can beg, borrow or steal if I'm going to broker some sort of agreement about international cooperation on this scale. If there's even a remote chance the problem could sort itself out, it would be to our advantage."

"Brigadier, *soon* in geological terms could be as much as several lifetimes." Joey sighed, took off his glasses and gave them a totally unnecessary polish. "Best guess? Expect the current extreme weather conditions to settle down and become more predictable within a week or so. Does that help?"

"I'll take it. I don't like the idea of seven days of storms and the damage they'll cause, but it gives me an opportunity to contact as many people as possible, persuade them to work with us on finding a way to correct the wobble we seem to have created in the Earth's spin—assuming it's not going to settle down itself, and we can't afford to wait and see. That's not an option."

"Seeing the effects of the storms might actually persuade folk to take us seriously, Brigadier. The most important thing is, we have to come up with a plan of action, a possible solution—and it *has* to be ready within the next week."

"Any preliminary thoughts?"

"This might sound more than a little crazy, Sir..."

"Desperate times, Doctor. Let's hear it."

"I need any reliable figures you can glean from anywhere in the world—especially the Southern Hemisphere—and remote access to fast computers to process and interpret them.

"Remember the eddy effect I mentioned? If we can find a way of breaking up the directional flow by constructing an obstacle on the seabed *upstream* of the Mariana Trench site, diverting the stream north and south, it would kill the momentum of the water mass in the same way we use breakwaters and groynes on beaches to control surface tides and protect coastlines."

"That's...easy to understand, Doctor. But will it work? We're not dealing with the erosion of the North West English foreshore here. To start with, this obstacle would have to be constructed in the deepest recorded part of any of the world's oceans."

"Brigadier, we managed to place a considerable number of extremely dangerous missiles *exactly* where we needed them, at exactly the same depth. We then detonated them, and there were no mishaps or casualties. Think of that as a test run if you like. I believe we can do this."

"And the materials needed for this...breakwater, whatever you decide to call it. Even if we ignore for the moment the sheer volume and the shipping needed to transport and dump it—we're talking telephone numbers of tonnes of ballast, presumably—just manoeuvring the cargo vessels is going to be a logistics nightmare."

"The fact that it's an isolated location, far from any major landmasses could actually be an advantage, Brigadier. But it will mean every country which has *any* cargo vessels available has to be involved. It's going to make the evacuation of the beaches at Dunkirk look like a walk in the park, I realise that. But as you said, it's desperate times, and it calls for drastic measures."

"And the ballast itself?"

"Red Adair once said, 'Fill the hole with whatever junk you've got to hand and cap that son of a bitch.' He was the best oilwell troubleshooter ever known. I think we should take him at his word.

"The whole of the industrialised world has a problem with waste disposal. Scrap metal mountains, building rubble— just about any inorganic rubbish which is solid enough to sink instead of floating. We could use this as an opportunity to clean up the environment, worldwide."

"There are very strict laws about the dumping of waste materials, Doctor, but I understand what you're saying. This is a unique situation, outside anyone's experience. A week is nowhere near enough time to get a general agreement, but you've given me breathing space, time to talk to others. I'll continue to get you as much data as I can from around the world. Keep me informed of any change in the weather patterns, and especially if the wobble in the Earth's spin looks like getting worse."

True to form, Groth ended the transmission without further ado.

CHAPTER THIRTY

NAVAL COMMAND, AUSTRALIA. *All shore leave has been revoked; all available crews instructed to report to their vessels within twenty-four hours. Merchant shipping has been ordered to offload any cargo on board and stand by. All tourist routes are being held at their current docks and harbours. Those at sea will make landfall at the nearest available port."*

"Situation report, Japan. All naval vessels have been deployed at sea, leaving harbours clear of military vessels. Commercial vessels have all been contacted, many of them in the southernmost regions of the Arctic following established seasonal fishing routes."

"Thank you, Japan. Your fishing vessels are to remain as far south as practical. We can't use their cargo facilities without asking them to dump their cargoes, which would be a waste of food resources, but they must not enter the operations zone until we can give an all-clear. Confirm."

"Understood. The message has been relayed and acknowledged."

"Royal Navy, on behalf of the Joint Command, European Flotilla. Every available NATO vessel is fully crewed and on standby. Reservists have been contacted and given notice to report to regional centres. Smaller vessels will continue commercial fishing in the North Atlantic and the North Sea, as they will not interfere with planned operations further south."

"This is the US Coast Guard, Washington DC. Torrential rain and winds up to one hundred twenty mph have caused major structural damage in Haiti, the Bahamas and Cuba. There has also been severe damage along the east coast affecting all areas as far north as New York. The hurricane season has arrived earlier than anticipated. We're trying to mobilise all our larger vessels away from ports and harbours, into deep waters where they will be safer and available for deployment as required."

"Except this *isn't* just an 'early hurricane season'," Pete Whelan muttered, mostly to himself, and stretched. Cooped up in a disused army base in Tauranga, he'd all but forgotten what a bed—any bed but especially his own—looked like.

"We could have used some of that rain here these past few days." his PA said.

"True enough, Marc." The bay, usually lush and green with an abundance of rainfall, since the detonation in the Pacific had been drier than midsummer in Wairarapa. "But if we'd called in a fire control team, we'd have been obliged to give 'em a map ref."

"And someone would know this place actually exists. Jaysus, is the security still that tight? We're going to have to go public sooner or later."

"So let's make it later—the later, the better. Faced with a choice of bead-wearing hippies singing bad folk songs or skinhead thugs tossing bricks at anything that even hints at being vaguely military, I'd have 'em all lined up against a wall and shot at dawn."

"Come off it, Pete. I know you better than that. Deep down, you're just a big soft pussycat."

"Who's tanked up on Super Lava Java and hasn't slept for about a week. I know these reports are all crucial bits and pieces of the jigsaw, but there's just too much to process."

"Which is why the brigadier requisitioned all these state-of-the-art computers and top operatives to run them. Nobody expects you to run every programme yourself or know the details of every scrap of intel that comes our way. Fer Chrissakes, Pete, go and lie down before you fall down. You're no use to anyone like this."

"Okay, Pete agreed reluctantly. "Can you do me a favour and get in touch with my brother Dave? Give him everything we've got—and I mean, everything, no matter how obscure or insignificant it might seem. He's got Doctor Joey Hart at his shoulder, and there's nobody in the world who knows more about climate conditions and seismology. Our Dave has a way of spotting things others sometimes miss. He's not a scientist. He isn't going to bother *proving* something or finding a logical explanation, but who knows? His instincts and Doctor Hart's expertise between them just might give us an angle we haven't explored yet. I'll go and crash for a few hours, though I daresay I'm too tense to sleep."

Pete's body had other plans, however, and shut down immediately his head touched the pillow.

After calling Dave and looking in to make sure Pete was comfortable, Marc collated all the available data and made one final check for anything which might have arrived within the last few minutes before forwarding the file to Doctor Hart.

* * *

"Who on earth is *peewee*?" Joey mused aloud, frowning at the monitor, which displayed his email inbox. His finger was almost on the *delete* key when Dave shouted.

"Joey, wait! It'll be from my brother, although why he sent it from his personal account, I don't know."

"Peewee?"

"*Pe*-te *Whe*-lan." Dave looked over Joey's shoulder as he opened the message and clicked on the attachment.

Columns of figures interspersed with graphs and weather maps scrolled across the monitor screen. "Anything there we didn't already know?"

"Hmm. Not sure. I need a few minutes to crunch them, put them in context. Some of these were only logged within the past hour, so they're up to the minute—certainly more recent than the figures we've been using."

Brenda came to the console. "I've finished translating the reports from *Météo-France* and given them to Tom to add to the spreadsheet, Joey. And I've replenished the coffee."

"Thanks, Brenda. I don't know what we'd have done without you this past week."

"I don't know what I'd do without you, full stop," Dave said, smiling at her over his shoulder. Returning the smile bashfully, she leaned against his back and put her arms around his waist. It seemed an eternity since they'd had an opportunity for a moment of affection, and she wasn't inclined to pass up this chance.

"Those lines on the weather maps that look like the loops and whorls of a fingerprint. I know they're something to do with areas of high and low pressure, but I can't remember the proper word for them."

"Isobars," Joey said. "They show what direction the next weather pattern is coming from and the region it's likely to affect."

"So where they're closer together, that shows high pressure? It's a bit like reading a knitting pattern. More stitches per inch, more tension in the wool."

"That's a valid comparison, although weather systems aren't constant."

"But could you use that information to predict where and when the pattern—if there *is* one—is likely to repeat itself? That's what I'd be doing if I was knitting with more than one colour or, say, using a cable stitch."

"We can give it a try. We've tried everything else." Joey sat up a bit straighter in his chair, grateful for a suggestion of something different, a new challenge. He ran some calculations, factoring in the relevant variables—latitude, elevation, landmass and so on—and transferred the results to the weather map. A fresh set of isobars superimposed themselves over the ones already on-screen. Joey highlighted them and changed the colour from black to red. The overall shape was similar, but they were more tightly packed and further apart.

"Interesting. If this is accurate, we can expect the areas of high pressure to be more intense but with longer periods between them—put another way, heavier rain but for shorter periods and less frequently."

Dave stepped around Joey to take a closer look at the map. "Does that mean we'll see the weather improve for a few days, then get battered with another storm more damaging than the last one? And then again, only worse?"

"That could happen, but we're in uncharted territory here. I can't be certain each storm's going to be stronger than the one before, but I expect it to get worse before it gets better. At the same time, I can't predict how *much* worse it's going to get before we see things easing off. The period of calmer weather in between the storms, though—that's much easier to predict."

"How long was the last calm between storms?"

"Three days."

"And that blew itself to a standstill during the night. So, counting today as the first day, the next big storm can be expected in, what? Four days from now? Five? Longer?"

"Say four, then we're on the safe side."

"Best get on the horn to Groth. I told him he had a week, and he baulked at that. If we've a maximum of four days to prepare for a blow bigger than the last one, he's going to have to mobilise a shitload of bodies and equipment and get anything essential out of the way or permanently tied down."

***

"Is this our own little 'calm between the storms', I wonder?" Brenda arrived with a fresh set of full coffee mugs. Joey pushed himself gratefully away from the console and stretched slowly for the nearest one. He winced.

"I must remember to stand up and move about once in a while. I'm starting to feel like Quasimodo here—I've even got ringing in my ears." He stood and took a long drink. "That's better. Thanks, Brenda, and you're right. We've done all we can for now—brought Groth up to date with the latest from the Southern Hem, made an educated guess at the timeline—so we're back to maintaining the 'eyes and ears' remit we were originally given. Watch the screens, stay alert, try not to miss a trick."

"Joey, this might sound…well, not very scientific. Probably because I'm not a scientist." A frown furrowed Brenda's brow for a moment before she continued with a small smile of embarrassment. "We know where the shock wave originated. Can you work out how long it will take for it to travel right around the globe, back to where it started?"

"I haven't looked that far ahead, but I imagine so. Why do you ask?"

"I'm still trying to understand it all…and thinking about knitting patterns gave me a clue."

Joey's fingers suddenly sprouted a pencil and a scratchpad flopped obligingly open in front of him, although Brenda could have sworn the table was clear and empty. "Tell me more about knitting patterns."

"Well, when you're knitting, it doesn't matter *how* big the garment is. Every stitch is the same size as the one before it and the one after. If you need different-sized stitches, you use different-sized needles or thicker, heavier wool, but each *row* still has evenly sized stitches. When the garment—let's say, a sweater—is the size you want it to be, you cast off with a row of special stitches that stop the whole thing unravelling."

One by one, the rest of the team came over for coffee and tuned in to Brenda's analogy.

"Which got me thinking—when this shock wave completes a full sweep of the globe and gets back to where it started, it's reached the end of the last row. Time to cast off. But what happens next? Is there now a massive wall of rocks and rubble rising *above* where the trench used to be? And if there is, how powerful will the surge of water be? Strong enough to demolish the rock pile? Or will the rocks prove a solid barrier and turn the wave aside to flow in a different direction altogether?"

"Shit, that's a whole new can of worms," Eddie said, "and I'd bet my next pay cheque on her being right."

Dave put his mug down and half-turned to confront Eddie, who hadn't realised he'd said what he was thinking. He held up his hands.

"Dave, no disrespect. I happen to believe Brenda's instincts are spot on. If we can work out what's likely to happen when this vast wall of water finishes lap one of the world's first global marathon, it may give us a clue what we can do next. It's our one chance to sneak ahead of the game."

Joey's hands blurred between three or four calculators, which he appeared to operate without even glancing at them or the monitor screen as he threw formulae and complicated-looking diagrams at it.

"There's one thing I'm not even sure I pointed out, but it works in our favour." He reached what appeared to be a natural pause in his never-ending calculations and looked around with a relieved smile—the first one any of those present could recall witnessing. "This isn't the wave's inaugural sweep. I took readings from the North of England *before* the tremors were noticed further south. Remember? I told you then, it was most likely a shadow or recoil wave, bouncing back south after juddering up against the solid ice foundation of the North Pole.

"The recoil had already lost some momentum, and this is the second 'bounce'. In other words, it's tapering off steadily, moving more slowly. I still need to check some figures, but my gut feeling is, this could be the final shudder before the worst of the underground and undersea tremors settle. They won't cease entirely for some time yet, but they'll be less violent, more predictable and, more to the point, easier to control."

"That's a bold statement, Doc," Tom said. "You sure about that?"

"This isn't wishful thinking. It's solid, empirical, scientific fact. The data indicates there's no significant force left in the wave this time around. Even if there *is* some sort of rock wall or barrier where the trench used to be, the wave's going to wash around it and settle."

"Does the brigadier know this?" Harry cut in, a heartbeat faster to react than his SAS teammates.

"Not yet. Brenda's knitting-pattern analogy was just the kick in the proverbial I needed. I wanted to have something positive to report, and now I've got it. I'll get in touch with him once I've summarised my findings."

CHAPTER THIRTY-ONE

A RE YOU SAYING we should sit and wait?"
"That's what my figures are telling me, Brigadier. It's easier to understand if I translate them onto a graph. You can actually *see* the difference. You don't need to understand the maths involved."

Joey punched a key to send an image to Groth's computer. "The timeline is left to right, of course, and you'll notice the earliest waves, showing an area of high pressure, are bigger on the left then become progressively smaller. There's no doubt in my mind. The aftereffects are decreasing. The momentum is spent. We can start thinking about mopping-up operations—not that they're going to be easy to organise. There won't be any part of the world that hasn't been affected by the events of the past week."

Groth was silent for a few moments, but this time, Joey and the rest of the team at Bidston Hill could see him on the computer screen. He wasn't idle. His hands flipped impatiently through a ring binder on his desk, clearly searching for a specific entry. Suddenly, he stopped and bent closer to read something before addressing the camera again.

"Doctor Hart, what about the possible wobble you mentioned? Is it still affecting how smoothly we spin around the planetary axis? Has the angle itself been altered, either temporarily or permanently? How can we ch—" Groth stopped in mid-sentence. "Sorry, Doctor Hart. I've a hundred questions I need answered, and I'm giving you no chance to reply. Work on those two thoughts while I create a list of points, then triage them into some sort of order of importance."

Completely out of character, Groth didn't end the transmission abruptly, but looked at the screen and waited. Joey took the hint.

"Understood, Sir. I'll do as much as I ca—"

Joey just had time to notice the swift movement of Groth's right arm as he clicked the mouse, then the screen went blank. The brigadier might not have had the final word in this conversation, but he was clearly still in control of the situation.

* * *

"Doctor Hart, our problems might not be over yet. Not quite, anyway."

Joey muttered a curse and reached for a notepad.

"Understood, Brigadier. Go ahead."

"Three reports, three different regions, almost simultaneous and all reported within the last hour.

"Report from Grimsby, Yorkshire. Ground tremor resulting in a section of cliff breaking off, at least six houses destroyed. No report on casualties yet, but we must assume the occupants have been killed.

"In Japan, a strong tremor has caused the collapse of a road tunnel at Sasago, about fifty miles from Tokyo. Fatalities expected, but so far search-and-rescue ops have not begun.

"The third report is from the Philippines, relayed through our sources in New Zealand. The island group has been hit by severe typhoons, and almost all communication has been lost. This has been included because it mirrors similar events in New Zealand and Australia in recent weeks."

"Acknowledged. Brigadier. I need one more piece of information. I need to know the *directionality* of these incidents. If I'm right, the first two were north to south, and the last one was moving south to north. Can you confirm?"

"Stand by."

Groth muted his audio, and Joey and his team watched the dumb show on the monitor as the brigadier spoke to someone off-camera, then switched audio back on.

"Confirmed, Doctor. How does that help?"

Joey nodded. "I said the worst was over, and I stand by that assertion, but we can expect aftershocks for a while yet, possibly as little as the next twenty-four hours, but it may be longer. The point is, in all three events the shock waves were travelling *towards* the Mariana Trench. Once they meet—as they must, either at the trench itself or somewhere close by—they will effectively cancel each other out. That's basic Newtonian physics. Equal and opposite forces, as we were taught in school science lessons."

"Is it really as simple as that, Doctor?" There was an edge of distrust in Groth's usually expressionless voice. Perhaps the strain and stresses were getting to him, but Joey had no doubt in his mind. He took a deep breath and seemed to discover a hitherto-untapped source of adrenaline-fuelled energy.

"We're out of the woods, Sir. I'm certain of it. We can start planning the next phase, and I've had time to chase up some preliminary figures about the two questions you left me with."

"I'll come back to those in a moment, Doctor, but you sound confident. Do I take it you've something positive to tell me?"

"I believe so, Sir, but establishing some sort of evacuation of badly hit regions such as the Philippines should be high on the list. Where are the nearest groups of shipping which were ordered to stand offshore after detonation day?"

"That's classified, but I take your point. We have vessels moored within a few hours' sailing distance."

"I'm not trying to tell you your job, Sir." Joey couldn't help himself.

"Very wise, Doctor. However, you've been the eyes and ears of the whole operation from the very beginning. We couldn't have managed without you. I'm authorising the immediate release of every vessel with hospital facilities and capacity to rescue flood victims in the Philippines and provide specialised assistance to Japan. We're reasonably strong on the ground in Northern England. We can send in REME squads with the engineering and rescue skills to deal with the landfall in Yorkshire. We can ease off, downgrade from Condition Red, lift military law and travel restrictions. I have to ask you to remain on duty for a while yet, but I'm sending you some relief staff to ease the burden."

CHAPTER THIRTY-TWO

A WEEK BECAME TEN days, then twelve: twelve days of unremitting storms and other foul weather conditions, which had to be dealt with as they arrived and in most instances with little or no warning. A deep blanket of snow had covered most of Scotland for most of August, stretching into the North East of England. Further south, where the climate was a few significant degrees warmer, rain was the problem rather than snow, with some parts of the country experiencing landslips as the thoroughly Devon and Cornwall were hammered mercilessly with twenty-eight inches of rain in a single day.

Further sizeable sections of Dover's famous cliffs simply sheared off from the constant battering of tidal bores travelling north, made worse by pinballing backwards and forwards across the narrow channel separating the UK from the northern coastlines of France and Belgium. The year would eventually be named experienced in the UK since records began, and satellite pictures taken in the aftermath of the clean-up operations would show significant and permanent changes to the British coastline, mostly in the South West of England and in North East Scotland.

The leader of the Conservative Party won a certain amount of respect from the media and possibly bought a few begrudged votes from the electorate when he went to the queen and asked for permission to form a national government for as long as it might take to restore some semblance of order in the UK, citing the War Cabinet of the 1940s as historical precedent.

It was no surprise when the petition was granted. Less than half of an apathetic electorate had bothered to turn out at the last General Election, and the Tories had only been able to tread water thus far with the reluctant support of the runner-up Liberal Democrat party. Basking in the glory of the newly coined title National Minister, the Tory leader was able to draw on the best talents available sitting in the House of Commons. Bickering between various shades of red, blue, green and other party-political differences ceased overnight. An unexpected bonus soon followed. People rallied around, showing the 'war spirit' of an earlier generation, and the true meaning of the soundbite, coined by a minister with a large personal fortune and therefore much maligned by the press, 'We're all in this Together' became a reality.

* * *

"Mayor Anderson has invited us to a private meeting in his office. He's got some interesting news he wants to share with the 'Eyes and Ears' group before it's announced publicly. He says he wants to thank us all personally for our contribution." Dave passed the letter across the breakfast table for Brenda to read.

"I'm guessing he's also written to Eddie and Errol. I wonder if we'll get to meet Brigadier Groth—even find out the real names of Tom, Dick and Harry."

"That's probably covered by some obscure clause of the Official Secrets Act. You know—'If I tell you, I'd have to kill you afterwards,'" Dave responded gravely. The phone rang, sparing him from becoming the target of a well-aimed cushion.

"Hello?" … "Errol, hi. Have you also got a letter?" … "Yes, that's kind of you." … "Eleven o'clock? Fine, it's only ten minutes or so from here." ... "See you." Dave hung up and grinned at his wife. "Errol's got a flash company limo. He says he'll collect Eddie and Joey, then come for us. He's even providing a chauffeur."

* * *

"All the time we worked together, even cooped up in the bunker, you never once told us you had a regular job as well as playing a mean trumpet, Errol."

Errol shrugged at Dave's observation as their group reached the doors of the Town Hall. "Someone had to tout for business, answer the phone, sign a few cheques, and Paw said it would keep me off the streets and out of trouble. But the job has its own small perks."

"Small?" Dave glanced back across the car park. "That limo needed *two* parking bays. Did you remember to feed both parking meters?"

Errol was momentarily at a loss, unsure if he was being teased or not, but at that moment, Mayor Anderson appeared in the foyer, taking each of them by the hand and thanking them personally before leading them through to his office. Brigadier Groth was already there, standing at ease; he greeted the team with a formal nod as they entered.

"You'll notice I've cleared the room of lackeys and pen-pushers." He gestured for them all to take a seat around the highly polished oak table. "The only thing I'm going to ask of you is a promise not to repeat any of this, anywhere, until it's made public."

"When might that be?" Joey wanted to know.

"Less than twenty-four hours is all I can say for the moment. There are quite a few people looking to claim a share in the glory of some really good news for Liverpool." He looked around the table. "Our first priority, nationally, is to take care of the most urgent repairs and rebuilding work needed all over the country, especially in the South and South West, which suffered the worst of the coastal erosion and flooding."

"I've seen the aerial shots," Brenda said. "Devon and Cornwall—what's left of them—are a totally different shape." She'd already started re-assessing her classroom notes for geography lessons once the new academic year began.

Joey nodded. "I hear there are plans to offer full-time employment to anyone prepared to pick up a shovel and roll up their sleeves. Even on a fixed-term, twelve-month contract, it will put more money in the pockets of people who are currently living on benefits."

"And make the Government look good by reducing unemployment statistics," Dave cut in. "But that's beside the point. I'm in favour of anything which makes for an easier life."

"Might suit me, though." This very quietly from Eddie, who'd spent most of the month since emerging from the underground bunker scouring the classified ads for job opportunities. He shrugged. "Well, I can still swing a shovel. Just because I've been flying a desk for the last few years doesn't mean I actually *enjoyed* the job."

"Easy, Ed. We all know you're serious. But let's not get sidetracked. The mayor brought us all here for a reason, and I don't think we've quite got to it yet. Am I right?"

The mayor nodded once more. "When I said, 'Good news for Liverpool,' I meant *specifically* Liverpool. But I've also been told—unofficially—those applicants from regions of the country which have higher unemployment rates will get a helping hand if they need it. The benefits for Liverpool as a region will be seen in the immediate future, but we won't have to wait to get things started.

"Effective immediately, Bidston Hill and the weather research facilities will be extended and improved and become the Hub of a national Meteorological Service. Funds will also be made available to extend and improve weather stations around the UK, which will all report to the Hub. I'm reliably informed that someone has leaned heavily on other countries in Europe, and we can expect both an increase in funding and improved weather data from that source, too."

"Not a moment too soon." Brigadier Groth's comment was carefully neutral, containing no hint of censure or blame. Those were the first words he'd uttered since entering the room, other than a courteous acknowledgement when Mayor Anderson had thanked him for his involvement, but Dave sensed there was considerable power and authority behind the man in pristine, perfect uniform. There was no sign of Tom, Dick and Harry nor any explanation for their non-appearance. Dave had to assume that they were gainfully employed elsewhere and unable to attend.

Mayor Anderson seemed slightly flustered by the brigadier's words, despite their apparently non-judgemental nature.

"I agree with you, Brigadier. It's time we insisted on more cooperation from our European allies, and I'll be making that one of my personal priorities."

"I'm glad to have this opportunity to thank the civilian members of the team which functioned so well and at such short notice," Groth replied. "We'd have been lost without them."

The mayor nodded. "Hear, hear. And there's more good news for the whole of Liverpool. Europe has agreed to allocate Objective One funding for the development and expansion of Merseyside's docking facilities. In effect, we should be able to offer state-of-the-art cargo operations as well as the Cruise Liners Turnaround Terminal. This information *must* stay within these walls until certain interested parties decide to go public, but there's a gentleman's handshake on the deal, and I can assure you all, it won't go sour."

Errol had been fidgeting in his seat for several minutes and seemed to come to a decision. Slowly, almost reluctantly, he raised his hand. For some unaccountable reason, Brenda had the image of a naughty child 'fessin' up to his teacher for a minor misdemeanour.

"My father's board of directors contacted me last night by email. They're impressed with the way Liverpool—the facility at Bidston Hill in particular—has performed throughout this real and present danger to the whole planet." He broke off with a grin. "And I can guess which member of the board insisted on using *that* melodramatic phrase. Still, the whole shootin' match had a lot of media coverage in the States this past month.

"As a result, the board authorised me to offer financial backing and any practical assistance you may require to rebuild and repair throughout the region. They believe Liverpool has the potential to be a major port for both cargo and tourist trade."

"Eddie, you're our number-cruncher. What's your take on this?" Dave wanted to know.

Eddie waved one hand briefly as he juggled numbers in his head. It could have been a plea for patience or a signal of total surrender. After a few seconds, he took a deep breath and glanced around.

"The finances we're talking about, nationally and from Europe, are promising in themselves. Further investment from the US, courtesy of Errol's family business, is really the icing on the cake. I can't factor it into the overall picture without some idea of the size of the investment, but it will certainly sweeten the deal."

"I have a suggestion for you," Errol said. "It's something I'd have to put before the board, but I think they'll be amenable. One of our subsidiaries specialises in site clearances. I propose we invite them to tender to dredge and maintain the riverbed, keep it navigable for the cruise terminal and make it possible to develop a commercial harbour. Like I say, the company is more than willing to offer practical assistance as well as finances. By improving and maintaining shipping lanes on the Mersey, they're creating employment for their own workforce as well as performing a vital service for Merseyside. It's a win-win for everybody involved."

"Lady and Gentlemen, if there's no further need for my presence...?" Brigadier Groth half-rose from his chair.

"We're grateful for your time, Sir," Joey murmured in deference. "Permission to email you with details of any significant developments?"

The brigadier nodded his agreement and slid his chair neatly back into position. With the same formal nod he'd used to greet them, he turned smartly and almost-marched out of the room.

"Do we have a sitrep on publicity?"

"Sure, Eddie, but no need for the military jargon now the brig's left us." Dave grinned. "In brief, there isn't a lot we can do before whoever is calling the shots gives us the green light to beat the drum and, hopefully, bring home some new business and investment. I've made notes, but that was before Errol threw his company's hat in the ring."

"'Scuse me, but the hat you're a-talkin' of belongs t' ma paw. I'd never try to claim the company as ma own," Errol drawled in a not-too-serious attempt at self-mockery.

"Noted, Errol. The offer makes a significant difference, and I'll have to find a way to show how much our position is improved, but there's no rush to get that done. I can have a statement ready as soon as we get the go-ahead."

"You'll have to excuse me as an ignorant Yank if this is a dumb question," Errol cut in again, but this time, there was no frivolity in his voice. "I've never completely gotten the hang of your political system in the UK, but back home, the statement you're talking about would be delivered by the president and simulcast on every TV channel. We call it a State of the Nation address. D'y'all have anything even like that in the UK? And if so, my next question is, who's got the *chutzpah* to carry it off? Surely not the present prime minister?"

"Hardly!" Dave said. "And offhand, I can't think of any of the current shower of House of Commons deadbeats who *could* pull it off."

"Nor me, Dave, but I can see you doing it."

"Me? You've *got* to be joking. My old Latin teacher'd be spinning at a rate of knots in his sarcophagus at the very idea. He warned us that becoming a 'paid politician' was the worst fate that could possibly befall *anybody*."

Dave's horrified rejection of Errol's proposal produced a ripple of genuine laughter that stilled abruptly when the door flew open and Brigadier Groth re-entered, clutching his mobile.

"We're not out of the woods yet. It's fortunate none of you have left, and I have to remind you that you've all signed the Official Secrets Act."

He paused, closed the door and made sure it was locked before moving closer to the table but didn't resume his seat.

"My taxi didn't even make it as far as Lime Street Station, which is fortunate, as I'd have been obliged to turn around and recall this team."

"Sir, all the tests over the past four weeks—"

"Confirm a job well done, Doctor Hart. Yes, the Enemy Within has been dealt with, and the world already owes you for that.

"Now there's a new and completely different problem, one which I'm sure you can deal with just as well. No interruptions, please." Groth raised his hand against Joey and Dave's simultaneous intakes of breath. "On this occasion, at least we have the...luxury, I suppose, of having rather more time available, but we're going to need every hour of every day.

"The intel I have on this is unquestionable and comes from multiple sources. We managed to prevent our planet blowing apart due to pressure from within. The work you did as a team was extraordinary, magnificent. Choose whatever adjective you like, none are good enough to describe your efforts, especially working against such a desperate timetable. This time, we must look outwards, or upwards, not down below the deepest known rift in the seabed.

"Radar telescopes have detected a mass of unimaginable size at the extreme limits of our vision. Calculations confirm it's heading our way, and the likelihood of a direct impact is very high—almost guaranteed, in fact.

"A mass this size will inevitably influence gravitational forces, even if it doesn't actually strike Earth. We have a time slot of approximately one year—a full orbit of the sun—before these effects will start to be felt. That is all the information I have at this moment. A more detailed report will be available later this evening. You have a track record of working well as a team. Your comments, please."

For an optimistic fraction of a microsecond, Dave dared to hope the brigadier was testing them for some unfathomable reason only he could justify, but Groth stood ramrod-straight and silent, his body language unambiguous. He'd made his statement and demanded a response.

"This is déjà vu, all over again." Errol's slow drawl broke the silence just as it was on the verge of becoming unbearable.

There was a hint, but no more than that, of amusement in his voice as he continued.

"With respect, Sir..." Joey began. "Yes, we managed to function as a team for the duration of the emergency we all lived through. I'm in the privileged position of only having myself to consider, and the finances to do as I damn well please, but that's not the case for everyone else. Dave and Brenda, for example. They've had no privacy, no time to themselves since it all began, and we all have family somewhere out there."

"Perhaps we do—at the moment," Groth agreed. "But family and a lot more besides will become meaningless twelve months from now unless a solution to this new threat can be found and implemented.

"We can learn from experience. This threat isn't the same. It's approaching from above, or from somewhere outside our solar system, not from the planet's core. This time, we gain nothing from keeping it all under wraps. Everything has to be done openly and with total cooperation and agreement from every side. Otherwise, human nature being what it is, sooner or later, someone will attempt to throw a spanner in the works, and we can't afford the luxury of delay.

"Frankly, there isn't another team I'd trust—not one which has already gelled as a unit, doesn't need to be assembled and trained to work together, and has a mix of skills and non-technical instinct, which you've already proved you have between you. Some of your outside-the-box guesses have been crucial and came at times when a large slice of random luck was sorely needed."

The brigadier looked directly at Brenda as he said this. She blushed and accepted the implied compliment.

"We're starting from a stronger position, with more time to plan and the resources of the whole world available. I need the best team to coordinate the million and one things which will have to be tackled along the way, and *you* are the best team."

Eddie had been slumped in his chair throughout the exchange. Since he'd joined the others in the Bidston Hill bunker, he'd more than pulled his weight but somehow managed to remain isolated, a loner.

Now he raised his head from his arms and looked around. "Yous all know the score wi' me," he said in a monotone. He paused as if reprimanded by an invisible advisor, then blinked, squared his shoulders and continued in a far crisper, more decisive manner. "I appreciate I've been a bit of a wet blanket most of the time. Even before I began that long drive home from Spain, I knew there was no job waiting for me and an empty house I couldn't afford payments on unless I found another job right away.

"Being on this team's what kept me going, you know? Showed me I still had some *real* mates," he said with a special nod at Dave. Brenda, sitting next to Dave, felt guilty being included in Eddie's grateful acknowledgement but didn't interrupt. Eddie clearly wasn't finished yet.

"So I'm all for it—carrying on as a team, that is. 'Cause even when—*if*—we pull this off and I get to go home, I'll not be surprised to find the house repossessed and a few broken bits 'n' pieces of furniture dumped in what used to be my back garden. You can count me in, Brig...Sir." Eddie sank back in his chair and pulled out a large handkerchief, blowing his nose long and hard to cover his embarrassment.

Groth looked at Dave, who automatically reached across and squeezed Brenda's hand. He felt the tiniest trace of confirmation in Brenda's fingertips and didn't need to see the positive nod she gave Groth when his eyes flicked from Dave to her. "If you're satisfied with what we've achieved to date, Sir, we're happy to carry on."

The whole interchange had taken only a few seconds, but it was time enough for Eddie to regain control of his emotions.

Groth cleared his throat. "Doctor Hart. Probably the most important person on the team—I daresay the leader—but we haven't heard from you. Do you have anything to add? Any commitments, personal matters, family or housing problems you need to organise?"

"No, Sir. Last time I checked, every direct debit I set up with my bank is still being paid, and on time, and what family I have is spread around pretty thinly. There's just one suggestion I'd like to make."

"Name it."

"Critical readings from weather stations in any region which is still reporting extreme weather conditions. Local temp, wind speed and direction, barometer readings. I need them at regular intervals—hourly would be ideal, but that's probably asking too much. It's pertinent to my current research."

Groth said nothing but nodded for Joey to continue.

"I propose we move back to the Bidston Hill site, if they'll have us, and base the whole operation there. My lab at the university doesn't have all the equipment and facilities we'd need. We also need a plan of action. You said the mass is expected to come crashing through our solar system in twelve months' time. Realistically, we have to be in a position to launch something powerful enough to destroy it—or at very least turn it far enough to prevent a direct hit—in a far shorter time than that. Six, eight months tops, I'd say."

"Agreed," Groth said. "And this time, we'll all be in the one place, which will save time and improve security. I'll make a few phone calls. I suggest you pack whatever you feel you'll need and be prepared to move out within—" he looked at his watch "—two hours? I'm sure I can have the transport available by 1800 hours."

* * *

The transport vehicle was a standard military wagon, driven by Tom. Dick and Harry occupied the passenger seats. When they arrived at Bidston Hill and unloaded their personal gear, they entered the observatory through the discreet side door facing the riverbank. The three-man security team wore their usual combat fatigues, devoid of nametags or other ID labels. For the first time Dave could recall, they carried weapons when they climbed out of the cab and stood easy inside the access door.

The civilian day shift was assembled in the largest available room. Once Groth had confirmation that all staff members were accounted for, he sorted the sheep from the goats. Everyone with any sort of family at home was dispatched, with an assurance of full pay, and told to await instructions regarding future shift patterns. A skeleton crew of eight singletons remained. Groth had a stark ultimatum for them.

"Your colleagues with family commitments will continue to receive full pay until further notice. If any of you choose to leave now, you will be treated in the same manner, and there will be no recriminations or penalties imposed once the present crisis has been resolved.

"We will need all the extra manpower we can retain. If you choose to remain, you will be required to sign the Official Secrets Act and observe all the terms and conditions this entails. I can only reveal the details of this operation to those who opt to remain and realise that I am, in effect, asking you to sign a declaration of commitment without knowing precisely what you're agreeing to, but I'm afraid I have no easy option to offer. This is an international emergency that will require liaison through key personnel around the world, and there is a need-to-know affecting not just national security.

"I am prepared to allow you a few minutes to reflect, but I must have an answer this evening. You can discuss the matter as a group if you wish, or retire to think about your options in private, but I need to know what you decide by 1900 hours." He looked at his watch. "That's thirty-four minutes from now. You can leave to collect your belongings from home, but please ensure that you have everything you require with you when you return. This facility will be in lockdown until further notice."

The group of technicians glanced at each other. None of them seemed inclined to stand up or leave the room. One of them murmured something, and they formed an untidy, heads-down rugby scrum. Less than a minute later, there was a flutter of movement which looked suspiciously like a swift rock-paper-scissors decision. One of the group stood.

"My colleagues have asked me to inform you of our decision. We're in."

A brief ripple of applause from the rest of the group confirmed the decision was unanimous.

The brigadier nodded in acknowledgement. "Excellent. Now, while I supervise what needs installing for efficiency, is there someone with a good grasp of the basic supplies in this bunker? We'll start with food—canned, dried, salted, I don't care as long as it hasn't spoilt and still has a decent shelf life. Bottled water. First-aid supplies..."

* * *

"Does the brig ever *sleep*?"

"Errol, I'm not even sure if he eats or uses the bathroom."

Dave had slept half a dozen times since entering the bunker and was convinced someone had ripped a fortnight off the calendar outside their triple-bolted microcosm. Groth had insisted they all remove their watches and refer only to the clock times displayed on computer screens and wall clocks mounted in every communal room.

"He must have a wardrobe master's storeroom full of identical uniforms," Errol remarked. "He's always perfectly dressed. I swear you could get a nasty cut from the crease on his pants."

"Trousers," Dave said automatically. "In the UK, pants are your undies. That or a slang word meaning 'rubbish'."

"Damn. I knew that. I've lived here long enough. But here's another thing. He never has a five o'clock shadow. When does he disappear long enough to shave or change clothes?"

Groth had been ever-present in the control room, or so it seemed. Phones rang non-stop, yet whenever the operator was struggling with a difficult or reluctant caller, he was invariably there to bark a command and ensure he got what he wanted.

Days, provisionally demarcated by sleep periods, flowed one into another. Coloured pins appeared on a map of the world, predominantly red to begin with. Gradually, they were replaced with different colours. Some went directly to green, others became yellow for a while, but by the end of the seventh or eighth sleep, the tempo of the changes had picked up. Most pins were now green, and the remaining red pins were few. Tom, Dick and Harry took responsibility for plotting the precise position of each pin. They referred to printouts for this. The coordinates were twelve-digit figures as opposed to the six-digit navigation standard.

"Strange how many weapons were overlooked when we asked for contributions to seal off the Mariana Trench," Groth mused as the last red pin in the Australasian sector turned green.

"But will we have enough firepower?" Dave took a mug of coffee from the tray Brenda was carrying. Groth hesitated a moment, then helped himself to a bottle of water.

"The sooner we can get a first wave of missiles into position and programmed the better."

Dave felt honoured. He hadn't really expected an answer. The brigadier stuck rigidly to his guns as far as the need-to-know mantra was concerned.

"Once my weapons team has worked its magic, we can calibrate the onboard guidance systems and send this lot on their way. That will create some breathing space." Groth suddenly clammed up, as if realising he was very close to contravening his own strict rules.

"Breathing space?" Dave said, papering over the split-second hiatus as if he hadn't noticed it. "You mean there are *more* weapons? Why not send them all at once?"

Groth sighed. "Because they're still under construction. Everything you see on the map is already in a silo or on a ship. One of the first things I did was to authorise production of more missiles at every munitions factory with the necessary equipment and personnel. With any luck, we should have a similar number of MLBMs—that's modern large ballistic missiles—ready to go in under a fortnight. Travelling such vast distances, they'd catch up with the first-wave weapons long before they reach the target zone. Following closely in the wake of the first wave rather than catching it up will also work to our advantage. The last thing I want is to nudge one and set off a harmless chain reaction in the middle of nowhere. And now I've broken my own rule by telling you something you don't 'need to know', I probably ought to shoot you, but as long as you give me your word this will go no further, I'm prepared to give us *both* a break."

"Thanks—I *think*." Dave risked a quick glance in Groth's direction and decided to push his luck. "Does that mean you've had positive responses from all the places on the map marked with green pins?"

"Not quite that simple, but in essence, yes. We still have the problem of getting them to suitable launch sites, but that is all I can tell you. We've reached a stage where I can make a start on that. Would Eddie be prepared to help me crunch some numbers—pretty big ones?"

Dave was caught flat-footed at the sudden change of topic but nodded anyway. "I'm sure he'll be only too glad to help. I'll send him to your office right away."

* * *

Dave didn't see Eddie until three sleeps after he'd relayed Groth's request for assistance, and even then, it was purely by chance. Eddie stumbled out of the CO's requisitioned office bleary-eyed and unshaven as Dave collected empty and unfinished coffee mugs abandoned around the ops room.

"Don't ask how it's going—you know I couldn't tell you even if I understood a tenth of what's going on, which I don't. And don't tell me I look like shit warmed up. I know that already.

"But for what it's worth, you were right about himself not needing sleep. Just before every shift change, he disappears into a back office, runs a shower, then comes out in a fresh, crisp uniform. He must have at least a dozen of 'em hung on a rail in there. He's a real bundle of energy, and he never breaks into a sweat. He's an inspiration, seriously. You feel you just have to pull ye finger out and work as hard as he does, d'you know what I mean?"

Dave thought he did know. He'd met a few happy workaholics in his time. He spotted one more coffee cup attempting to avoid detection and eased around his friend to capture it.

"You'll feel better once you treat yourself to a shower and a change of clothes, Ed. I'm sure *the Groth effect* is more to do with the psychology of keeping up appearances than anything else. Anyway, it'd be a waste of your time trying to explain even the simplest maths equations to me, so sod off, get yourself under a shower. I'll speak to you *after* you've had a well-earned kip."

CHAPTER THIRTY-THREE

D AVE AND ERROL were assigned different shifts, and both checked in regularly on Eddie, who slept a full twenty-four hours before showing signs of life.

"I swear it was the smell of the coffee that woke me as soon as you opened the door," he said as he accepted gratefully the super-strength, military-issue brew Dave offered him.

Dave grinned. According to folklore, army coffee was strong enough to wake the dead and persuade them to run a couple of marathons.

"For the record, you've been out of it for a full day, Ed. No panic, we're not short-handed, and the brig has called a timeout. There's a briefing for all three shifts at noon. That gives you time to shower and shave before you grab a bite to eat."

Brigadier Groth's public speaking technique mirrored very closely his telephone mannerisms. Once all personnel had been accounted for, he began without preamble.

"This is the first occasion you've all been together in one room at the same time. I'll start by thanking every single one of you—three teams of forty, if anyone's counting—for your input over the six weeks since you volunteered to be sealed in this bunker without knowing when or even if you'd be able to re-join friends and family. A simple 'well done, and thank you' seems inadequate, but I'll say it anyway. Thank you, one and all.

"To business, then. The map on the wall is easy enough to interpret." He gestured at the display with the swagger stick which was an inevitable part of his habitual pristine parade-ground uniform. Every pair of eyes turned to study it. He allowed them a few moments to drink it all in before continuing.

"We reached a Green for Go status just over twenty-four hours ago. Those of you who were on duty the last two shifts will have noticed that we've had far fewer calls to deal with. That's because we're at the end of the preparations stage. We're now very close to a launch date, with time on our side, and it's all due to your hard work."

What sounded like a suppressed sigh of contentment rustled around the command room, stifled by a peremptory double-tap of swagger stick against podium. Groth wasn't finished yet.

"Depending on local weather conditions more than any other factor, it will take another few days for all the weapons to be delivered to their launch silos around the world. Some of the larger sites will receive sufficient weapons to be able to fire a second salvo, but you don't need to know the logistics of that, other than identifying which sites will be firing and tracking them until they disappear from your screens.

"Starting with Woomera, which will be at the most advantageous position, firing will commence at 0000 hours Zulu—or midnight in London for the civilians among you— on a day which will be confirmed once we are certain all the missiles have been successfully delivered and installed.

"Every hour, as the next time zone reaches the position Woomera was in, the strike locations in that zone will fire their missiles. Twenty-four launches spread over twenty-four hours. The largest single strike in peacetime, made possible by your efforts. The future of this planet rides on it being successful.

"A sobering thought and a tremendous responsibility. I'm sure some of you will have asked yourselves why so much firepower was being assembled and what the effects of such a massive detonation might be, but if you'd been *told* this, or indeed guessed, during the preparation phase, it would only have served as a worrying distraction when you needed every available moment to concentrate on your professional skills.

"There is also this to consider." He paused and looked around the room to make sure he had everyone's full attention.

"By calling for every country's known stockpile of 'Weapons of Mass Destruction'—a term with which the news media is enamoured and, in this case, has made our job easier to sell to the public—and firing them all at a target far from our home planet, we are in effect making this world a safer place. Irrespective of whether certain countries withhold a cache of undeclared weapons, there will still be far fewer in the world than there are today, even following the recent weapons purge to collect sufficient power to collapse the fault in the Mariana Trench.

"We have already demonstrated these missiles are more than weapons for destruction. They are powerful tools in our planet's defence. There is every chance that a genuine, permanent peace may be brokered, and war could become a thing of the past. That, ladies and gentlemen, is the legacy of your efforts for your children and grandchildren to enjoy."

There was more than a suggestion of emotion in Groth's voice as he ended his impromptu speech, delivered without hesitation...and also without notes of any sort. The full complement of volunteers spontaneously broke into cheers and applause, many offering the brigadier their own civilian idea of what a smart military salute *ought* to look like.

* * *

The drum-tight security surrounding the unique World Summit was reflected in the fact that it was three full days before anyone—even the most obnoxious and persistent wolverines of the tabloid press—realised that none of the 250 participating world leaders had been seen in public or in their respective offices.

Naturally, a brilliantly inventive press statement had been prepared in advance, a masterpiece in sound and fury, signifying nothing and containing precisely zero information. Crucially, this bought a further forty-eight hours of debating time; by Friday evening, there was a broad consensus of agreement.

"We have been given adequate time to prepare ourselves, but we must respond swiftly. Every country in the world must contribute what they can. Our whole planet is under threat. Working together, without panic or alarm, is the only way we can succeed."

The US President was first to fold and admit that his administration had 'revised their records' and in the process 'discovered' there were still some tactical missiles that had been 'overlooked' when they had made their contribution to the sealing of the Mariana Trench.

Similar discrepancies were swiftly found in the records of other countries, which surprised nobody, and an amended, more truthful stocktaking of the planet's arsenal was swiftly compiled, together with a list of suitable launch sites and the rocketry needed to launch the weapons.

Once the first barriers crumbled, the floodgates of unprecedented international cooperation opened wide. Time was suddenly too precious to waste on prevarication, posturing and near-paranoid distrust of a neighbouring country's possible intentions. The survival of the planet was all that mattered.

The ending of the year was uncharacteristically quiet. The commercial scramble of the festive period was more subdued than any since the austere years of World War Two, but the religious services of all denominations were noticeably better attended.

Early in January, with practical preparations well in hand, it was possible for the political delegates to extract themselves from the summit and return to their respective countries, where they were without exception welcomed as conquering heroes. They were in an ideal position to win the hands and hearts of the countries they had been born or elected to rule and encourage them to 'keep up the good work'.

The reduced rump of the summit, consisting of professional military minds, was now able to surge ahead with confirming the complicated logistics essential to the audacious project they had undertaken.

"We only get one shot at this. We've neither the time nor the resources for any field tests," Groth said at the end of yet another intense, somewhat bad-tempered meeting. "It's got to be right, first time."

Pete Whelan was in on the meeting, by Skype video link.

"You saw the model I put together," he said. A three-dimensional cube appeared on-screen at Western Approaches and key locations worldwide. "I got the idea from Spock playing 3D chess, with eight boards and two hundred and fifty-six pieces. Each piece on the schematic represents a launch site somewhere in the world." The display had been put together to simplify the technical aspects of the operation for presentation at the summit.

"As we discussed, the tilt of the planet's axis means that sites in the Southern Hemisphere will be best placed for the main strike, with a window of early March as the optimum time for the launch date..."

"You make it sound childishly simple, Doctor Whelan," Groth remarked blithely, gathering his papers.

"Oh, it's complicated, Brigadier, no question. But Doctor Hart and I agree. The computer model has made it possible for us to run some test firings, and we're confident we've covered all the bases. It *will* work."

***

17ᵗʰ *March, 0000, ACST: Woomera range, Australia*

"First Base, Australia. This is Whisky Alpha. You are clear to fire. Confirm."

"Whisky Alpha, this is First Base. Stand by."

Thirty tense seconds ticked past. From the throats of hundreds of refurbished concrete silos, the silver spears carrying the first wave of the Southern Hemisphere's contribution rose on pillars of flame and leapt into the cloudless sky, accelerating out of sight in seconds. Their flight path was recorded on every conceivable form of tracking device. The timing of the launch of each missile was crucial. Each had been calibrated to reach the same target zone while maintaining a safe distance between them to avoid mishaps and collisions.

Back on the ground, crews were already in action reloading the silos with a second volley, timed to be released a fraction short of twenty-four hours after the first. In the command bunker, the calibrations were already being adjusted to allow for the Earth's rotation and the slightly different orbital position as the planet continued its unchanging swing around the solar system's fulcrum, ninety-six million miles from the launch site. Considering the distances involved, the slightest miscalculation of trajectory at the launch site was unthinkable.

"Launch complete. All missiles successfully deployed. Repeat. All deployed."

Over the next twenty-four hours, waves of missiles rose on cue and in perfect formation from sites all around the world, kept at a safe distance from each other by tiny, delicate in-flight controls made possible by Pete Whelan's *StarChess* computerised graphics.

The former members of the Eyes and Ears team sat in a crowded bar at the Ship & Mitre, watching the missiles rise and disappear on a giant TV screen, which was strictly contrary to the real ale pub chain's entertainment policy. There was no soundtrack or commentary to accompany the streamed images on the screen, and although the pub was filled to its utmost capacity and beyond, there was little conversation beyond an occasional murmur between friends.

"Guess it's all in the lap of the gods now," Dave said. Brenda didn't reply but squeezed his hand a little harder, then winced and wriggled free, chafing her palms to counter the pins and needles as the pressure of Dave's grip loosened and blood started to flow back into her fingers.

"It looks as if your brother's done a mighty fine job with his *StarChess*," Errol commented. He opened his cigarillo etui, then frowned and put it back in his pocket. Somehow, it seemed too much trouble to barge his way through the crowd to reach the door and stand outside for a smoke. Maybe it was time to kick the habit once and for all.

"Listen, Dave. Assuming this one-off roll of the dice works, and we have a future to look forward to, I think I can persuade my father to invest a generous amount of research funding into development of your brother's software. It could be extremely useful in logging and mapping on a grander scale than we've ever considered before, especially if we ever want to expand our horizons beyond the Third Rock at any time."

"Name a price, I'll buy a ticket on the first flight." This from Eddie, who hadn't seen much point in making plans for an uncertain future, not until or unless there was a positive result and the mad gamble of staking the planet's continued existence on one, single *putsch* succeeded.

"You buy the next round of drinks, and maybe we got ourselves a deal," Errol replied with a grin. "You can begin by explaining just what skills an ex-banker could possibly have to offer anyone recruiting a team to colonise another planet."

It was close to ten p.m. GMT on Sunday, 17ᵗʰ March. So far, silos in twenty-two of the world's time zones had released the missiles they had available. Woomera and several of the larger bases had re-armed and would fire a second volley as they circled to face the optimum direction once more. Before the end of the week, the first-strike volley would pass beyond the scope of even the most sensitive tracking equipment, but the data being continuously transmitted from every missile already fired was encouraging.

"I can assure you, we'll know if we hit it," Joey had said time and time again over the past six months. "An explosion of that magnitude would be impossible to miss—especially when we know what part of the universe we ought to be looking in."

"But what if you're wrong, Joey? What if we *don't* see anything? What if our sensors and computer programmes *don't* show us what we all hope to see? What then?" Brenda was clearly petrified at the thought.

"If we have no readings, no signals whatsoever, it could mean a total miss, but I can't see that happening. Even if we only manage to break up this rock into smaller pieces, it becomes less of a threat to our continued survival. Hell, even if we don't damage it at all but deflect it just a degree or two from its present course, that should be enough for us to live and fight another day. It may still affect our climate for a while, or even permanently, depending on how far away from us we can nudge it, but if we can avoid a direct hit, we've achieved something worthwhile."

"So if we're still here on Midsummer's Day and aren't freezing our balls off in green snow falling from a pink sky, we can thank the Lord and pass the gravy?" This came from Errol, slouched back in his chair with a devil-may-care glint in his eyes.

"That's three months away, Errol, and we'll know for sure in two, so yes, that about sums it up. Though personally, I'd have tried to dress it up in more scientific terms."

One by one, the dots on the TV screen which represented the missiles hurtling through space winked out of existence as they passed the limits of the recording devices' ability to receive signals. A vivid imagination and a leap of faith would be needed to extrapolate the most likely course of their onward thrust, and over the next two months, many people who had never considered themselves to be religiously inclined would discover they were praying for the miracle of success.

* * *

Beyond the limits of the unique blend of breathable gases which had shaped the development of the flora and fauna indigenous to the third planet of an insignificant star in one of billions of galaxies, well-ordered, rank after rank of the most powerful weapons the dominant life form on that world had ever constructed hurtled through the silent, lightless vacuum of nothingness, seeking an impossibly small target in the vastness of infinite space. The payload was easily identified as solid, physical, measurable megatonnes of destruction, but they also carried the unquantifiable, immeasurable, weightless hopes and prayers of a whole species.

ABOUT THE AUTHOR

Born in the Year of the Tiger, Paul has always had the feline instinct to roam.

After spending most of his teaching career as an eternal supply teacher throughout Europe, Liverpool's siren song was too strong to resist, so Paul came home and got himself a 'proper job' writing books.

Just one dream still unfilled: to buy a horse and caravan and hide on the country lanes of Roscommon.

BEATEN TRACK PUBLISHING

For more titles from Beaten Track Publishing,
please visit our website:

https://www.beatentrackpublishing.com

Thanks for reading!

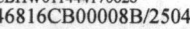